Acclaim for the authors of
Regency Christmas Liaisons

CHRISTINE MERRILL

"A lovely Regency romantic story with engaging characters and a plot that will tug at your heart."

—Vikki Vaught, author and blogger,
on Vows to Save Her Reputation

SOPHIA JAMES

"Harlequin is publishing some of the best historicals in the industry these days."

—Frolic Media on
Their Marriage of Inconvenience

MARGUERITE KAYE

"One of my favourite authors... [Marguerite Kaye] can be relied upon to create interesting characters and situations that are firmly grounded in their historical settings, while also crafting a compelling and emotional romance between her hero and heroine."

—All About Romance on
A Forbidden Liaison with Miss Grant

Christine Merrill lives on a farm in Wisconsin with her husband, two sons and too many pets—all of whom would like her to get off the computer so they can check their email. She has worked by turns in theater costuming and as a librarian. Writing historical romance combines her love of good stories and fancy dress with her ability to stare out the window and make stuff up.

Sophia James lives in Chelsea Bay, on the North Shore of Auckland, New Zealand, with her husband, who is an artist. She has a degree in English and history from Auckland University and believes her love of writing was formed by reading Georgette Heyer on vacations at her grandmother's house. Sophia enjoys getting feedback at Facebook.com/sophiajamesauthor.

Marguerite Kaye writes hot historical romances from her home in cold and usually rainy Scotland. She has published over fifty books and novellas featuring Regency rakes, Highlanders and sheikhs. When she's not writing, she enjoys walking, cycling (but only on the level), gardening (but only what she can eat) and cooking. She also likes to knit and occasionally drink martinis (though not at the same time). Find out more on her website, margueritekaye.com.

REGENCY
CHRISTMAS
LIAISONS

Christine Merrill
Sophia James
Marguerite Kaye

HARLEQUIN
HISTORICAL

HARLEQUIN®
HISTORICAL™

Recycling programs
for this product may
not exist in your area.

ISBN-13: 978-1-335-40743-6

Regency Christmas Liaisons

Copyright © 2021 by Harlequin Books S.A.

Unwrapped under the Mistletoe
Copyright © 2021 by Christine Merrill

One Night with the Earl
Copyright © 2021 by Sophia James

A Most Scandalous Christmas
Copyright © 2021 by Marguerite Kaye

All rights reserved. No part of this book may be used or reproduced in
any manner whatsoever without written permission except in the case of
brief quotations embodied in critical articles and reviews.

This is a work of fiction. Names, characters, places and incidents
are either the product of the author's imagination or are used fictitiously.
Any resemblance to actual persons, living or dead, businesses,
companies, events or locales is entirely coincidental.

This edition published by arrangement with Harlequin Books S.A.

For questions and comments about the quality of this book,
please contact us at CustomerService@Harlequin.com.

Harlequin Enterprises ULC
22 Adelaide St. West, 40th Floor
Toronto, Ontario M5H 4E3, Canada
www.Harlequin.com

Printed in U.S.A.

CONTENTS

CONTENTS

UNWRAPPED UNDER THE MISTLETOE

Christine Merrill

To Chaos and Mayhem.

I've put you in a story.
Now please get off the keyboard.

Dear Reader,

Regency Christmas parties wouldn't be the same without punch.

Unlike the mild or nonalcoholic fruit punches we see today, Regency punches were alcoholic and strong enough to raise spirits and loosen inhibitions.

If you want to make your own, just remember:

One of sour,
Two of sweet,
Three of strong and
Four of weak.

Those are the proportions of lime juice to sugar to dark rum to water that will get you a Regency punch. Or try any of the recipes in *Punch: The Delights (and Dangers) of the Flowing Bow*, by David Wondrich.

Merry Christmas!

Christine Merrill

Chapter One

Daffy Bingham had been born a spinster with an affinity for cats.

Technically, all women were born innocent. But there was something about little Daphne that made everyone assume that the condition was likely to stick until she died alone at a ripe old age. Just as her cousin Geoffrey was born Viscount Mawbry and his sister was born Lady Honoria, Daphne was born a spinster.

To begin with, her parents, Mr and Mrs Bingham, had the misfortune to die of ague when she was still an exceptionally healthy baby, leaving her as the poor relation that the Duke and Duchess of Twinden were obliged to take in. This is not to say they did it ungraciously. They loved Daphne in the same, absent-minded way they loved their own children. But she was a poor relation, none the less.

Then came the unfortunate nickname given her by Geoffrey when he was a lisping child of three. The family proclaimed it adorable and agreed that thenceforth she was to be Daffy. But what was adorable when one was five was quite another matter when one reached adulthood. And though Geoffrey grew to be a stalwart Geoff, and Honoria was sweet enough to be called Honey, the sensible Daphne remained trapped for ever as Daffy.

Good sense was another excellent quality in a spinster. Despite her name, Daffy had it in excess. Eight years ago, she had been given a season. But even from the first, the Duchess had doubted that it would take. Men liked to believe that they were rescuing women by marrying them. But Daffy Bingham exuded an unfortunate confidence that implied she was quite capable of taking care of herself, and any others that might happen by.

Daffy was the sort who always seemed to have an extra handkerchief when another, more delicate lady was in tears. She also had a pin to do up the ruined hem that had brought on the crying. And should the surfeit of emotion bring on a swoon, Daffy had hartshorn in her reticule.

Daffy never swooned.

Nor did she need a young man to get her a lemonade after a vigorous dance. She was rarely asked to stand up, but when she did she danced well and was never over-taxed. In fact, she was as strong as an ox.

Though her affinity for cats was often commented on, the supposition was not quite true. It was more accurate to say that cats had an affinity for her. Though Lady Honey could get robins to land in her hand when strewing breadcrumbs in the garden, birds were presented dead at Daffy's feet by adoring moggies everywhere. When they were *enceinte*, they had their kittens in the drawer where she kept her spare handkerchiefs. And when she sat down they hopped into her lap and snuggled into her knitting, confident that their naps would not be ruined because Daffy Bingham was never going to go anywhere.

They made her sneeze.

But she allowed them to remain because she was not the sort to inconvenience another person, even when that person happened to be a cat.

According to the Duke, it was why her current behaviour was so disconcerting. A girl so practical in all other ways should not be given to taking things that did not belong to her.

'Especially at Christmas,' the Duchess added, wringing her handkerchief into a thin rope of anxiety.

'It is bad enough the rest of the year,' the Duke huffed. 'We're constantly having to retrieve the shirt studs and eardrops from her room after she's nipped 'em. It's ungrateful, that's what it is.'

As a thief taker, Charles Pallister was well aware that a family's meagre charity might drive a poor relation to pilfer items from around the house. What he did not understand was what these people expected him to do about her. 'Have you spoken to her about the problem?' he asked, seeking the most direct solution.

'Multiple times,' the Duke said, frowning. 'It has done nothing to curb her behaviour. It is dashed annoying.'

'We have made allowances. She is family, after all,' the Duchess said with a shrug. 'Not close family, of course. Still, every family has its quirks, and allowances have to be made. But now,' she added, 'we have guests. A house full of them. And if their possessions go missing? Well, we cannot have that.'

'I see,' said Charles, from his place in the wing chair by the fire. 'But still, the matter is an unusual one. It is typically my job to find the culprit, run them down and drag them to justice. In this case, the first two steps are not necessary. What precisely is it that you wish for me to do with a thief you have already caught?'

The Duchess gave her handkerchief another twist. 'We thought, perhaps, if you spoke to her...'

'Threatened her, you mean,' Charles replied with a bland expression. Hanging was a common punishment for thieves. Apparently, he was here to put the fear of God into some poor old woman for nicking the silver. There were days he hated his job.

'Not in front of the guests, of course,' the Duchess added.

'We want no one alarmed,' the Duke said.

'Except Miss Bingham,' Charles replied.

'Only to the extent that she does not embarrass the whole family with her behaviour. If you can watch her closely and keep her from stealing, that would be even better,' the Duchess said.

'We will introduce you to the party as a distant cousin,' Twinden said triumphantly. 'No one need know who you are.'

'I doubt Miss Bingham will find that particularly alarming,' he reminded them.

'You will have no reason to reveal yourself to her if she does nothing wrong,' the Duchess informed him. 'Perhaps you can stop her with a gentle warning, as if from a friend.'

'I am to befriend her now?' he said, trying not to let his frustration show.

'But if she walks off with someone's diamond tiara,' the Duke said with a grim look, 'something will have to be done.'

'So, you simply wish me to prevent any thefts at this house party, in any way possible,' he said, relieved to find some clarity. He was normally far more interested in punishment than prevention. But the behaviour they described could be a sign of a weak mind rather than a bad character. He did not have the stomach for persecuting gentlewomen for actions that they might not be able to control.

'Stopping her would be ideal,' the Duchess replied, relieving the pressure on her tortured handkerchief. 'Watch over her, when we cannot, and see to it that she does nothing to embarrass herself.'

'Or us,' Twinden said with a frown. 'I have had enough nonsense from her to last a lifetime. If she cannot control herself until Twelfth Night, drastic action will need to be taken.'

Taken by him, Charles supposed. If he did not want to haul an unfortunate old maid off to the asylum for Christmas, he had best keep on his toes. 'I will see to everything, Your Grace,' he said with a reassuring smile. 'As of today, I am your estranged cousin visiting for Christmas. And Miss Bingham shall be no trouble at all for any of us.'

'You are under the mistletoe,' the handsome young Lord Beverly said, a slow smile spreading across his face.

His quarry looked up, feigning surprise, just as all ladies did when caught thus. It would not do to make a gentleman believe that there was anything contrived in the moment. The fairer sex did not ask for kisses, no matter how much they might want them.

'You must pay a forfeit,' he said, his eyes smouldering into hers.

She fluttered her hand before her chest, gave him a hesitant look, then smiled. 'If I must, I am most happy to pay it to you, my lord.'

His lips came down on hers as he plucked a berry

from the kissing bough. His hand lingered above them, just as his lips lingered in the kiss. Slowly, he reached for another berry.

From a darkened corner of the room, Daffy cleared her throat.

The couple jumped, embarrassed at having been caught. They had not noticed her. But then, people rarely did.

'Leave some berries for the other guests, Lord Beverly,' she said.

'Of course, Miss Bingham,' he said, retreating from the doorway.

Lady Honoria retreated as well, giving her a single exasperated look before departing. The poor thing had been trailing after Beverly for days. Now that success and Beverly were in her grasp, Daffy had come to spoil it all.

Daffy sighed. It was not as if she wanted to be the one who killed all the Christmas joy. But someone had to do it, and she was a born chaperone.

Since she had been the one to decorate the house, she knew where all the temptations lay. She had put the most impressive arrangement of mistletoe in this out-of-the-way corner of the house, knowing it would attract young couples who wanted a moment of privacy. She allowed them that moment, two at most, before she was honour-bound to put a stop to it and send them back to the party. There would be no forced weddings on her watch. Above all, Daffy was more sensible than the name that had been forced on her.

She stood and stretched her legs, running a satisfied hand over the boxwood garland on the library mantlepiece. Between that and the candlelight, the room looked and smelled wonderful. It was a shame that she was too old to enjoy it as the young people did. But she'd had her turn eight years ago. Stolen kisses at Christmas had been very nice, she remembered with a sigh. She'd not had many of them, and the few she'd got were cherished memories.

But she had put that behind her now and was quite content with what she had, which was knitting and books and peace for Christmas. She did not have to dance and make merry if she did not want to. No one minded if she sat by herself, whether she stayed up late or retired early. For the most part, her time was her own.

A cat rubbed against her ankles, and she stared down at it with a frown. She did not exactly dislike the animals, but Twinden House had far too many of them. The manor was full of mice, and someone had decided that something must be done to keep down the nuisance. But she sometimes thought that the cats were nearly as big a problem as the rodents.

No matter what room she was in, there seemed to be one waiting to sit with her, rub against her, or stare at her expectantly as if it thought she might pull a morsel of meat from under her chair. Like it or not, they had made her their queen. Probably sensing that she had no one else.

After a long, serious look at her, the current feline, a blue-grey beauty with a question mark tail, hopped up onto the mantle and strolled along the garland, giving a speculative sniff at the holly berries.

'You will poison yourself, you little fool,' she said giving him a stroke and a gentle push away from danger.

As if he agreed, he turned up his nose and strolled in the opposite direction.

'Daffy, come out to the hall,' Honoria whispered from

the doorway. 'Cousin Charles has arrived.' Honoria had been almost as excited at the prospect of this unintroduced cousin as she was at entrapping Lord Beverly. She had been speculating as to his age, wealth and possible good looks since the Duchess had surprised them with the news of his impending arrival almost a week ago.

'He is in Father's study,' she whispered again. 'And we are in just the place to see him come out.'

'Under the mistletoe, you mean,' Daffy said with a shake of her head. Then she took the girl by the arm and moved her gently to the side. 'Even if he is as handsome as you hope, there will be time enough for that later. For now it will do you no credit to be too eager.'

Though she was not as eager as Honoria, she did admit to a certain curiosity about this Charles Pallister. She could not remember anyone in the family ever speaking of him before. It hardly mattered, really. She was not the one to set the guest list. But the late addition of an unattached male would leave them uneven at dinner and set all the young ladies in a flutter, trying to attract his attention. Someone was likely to be left sitting out. As a person who did that often, she felt sympathy for the fellow, whoever he might be.

Honoria sucked in an excited breath as the door to the study opened and her parents stepped out, followed by the man in question. Daffy had to admit, though he was not a nine days' wonder, he was worthy of maidenly interest.

Charles Pallister was not handsome as she'd have defined it in her youth, when she had swooned after equally young men who were delicate in body and soul. The man before them now had to be nearly forty. He was well past boyhood, for there were dashing blazes of silver at the temples of his dark hair. His cheeks were bronzed instead of rosy, darkened by years of riding and walking in the fresh air. His skin was a startling contrast to his eyes, which were a fascinating shade of silvery grey. They made her think that, if the room were dark enough, they might glow with a light all their own, like moonlight on water.

As he walked down the hall towards them, he carried himself with a confidence that she did not see in the other gentlemen attending the house party. He looked solid, as if he would be unmoved by the most violent storm, and not stopped by man or beast if his mind was set on a goal.

He was almost abreast of the doorway where she stood beside Honoria. As he passed, he glanced in their direction, his eyes seeming to catalogue every detail of their persons, as if storing the information for later, when proper introductions could be made. Then they flicked upwards to a spot a few inches above Daffy's head, and he smiled.

She looked up as well and found she was standing dead centre under the kissing bough, as if waiting for a kiss from anyone who passed by.

Honoria giggled, and Daffy stepped back, treading on her own hem in her rush to change position. She needn't have bothered, for Charles was already halfway up the main stairs and heading to his room to change for dinner.

In his wake, she was left... Goodness, was she actually flustered? Even the idea made her want to laugh. She had not flirted or been flirted with in at least five years. Then, it had been more of a joke than anything serious. But even if he was amused by what must have appeared a shameless request for a kiss, Charles Pallister had looked at her with appreciation, and nodded in a way that said, I will be speaking with you later.

It was probably because he recognised her as family. They must have met at some earlier point in time, though, for the life of her, she could not remember ever seeing him, or hearing his name mentioned. And surely, she'd have remembered those eyes.

She shivered, drawing her shawl a little closer around her shoulders. No matter what, it was going to be a more interesting Christmas than she had imagined.

Chapter Two

$\infty\infty\infty$

After he had washed and dressed for dinner, Charles came downstairs and joined the guests mingling in the drawing room in preparation to proceed to the table. He had been assured that Miss Bingham would be amongst them. It was suggested that he would not need a formal introduction to her as they were supposed to be family and, after all, *it was only Daffy.*

This explanation had left him feeling slightly defensive on her part. It must not be easy to be so taken for granted in a family that common courtesies were deemed unnecessary. Of course, he shouldn't have been surprised. This was the same family that would call out the law on the poor lady rather than trying to break her of her bad habits by showing her kindness.

He put on his most amiable smile and scanned the room for a tallish woman with short, sensible hair. From the description he'd been given of her character, Charles pictured a nervous woman, rather gaunt and awkward. One of those creatures that seemed to lurk at the corners of ballrooms, all elbows and opinions. Her hair would not be grey, of course. They had said old but not ancient.

But perhaps the first light of youth had already begun to fade from it, leaving it a muddy brown or an ashy blonde.

He noted and rejected at least half a dozen girls before coming on the only one that could possibly be her, and when he did he had to force his eyes away, lest she see his amazed stare.

It was the woman who had been standing beneath the mistletoe in the hall earlier. He had not precisely leered at her. But he had definitely given her a teasing glance to remind her what he might do if she did not move. She had blushed most prettily. He had felt quite pleased with himself about it and gone up the stairs planning to dance with her later.

Normally, he would not have dared to force his company on an employer's guest. But he would need to do just such a thing if he was expected to blend in with the crowd as Cousin Charles. It would not do to relentlessly stalk a single member of the party until everyone noticed the attention he was paying her.

And, in truth, it would be a relief to break up the grim nature of his career with a little dining and dancing. Though there was a satisfaction in bringing miscreants to justice, it was not as enjoyable as it had been when he had been young and sure of the fairness of the law. Since, he had seen too many people like Miss Bingham and felt too much sympathy for their situations.

Which left him to wonder what he was to do with this surprising development. Daffy Bingham was not some comical old maid. She was exactly the right height, with a set of curves that said she saw no reason to starve herself to delicacy for the sake of any man's opinion. Her hair was cut short, as expected, probably to save on the efforts of the lady's maid that would always get to her last, if at all. But what was there was a rich chestnut-brown, with untamed curls that begged to be touched.

Her eyes, which he had imagined in a perpetual squint, were wide and the smoky green of moss. Right now they scanned the room, taking in all the action but expressing no approval or disapproval at the riotous celebration. There was no wistfulness to show she wished to participate, nor jealousy that she was forgotten. She was simply, delightfully, *there*.

For a moment, he was frozen in place, listening to the beating of his own heart and unsure of how to move or what to say to introduce himself to her. Whatever he said would be a lie, of course. He was familiar with lying to further his pursuit of wrongdoers. But he had never liked it less than he did today.

What did the Duke and Duchess expect him to do about a woman like this? If she was a thief, she must be a very subtle one. She did not seem interested in the jewels that were displayed on ears and throats all around her. If he had been of a mind to take things, he'd have chosen the diamonds on the Dowager who was currently standing right beside her, or the ruby stickpin in the cravat of the Earl on her other side. Instead, she was looking at…

Dear God, she was looking directly at him.

He took a stilted step in her direction before he could find his footing again and stroll normally, falling into his character of long-lost cousin, coming to make nice with a distant relation.

He was coming her way.

It was ridiculous to read too much into a single shared glance in a hallway, but she could not help it. The memory of it still had Daffy tingling to the tips of her toes.

It was most unlike her to be so affected by a gentleman guest. There had been dozens of them in the time she had lived here, and there were at least half a dozen eligible men in the house with her right now.

But none of them had looked at her the way Charles Pallister had.

It was probably because he did not know who she was. Once he realised that there was nothing to be gained by flirting with her, his attention would turn to someone else.

By the time he had arrived at her side, Daffy had managed to compose herself to reveal no trace of the anxiety she felt at his presence.

'Miss Bingham?'

She tried not to start at the sound of her own name, for it was clear that he knew exactly who she was. Then she offered a smile and a curtsey. 'And you are Mr Pallister.'

'The cousin from Gloucestershire,' he said and nodded back, bowing politely over her hand. 'It is a pleasure to meet you.'

'And you as well,' she said, then hurriedly added, 'Any family, really. I have so very little of it, you see.' Hopefully, she was not seeming over-eager.

'I have no family either. Except for this, of course.' He clasped his hands behind his back and rocked once on his heels, as if accentuating the fact that he had already run out of conversation.

She hoped he did not expect her to carry the rest of it, for she had never been any good at making small talk. She smiled politely into the silence, then looked past him, searching for someone, anyone, that might ease the awkwardness of this encounter.

'I have never been to a great house at Christmas,' he

said, glancing past her as well. 'The decorations are really quite lovely.'

'Thank you,' she said, absently.

His eyes snapped back to hers, surprised. 'Are you responsible for them?'

She nodded. 'The decoration of the house is always left to me.'

'I had thought the servants, under the direction of the lady of the house...' His voice fell away as if he was not quite sure how to finish.

She shook her head. 'The Duchess is a lovely lady. But she has never been much for managing such things.'

'I see,' he said, as if she had revealed something more than she'd thought.

'And it is no bother, really,' she added. Although, if truth were told, it was quite a bit of bother. She had spent an entire day up on ladders around the house, fluffing bows and twisting garlands.

'The result is very festive,' he added.

'Thank you,' she repeated.

They fell silent again.

'I set the menus as well,' she added, because the silence was becoming strained again.

'Hmm.' She could not decide by the tone of the sound whether he was surprised, or not surprised at all.

To her relief, a servant sounded a gong signalling them to proceed to the dining room and she looked about hurriedly, trying to decide her place in the procession.

'May I escort you in to dinner?' he said, offering an arm.

'Thank you,' she said after a moment's hesitation.

He smiled. 'You are thinking that I do not have to feel

obligated. But someone must take your arm. I see no reason why it cannot be me.'

He was right. She had been calculating their ranks and deciding whether the pair of them were appropriately matched. She was tempted to tell him that he could do better, and direct him to one of the other, younger ladies. But, since all she knew of him was that he was a distant cousin, they were suitably matched until she could quiz him about his income and make some introductions for him.

For now, she took the arm he offered and let him walk her in to dinner. When they took their seats, he was beside her again.

She gave him an exasperated smile. It was not that she objected to his company, precisely. She was just not used to having so much polite male attention.

She should not have been surprised when Mr Pallister sat beside her at the table. As he had pointed out, there was no reason to believe that his rank was that much different from her own. But it confused her that the table was so easily balanced when she had assumed this late addition of a new guest would throw the arrangement into disarray.

Silently, she counted heads, trying to think who she could possibly have forgotten.

'What are you doing?' Mr Pallister sounded faintly amused, and she realised that she must have been bobbing her head as she counted.

She tried to come up with a plausible lie that would conceal the amount of interest she had in the week's matchmaking, then gave up. 'Your arrival was announced at the last minute and I was concerned that it would unbalance the table. But I seem to have miscounted.'

'You were responsible for the seating arrangements,' he said, surprised.

'Well...' she said, giving a flutter of her hands. It should have been the hostess's job to do such things. But she could almost hear the Duchess's voice when she had passed on the duty echoing again now:

Daffy, you are so much better at these things than I...

The man next to her glanced around the room, then announced, 'It seems perfectly fine to me.'

'Who could I have forgotten?' she said, almost to herself.

'Did you include yourself in the plans?' he asked, still sounding amused.

'I...' She never counted herself. She did not signify when she meant to spend most of the evening with her knitting, sitting out of the dancing and games.

'It is most kind of you to be concerned about the happiness of the other guests and myself,' he said, taking a sip of wine. 'But I do not think we need to be overly concerned about it. I am quite happy where I am.'

She could feel herself blushing. He glossed over the matter with such a skilful compliment that she felt not the least bit embarrassed at having rendered her own person as a nought on the party list. But it did make her feel a strange little flutter to know that he'd had no trouble seeing her. Sometimes it seemed that so few people did.

She took her first sip of soup, which was, as always here, excellent. She could see by his smile as he ate that he agreed. 'You will enjoy this meal,' she said with confidence. 'The Twinden kitchens are very fine. And for Christmas, Cook always outdoes herself.'

'That is...'

Behind them, there was a faint clearing of a throat,

and one of the footmen thrust a napkin in her direction, setting it just to the side of the plate. There was a hastily pencilled note along the hem. She read it with a sigh and eased her chair back, preparing to stand.

'Where are you going?' Charles said. 'The first course has barely arrived.'

'There is something wrong with the wine at the head of the table,' she said with a sad shake of her head. 'Either it is corked, or the wrong vintage.'

'Surely the footman can handle it,' he said with a surprised smile.

'The Duchess wishes me to see about it,' she said, smiling back, and stood up.

'Does she do this sort of thing often?' he asked, his smile disappearing.

'Not often. The servants are normally very precise, especially at meals such as this. If you will excuse me?' She gave a single, regretful look at the soup remaining in her bowl, and headed for the butler's pantry to take care of the problem.

Charles resisted the urge to toss his napkin aside and follow her. If she was the thief her family claimed that she was, this was the perfect opportunity for her to go searching guest rooms for stray baubles. It was also the worst time for him to chase after her without causing a great deal of disruption to their lowly end of the table.

He reached casually across to her plate and retrieved the napkin, reading the message on it and assuring himself that it was exactly what she had said it was. It appeared that Miss Bingham was responsible for most of the unpleasant and technical hostess duties and was only allowed to participate in the party if she danced attendance on the Duchess. He was not sure why, but he'd found it particularly irksome that she had been unconsciously pairing him off with debutantes, simply because he had arrived alone. It was not as if he was looking for a wife. But if he were, he would be quite capable of choosing for himself, and it would not be some green girl. It would be someone…

Well, he was not quite sure who it might be. But he was capable of making the decision for himself. And none of this answered the question of what he was to do about Miss Bingham.

She did not appear again for the rest of the meal, leaving him to make polite conversation with the vicar's wife on his other side, telling elaborate lies to the good woman about his family connections and his life in Gloucestershire.

Eventually the meal ended, and the party retired to the ballroom for dancing. The pianoforte had been tuned, and a creditable musician found, probably by Miss Bingham, to entertain the guests.

When he looked about the room, he found that Miss Bingham had re-joined the party without his noticing. She was in a seat on the far side of the room with the chaperones. Her knitting was in her lap and one of the many household cats was twining around her ankles and eyeing the silk thread trailing from her needles. She was doing her best to appear focused on her craft, as if she did not want to spoil anyone's fun by calling attention to her wallflower status. But Charles noticed the toe of the slipper that peeped out from under the hem of her modest gown was tapping in time to the music.

She stared down at the cat with a half-smile and he saw her mouth form the words, 'Don't you dare.'

The cat gave her a sceptical look, as if he did not believe she would lift a finger to him, should he become tangled in her work. Then he recommenced rubbing against her ankle.

Charles walked across the ballroom towards her, trying not to focus on the amount of ankle revealed as the cat pawed at her skirt. He cleared his throat to announce his presence, then glanced down at the cat and said, 'He seems to like you.'

She looked up, trying to contain her surprise at his appearance. 'I beg your pardon?'

'The cat. He seems to enjoy your company. I thought I might join you as well.'

'Oh.' Now, she looked back to her knitting, feigning a need for concentration. But it was clear by the smooth clicking of the thin metal needles that she was skilled enough to manage any distraction. As he watched, an elaborate pattern of red and white was growing as if by magic.

'Is that a gift?' he asked, wondering if it would be possible to finish such a complicated thing before Christmas.

'For myself,' she said without dropping a stitch. 'I have nowhere to carry it and scant little to put in it, but it is Christmas and I bought a few balls of thread for my own use.'

It made him wonder if this was the only gift she had been given. Such neglect might explain her desire to steal what she was denied. But for the moment, she seemed satisfied with the knitting. 'It is lovely,' he said. 'Or it will be, once you are finished.'

This made her smile. 'Are you an authority on ladies' reticules?'

'No. But I assume that you are. And that you would not make something you did not enjoy.'

She gave a small grimace of agreement but did not stop knitting.

'It surprises me that you would work on it when there is a dance going on,' he said.

'Idle hands are the Devil's workshop,' she said, then made another face, as if she realised that she sounded like the spinster he had been expecting to find. Then she looked up with an apologetic smile. 'A project makes the hours pass more quickly.'

'So does dancing,' he said, gesturing at the people standing up behind him.

'I imagine it does,' she said, giving him a puzzled smile.

For a moment he wondered if she was so hopelessly out of touch that she did not recognise the offer, or if, perhaps, he was so out of practice in Society that it had been unrecognisable. Then he held out a hand to make his intentions clear. 'Will you stand up with me, Miss Bingham?'

For a moment, she could not seem to find an answer. Had it really been so long since she had been anything more than a chaperone that she did not know how to have fun?

'Miss Bingham?' he repeated, reaching for her hand.

'Yes,' she said, breathlessly. Then she set aside her knitting and rose, taking his hand and allowing him to lead her onto the floor.

Daffy took Charles Pallister's hand, trying not to be a goose about something that should be simple and easy to understand. It was nothing more than a waltz, but, after so many years sitting to the side, it felt as intimate as a kiss to her.

But as they danced he was looking into her eyes as if there was something he wished to discover about her that no one else knew. She stared back, lost in the silvery depths of his, suddenly very aware of his hand on the centre of her back.

When was the last time a man had touched her in any but the most casual way? He was holding her as if she was something precious, gently but with a firm grip as if he did not want to lose her, now that she was in his arms. It made her feel small and delicate, which was very strange indeed.

When she thought of herself, which she rarely did, it was as someone capable of navigating her tiny slice of the world without a hand on her elbow to keep her from stumbling. But now she wondered if it might be nice to walk arm in arm, once in a while. She still would not trip, but how delightful to think that someone was there to note the fact.

He was smiling contentedly at her, as if her presence was all that was required to make him happy. She allowed one satisfied sigh and then made a point of looking past him, refusing to let her mind be carried away by what was likely nothing more than a polite quirk of the lips. There was no reason to believe that he would not look the same way at the next woman he danced with. And, since he would be gone in little over a week, a future between them was unlikely.

But that did not keep her from wondering how he had come to be here in the first place. 'How do we share a family connection?' she blurted, trying to put an end to the romantic silence she was imagining.

'Eh?' He seemed surprised by the question, starting as if he too had been spinning fantasies.

'You are a cousin, and so am I. But I have never heard of your branch of the family, nor did I know we had people in Gloucestershire.'

'I am from the Duchess's family,' he replied.

'Oh.' And yet she was sure that he had been described as a relative of the Duke. 'I am sure it is nice for her to have you visit.'

He laughed as if the idea had not occurred to him. 'I had not thought of it. I am not often greeted so warmly when I visit places.'

'Really?' she said. How odd that such a well-mannered and—dared she think it—handsome gentleman would not be welcome.

He spun her around, making her gasp in delight, then leaned forward as if about to admit to a dark secret. 'It is my profession.'

'You have a profession?' she said, surprised to find that he admitted to working at all.

'I am a thief taker,' he replied, touching his finger to his lips to warn her that it was a secret.

She stumbled on the next step, as if her dreams had been a solid floor collapsing beneath her. Then, as she always did, she got a hold of her emotions and found the rhythm without anyone's help. 'How interesting.'

'It is nice to have a few days where I need not concern myself with the indiscretions of others,' he said, ignoring her misstep.

'I am so happy for you,' she said weakly, resisting the urge to feel her pockets to make sure they were empty. 'And how did you find such a job?'

'I am the second son of an office clerk. My parents

had little to give me or my brother but the conviction that, with a proper education, we would be able to make our own way in the world. My brother and I both read for the law. But while he went on to practise it, I was more interested in enforcement.'

'I see,' she said, not seeing at all. 'But I thought you had no family. Your brother?'

'Has gone to the Americas,' he said almost too quickly, as if the absence was part of a story he did not wish to tell.

'You must miss him,' she added, embarrassed to have brought it up.

'It is an old wound, and fully healed,' he said, then changed the subject. 'And it has been delightful to dance with you, of course,' he said, beaming at her as the music came to a stop. 'I did not expect you to be such a charming partner.'

'Thank you.' She smiled back, for she could not help it. But she feared there was an edge of nervousness to the expression that she could not control. Thief takers were often dangerous men, barely more honest than the men they caught.

But she could find nothing frightening about the man at her side. And, though the family he claimed seemed humble, he had the Duchess as a branch on the same tree. He was leading her back to her chair now and shooing the cat from the cushion so she could sit down.

'May I get you a glass of punch?' he asked, offering a bow and another smile.

'I would like that very much,' she said, watching as he crossed the floor to the punchbowl. She liked it even better that he did not offer her lemonade instead, as if she was too young or too old to handle spirits. Right now she needed something strong to settle her mind.

The dancing had been delightful. She had never waltzed before, and it was quite magical that her first time had been with Charles Pallister. From the moment they had seen each other, she had felt a connection. Then he had sought her out before dinner, and been seated at her side, even though she had done nothing to arrange that.

And then he had made the strange comment about not expecting her to be as charming as she was. It implied that someone had spoken to him about her, of all people. And that she had exceeded his expectations.

Which meant that the Duchess had rearranged the seating specifically so the two of them could be together, and the Duke had likely talked about her when he had greeted Mr Pallister in his study.

She sucked a surprised breath through her teeth. They were matchmaking for her. It was the only thing that made sense. After all this time, they had finally found someone deemed acceptable husband material and had thrown the two of them together at Christmas to see if they would suit.

A part of her wanted to be angry at the manipulation of her life. But far more of her was flattered that they had bothered. She had been quite used to being thought beyond the pale as far as marriage was concerned. But Cousin Charles was both handsome and personable and she could not say she minded the attempt.

Even thinking about it, she could feel her cheeks growing hot and pink. Not only was he the sort of man whose head did not seem easily turned by the young and pretty girls who were visiting, but he had also been paying very specific attention to her.

She could not remember a time, even in her first and

only season, where a man had come across a full room to speak specifically to her. And as they had danced, she knew it had not been her imagination after all. He had been staring into her eyes, trying to make a connection.

His occupation was problematic, of course. But the Twindens must not have mentioned her curious problem or he would have shunned her from the first. Perhaps, if she were living somewhere else, she would no longer be troubled by her curious affliction. If she could manage to control herself for a few short days, she might never have to tell him about it at all.

And if she could not? Then there was no reason to spoil things a moment before it was absolutely necessary. She did not have to confess each ugly detail of her life until she was sure that what he felt for her was more than courtesy. Everyone was allowed latitude at Christmas. Even someone like her.

Chapter Three

The next morning, Charles was summoned to the Duke's study and informed that the Dowager Countess of Stanton was missing a diamond eardrop, and her daughter, Lady Priscilla, a string of pearls.

He cursed quietly to himself while promising the peer that all would be taken care of today. He had let Miss Bingham escape during dinner, but what choice had he in that? And, since it did not seem fair to keep her in the dark about his identity, he had warned her while they'd danced so she might be on her best behaviour.

She had not run in the opposite direction when he'd announced his business. But neither had she been unaffected. A part of him had expected her to drop his hand and run, just from the knowledge that he had a job. Living with a duke, she could not have been used to consorting with the working class.

The fear of rejection had been surprisingly acute. He was aware that he should feel nothing. In the past, he had viewed the thieves he was hired to chase as jobs and not individuals. But there was something about Miss Bingham, a combination of beauty and competence, that broke through any defences that he had set for himself. It made the job much more difficult.

Watching the way she had been treated at dinner, he had a hard time faulting her for taking revenge in small ways against the people who oppressed her. If he could convince her to give up the items she had taken, they might be able to find other ways to salve her bruised feelings.

Another dance was called for, at a minimum. He had enjoyed dancing with her. She had been feather-light as he'd spun her around the room and fitted in his arms as if she was a missing part of him. The music had not lasted for longer than five minutes, but it might have been a life-time for all the plans he had made for the two of them.

Initially, he had thought he could pretend that the waltz was part of his job. She could not trouble others while standing up with a man who had nothing worth taking. But he had not needed to ply her with punch, nor to talk to her for the rest of the evening, ignoring the other guests. He could have watched her just as well from the other side of the room.

Better, perhaps, for it seemed she had found a way to steal despite his efforts to prevent her from doing so. She could not have managed it all at dinner, for he could swear the Dowager had been wearing both her diamond eardrops during the meal. But one had gone missing, all the same. How had she done it?

Or perhaps it was not a case of how could she? Perhaps the question was, *who else had a motive?*

He smiled to himself. The missing jewels were a co-nundrum, almost as much as Daphne Bingham herself. And he could not resist mysteries.

* * *

The entertainment for the night was to be a tableau vivant of the muses dancing for Apollo, and as usual, Daffy was left to organise the details of it. To this end, she spent the whole afternoon gathering every spare bedsheet in the house, and a variety of pins and ribbons to bind them up into creditable Greek tunics that could be worn over the girls' gowns.

Much to the disappointment of the young ladies, she was not allowing any nonsense about showing bare legs for the sake of historical accuracy. She agreed that they could dispense with slippers if they so wished, but stockings would remain in place and the hems of gowns would not be hiked any higher than mid-ankle. Nor would she allow anyone to strip to shifts under the assumption that a length of linen in any way compensated for the lack of proper clothing.

This meant that the scene presented would be closer to a bunch of proper young ladies wrapped in sheets than the wild abandon of the picture. But it was necessary for someone to be the level head in the room. And, as always, that role fell to Daffy.

After supper, when the tableau was presented, the gentlemen clapped politely and declared the girls posing to be worthy likenesses for the goddesses they portrayed. The ladies blushed and giggled and accepted their compliments. And then they went back to the parlour that had been set aside as a dressing room to divest themselves of their shrouds.

As the ladies removed the wreaths from their hair and set about returning their dress to their normal, impeccable state, there was a commotion on the far side of the room.

'I set it here. I am sure of it.'

'Well, it is not here now. And neither is the bracelet I told you to watch for me.'

The Misses Felton were only a year apart in age and, while old enough to be out, had not completely rid themselves of schoolroom squabbling.

'Ladies,' Daffy said in her best warning tone. 'What seems to be the trouble?'

The younger of the two, Miss Sybella Felton, pointed an accusing finger at her sister. 'When we dressed for the tableau, I gave my jewellery into Ophelia's care. And now it is missing.'

'I set the ring and the bracelet right here,' the elder said, patting the top of a side table. 'But they are both gone.'

Daffy felt her throat tightening, and it was a full ten seconds before she could bring herself to speak. When she did, she said, 'Have you looked under the table? Perhaps they were swept to the floor in the rush to leave the room.'

It was a logical explanation, and really, the most likely one. Even so, she surreptitiously wiped her hands down her sides, feeling for any unexpected lumps in her own pockets, and was relieved to find none.

'They are not on the floor, or any of the other tables,' Ophelia insisted. 'And I am sure of where I put them.'

'Then they must have been picked up by mistake,' Daffy said, flushing with guilt even as she accused others. 'I am sure they will turn up by tomorrow.'

The girls looked at each other doubtfully and returned to their mutual recriminations, Daffy's consolation forgotten.

When the Feltons and the rest of the girls had gone

to join the gentlemen in the parlour, Daffy lingered behind, searching under chairs and behind cushions, praying that, just once, the items would reappear in the place they were meant to be. But tonight, at least, her wish was not granted. The jewellery was nowhere to be found.

Chapter Four

$\approx\!\!\!\approx\!\!\!\approx$

Miss Bingham was avoiding him.

He was not absolutely sure of the fact, since there had been no dancing the previous evening and therefore no chance to stand up with her. But when he had finished his interview with Twinden, he had tried to search her out, only to be told that she and the other ladies were far too busy preparing the evening's entertainment to mingle with the gentlemen.

She had been absent at dinner as well, running errands for the Duchess, as she had on the previous evening. He was tempted to walk to the head of the table and remind his employers that if they wished him to keep Miss Bingham on the straight and narrow, they needed to stop giving her opportunities to evade him.

Today, the rest of the party had left the house for sledding and skating, which gave Charles a perfect opportunity to search Miss Bingham's room for the missing jewellery. But as he passed through the main hall on the way to the stairs he discovered that, today of all days, Miss Bingham was easy to find. She was standing in the middle of the hall, supervising the servants in setting up the welcoming display of treats that would await the guests on their return.

The air was heavy with the spiced steam rising from silver bowls of mulled wine. At the centre of the table, Miss Bingham was arranging a towering display of oranges and walnuts ringed with greenery. At her feet, several of the house's cats were stalking in circles and generally making nuisances of themselves.

As she stepped back to admire the finished work, she walked into his arms, then started forward in surprise, causing one of the nuts to roll out of place and spoil the effect.

Charles snatched it before it could roll off the table and put it carefully back in its spot. 'Not out skating with the rest of the party?'

She cast a wistful glance in the direction of the windows before returning to her work. 'There is far too much to do here for me to waste the day on the pond, Mr Pallister.'

He caught her by the hand, pulling her away from the table, and gave her his warmest smile. 'Please. You must call me Charles. We are practically family, after all.'

She gave him a strained smile in return. 'Very well, Charles.'

'And I will call you Daphne,' he said, since she had not offered.

'Daffy,' she corrected automatically.

He raised an eyebrow and stared at her silently.

'It is what all my friends call me,' she said.

'It does not sound very friendly of them,' he said, and continued to stare at her, hoping for a response.

'It does not bother me,' she said hurriedly.

He wondered if that was true. Of course, it really

did not matter if she cared or not. It was unlikely that her complaints would change anything. 'Well, I prefer Daphne,' he said, looking her slowly up and down. 'She was a nymph beautiful enough to tempt a god.'

'I don't think…' She was probably about to say that it didn't suit her.

He cut her off. 'If I were you, I would not struggle against my compliments. My career has made me extremely tenacious, and I am not liable to be talked out of my opinions. It is probably for the best that you accept it and move on.'

'Thank you,' she said softly. A blush was colouring her cheeks. If possible, it made her even more attractive.

'And you are pretty, you know. If you do not realise it, it is something you deserve to be told,' he added. 'Frankly, I am amazed to find a woman like you not yet married.'

At first, she had no answer to this, other than a deepening of the blush. 'No one offered,' she said, then added, 'and I was needed here, of course.'

'Do you like living here?' he asked, fixing her with the sort of direct look he used when questioning prisoners. 'If someone had offered for you, would you have left happily, or reluctantly?' It was an innocent question and one that he would have asked any culprit, if he thought it might explain the reason for their crimes. But waiting for the answer left him feeling strangely nervous, as if he were not talking about her motives at all.

Her eyes were wide, as if she had never thought of the matter before. Then she said, 'Even when I had my season, I did not think leaving here was something I needed to worry about. I am just not the sort…'

Charles did his best to hide his frustration at this passive response to perfectly sensible questions. 'Did the Duke and Duchess offer a dowry?'

'They paid for my gowns,' she said quickly.

'So the answer is no,' he replied.

'They provided the trip to London, as well. And allowed me to accompany Honoria to Almack's when she came out five years later.'

'As a chaperone,' he pointed out. 'They did not get vouchers for you?'

'I was not the sort to be considered a catch,' she said primly.

'Nor did they offer a second season.'

'A second London season would have been very expensive.'

'Not so much so if you have a London property, as Twinden does, and a reason to be there other than launching a debutante,' he reminded her. 'Attending Parliament, for example.'

'But when the Duke and Duchess go to town, someone is needed to see to the running of the house,' she reminded him.

'They are called servants,' he countered. 'And you are a member of the family.'

'A poor relation,' she corrected him. 'Because of that, I do not expect much,' she said quietly, as if she did not enjoy the feelings that his questioning had raised in her.

'That is probably for the best,' he replied, 'since you did not receive much.'

She wiped her hands on the apron she wore, as if to signal the end of the discussion. 'My season was a long time ago,' she said, her eyes narrowing with annoyance. 'I have not thought about it in ages.'

'But that does not mean you have not thought of marrying,' he said. Was she really satisfied with such a small and unrewarding life? If so, why was she stealing? 'There are men to be found outside of London. A failed season need not set the course of your entire life,' he reminded her. 'Surely you have hopes for the future.'

'Future?' she said with an incredulous smile. 'Mr Pallister…'

'Charles,' he reminded her.

'Charles,' she amended, 'I am twenty-seven years old.'

'And that is a far sight from dead,' he said. 'You are likely to live more years than that before you pass on to Paradise. What are you going to do with the time other than fetching and carrying for the Duchess of Twinden?'

She turned away from him, busying herself with the table again, picking up a tray of cups and setting them down so that they perfectly matched the alignment of the tray on the opposite side of the punchbowls. 'I do not fetch and carry, as you put it, Mr Pallister. There is something called "knowing one's place". It is rather like "minding one's own business". I am well aware of both these concepts. Perhaps you might consider acquainting yourself with them.' Then she untied her apron, tossed it on the bench beside the front door and stalked up the stairs and away.

Daphne walked down the upper hall, hands balled into fists of frustration. Why did he have to bring up all the thoughts that she had done her best not to have? He wanted to know her plans for the future…?

She laughed bitterly, then looked around to be sure that no one had noticed her doing it. The last thing she needed was to display behaviour that reinforced the idea that Daffy Bingham was a little bit mad. The Duke had hinted that action must be taken if she could not manage to control herself. She was not sure what he had meant but she knew that Bedlam was the most likely place to send someone so ungrateful that she stole from the family that had kept her safe.

No matter what was happening, no matter what Charles suspected, she would not be angry with him or the Duke and Duchess. It was important that she be the calm, level-headed chaperone, the helper ready to fix whatever mess others had created. What good was she to anyone, otherwise?

But still, the anger bubbled inside her like hot water. She walked hurriedly towards her bedroom, where she could close the door and have her display of pique unobserved.

The gall of the man for asking her the obvious. She had no plans and there was no point in making them. She had been drifting through life, trusting that tomorrow would be like yesterday, and that the future would be the same as the past if she could just manage to behave herself. The only thing that would change was that she would grow older and further away from any hope that she might have had for a husband and children.

Thinking about that made her feel the exact opposite of what she wanted to feel: hopeless and desperate and out of control.

She felt silly to think she'd entertained thoughts about the Duke and Duchess matchmaking.

What did this interloper mean by asking her so many questions? And what did he mean by dancing with her and smiling at her and making her think of things that were best forgotten? He would be gone by Twelfth Night and she would most likely never see him again. In his wake, he would leave dissatisfaction, and she would be even lonelier and more confused than before.

She opened the door, walked through and closed it quietly behind her, imagining the satisfaction of a slam that she did not dare attempt. If she had her way, the upper floors would be ringing with the sound of it. People would poke their heads out of their own rooms in shock, then nod in sympathy at someone as wronged as she had been.

She thought of her missing dinners, imagining the taste of the courses that she had not eaten on that first night. By the time she had finished speaking with the butler, and assuring herself that the wine was fine, she had missed the majority of the meal and made do with a plate of cold leftovers from the dishes that had returned to the kitchen. There had been no need for her to leave the table. Last night, she had been stuck with the servants, watching each plate and bottle as they left the kitchen to make sure there would be no more complaints from the head of the table.

The rational part of her mind assured her that the Duchess meant no harm in what she did. She simply could not manage to be any other way. But it was much harder to be kind and rational on an empty stomach.

Perhaps she should lie down. But there was a black and white cat lounging in the centre of the bed. She shooed it out of the way, then picked up the pillow where it had been sitting, to brush off the stray hairs. Then she glanced down, horrified. There, in a jumbled heap, were the mismatched eardrops, the rings and beads that had gone missing over the last few days.

After the last time, she had sworn to the Duke that it would never happen again. She had been careful to check herself after each activity and made sure that pockets and dressing table were empty of things that did not belong to her. She even read from the Bible each night, to remind herself that it was a sin to steal.

And yet, apparently she had done it again. She had read in a book in the library about people so mad that they took things for the thrill of it, and others who committed crimes without knowing that it had happened. They were mad too, of course. And, though she did not feel as if she was losing her mind, she had to admit, in her heart of hearts, that she was not happy here. She could find no other explanation for what was happening than that she was somehow acting out of spite.

If she could not remember doing a thing, how was she to guard against it happening whenever she got upset? She did not want the belongings of others. What need did she have for mismatched jewellery? She certainly did not need another scolding from the Duke, nor did she know what she would do if he put her out, as he sometimes threatened to do.

And what would Charles Pallister think if he found she was the one who was stealing? To choose a profession such as his, he would have to be devoid of sympathy. There would be no more fond glances and shared jokes if she pleaded guilty to breaking the one commandment in his purview.

She sat on the edge of the bed, staring at the pile of baubles beside her. She could not be caught with them. If there was talk of searching the rooms, she knew full well that hers would be amongst the first visited.

She would have to find somewhere to put them until she could find a way to return them quietly to their owners.

For the moment, she scooped the lot into a pocket,

Then she checked in the mirror to be sure that her gown was not pulled out of line by the weight, and made her way back downstairs to hide the loot.

Chapter Five

He had made her angry.

Charles did not feel the least bit sorry about it. It was better that she learn to face her anger than to pretend it didn't exist. And Daphne Bingham, for all her polite smiles and quiet speech, was one of the angriest people he had ever met.

She was also a most intriguing creature, much smarter than the sort of people he was used to dealing with. If she was truly guilty, his announcement of his profession had done nothing to throw her off her bad habit of taking things that did not belong to her. Trinkets had continued to disappear with annoying regularity and he had been unable to stop the loss or detect how she was doing it.

He was not unfamiliar with the subtle ways of cut-purses and pickpockets, nor was he easily fooled by sleight of hand or misdirection. But he had never seen a success-ful thief with such still hands and placid demeanour.

She must be waiting until she was alone in the ladies' retiring room with her victims. Unless the punch here was strong enough to render him blind, she was not steal-ing while in the common rooms with him.

It was a conundrum. How was he to stop her if she was practising her craft in places where a gentleman was not allowed to go? And if he did manage to catch her, what was he to do with her? If, indeed, it *was* her.

He doubted that the Duke and Duchess truly wanted him to drag her away. They would lose too much free labour. It was clear that the family had plans for Miss Bingham that had nothing to do with the normal desires of a young lady. Some day there would be children of the Viscount and Lady Honoria to be tended. He easily imagined those duties falling to Aunt *Daffy*.

It served them right that they saved money on servants, only to spend it on a thief catcher when their choice of help ran amuck.

It was doubtful that he would change the minds of Twinden and his wife in regard to Miss Bingham, but he had hopes that she could change for herself. It was clear, by her reactions to a few simple questions, that she was not happy here. He had but to present her with an alternative and see to it that she took it.

He glanced up the stairs and saw her descending with none of the bravado with which she had ascended a few minutes ago. She was walking hurriedly, her eyes darting from side to side as if fearing observation. If she'd turned and announced that she was up to mischief, she could not have been more obvious. So he trailed behind her as she turned and walked into the library, where the kissing bough was.

He was only a few steps behind her when she passed through the doorway and arrived in time to see her thrust a hand into her pocket and produce the lost jewellery, heading towards one of the matched vases on either side of the fireplace.

He cleared his throat.

She whirled about, terrified at having been caught.

'What do you have there?' he asked, as if it were not obvious to both of them.

She stared down into her own hands as if she could not quite believe what she was holding. Then she sank to her knees, holding her diamond-dripping hands out to him as if she expected him to bind them and cart her away. 'I swear, I do not mean to do it. I do not even know how it happens.'

'If you do not know how it happens, how do you know you are guilty?' he asked, honestly curious.

She paused, confused, looking down into her hands. 'Everyone in the house knows that I do this. Lost things are always found in my room. If I am not taking them, how else could I have come by these?'

It was an excellent question, one with an answer that she might not like to hear. 'I suppose that the Duke and Duchess are the ones accusing you.'

Her lovely eyes were round and frightened. She nodded hesitantly.

'I thought as much,' he said. And now they were seeking to keep her off balance and frightened so she would consider making a life for herself outside of this house. Worse yet, they thought they could use him as their instrument.

Before he could reassure her, there was the sound of the skaters returning and someone approaching from the hall.

'Here!' he said, scooping jewellery out of her hands. 'Give it all to me.'

'What?' For a moment, she was too shocked to act.

'I will explain later,' he said, dumping it all into a

vase beside the fireplace. Then he grabbed her hand and pulled her to her feet, turning towards the door and smiling broadly at the people who were entering.

Skating and fresh air had done nothing to improve the mood of the Dowager. Since the loss of her eardrop, her face had been set in a perpetual scowl. Her daughter fluttered at her side, making solicitous noises as if trying to keep the peace.

'Any sign of the missing diamond or the pearls?' Charles said, his face neutral.

'The servants promised to search the rooms while we were gone,' Lady Priscilla said with a disapproving shake of her head. 'But they say they have found nothing.'

'I do not know why they are bothering with the common rooms,' the Dowager snapped. 'It should be the servants' quarters that they are examining.'

'It might not be them at all,' Daphne said in a weak voice. 'It might be an accident of some kind.'

'Are you saying I am careless?' the woman said, bristling.

'Of course not, my lady,' Daphne said hurriedly. 'I am sure it is no fault of yours.'

'Very well,' the lady said, giving her a look that clearly said she was unaccustomed to being questioned. 'But I am going to speak to the Duke about this.' Then she left the room in a huff.

Now that they were alone again, Charles dipped his hand into the vase and pulled out the diamond that the Dowager had been looking for.

'I honestly do not remember taking them,' Daphne said, shaking her head. 'They were in my room, under the pillow on my bed. But, for the life of me, I have no idea how or when they got there.' She looked at him, desperate for understanding. 'I do not want them. But there they were. This is not the first time that this has happened, and I fear it will not be the last. But I never intend to do it.'

Strange as her story was, he could sense she wasn't lying.

'What were you doing down here with them?' he asked.

'I had hoped, if someone found them here, it would be put down to one of the children playing tricks. No one would take the blame and the matter would be forgotten.'

'But now I will know where they came from,' he said, looking her directly in the eye.

'What do you mean to do with the knowledge?' she said, looking terrified but resigned.

What was he to do? It was a very good question. 'You have nothing to fear. I have no intention of acting against someone who has already punished themselves for the crime,' he said, giving her an encouraging smile. 'First, we must see that things get back to where they belong.'

'Can you help me?' she said, both surprised and desperate.

'Better than you know,' he said. He was not sure how he would manage it. But there was something strangely appealing about the challenge of reversing the thefts without discovery.

'Please do not tell me that you will let the servants take the blame for what I have done,' she said. 'I could not bear that.'

'I will see to it that things are put back in the correct rooms,' he said, dropping the diamond into his pocket and retrieving the rest of the jewellery that he'd hidden. When he had stowed it in his coat, he smiled at her in encouragement. 'It will all look like a horrible mistake and no one need be blamed.'

'Thank you,' she said, reaching out to take his hand.

'On one condition,' he added, unable to resist the opportunity.

'Anything,' she replied, and by the expression on her face she immediately regretted it. He did not blame her. It was never wise to allow such open-ended promises when negotiating with a gentleman.

He stepped under the mistletoe and waited.

For a moment, Daphne could not believe what he was asking of her. Such a thing had not occurred in years. She had not dared to hope that Charles Pallister would make such a suggestion, no matter how pleasant it might be. She must look a total fool, for she was sure she was staring at him and could feel her mouth gaping in surprise. But she could not seem to drag her eyes away from him. At last, she blurted out the obvious. 'You want me to kiss you?'

'That is the purpose of the kissing bough, is it not?' he said with a deceptively innocent expression. He looked up at it, then back to her. 'You say you have made the thing, and yet I suspect you've never tried it.'

'Not yet this year,' she said. It was a small lie, for it implied that there was some likelihood that she meant to use it in the future. 'And you are doing it wrong,' she said, relieved to be changing the subject.

'How so?' he asked, not budging.

'It is not for you to stand under,' she said. 'That would require a woman to kiss you.'

He glanced up again. 'And why would I not want that?'

'No girl would dare,' she said with a blush. 'It would be most unseemly.'

'But before, you said a woman would kiss me,' he said, smiling at her to make sure she knew who he was referring to. 'That would be far better than waiting for some slip of a girl.'

'It is all one and the same,' she said with a frustrated shrug. 'It is not proper for a female to make such a daring advance.'

He was staring at her now, as if waiting for her to understand something he had not actually said. Then he replied, 'If it is so improper, perhaps you should not have hung the bough at all. Or, at least, you could have included some instructions.'

She gave an exasperated huff. 'It has never been necessary before. Perhaps the problem is with the man under it.'

'Perhaps it is,' he agreed. 'Why don't you come here and show me how it is supposed to be done?'

She froze, unsure that she had heard him correctly. 'You expect me to stand under the mistletoe.'

'If you want my help,' he reminded her. 'It is that or come here and kiss me yourself,' he added in a reasonable tone. 'I have noticed that it is very difficult to get you to stand still under the thing long enough for a gentleman to make his move.'

'Only because no gentleman would want...'

To kiss a spinster. At least not out of anything other than pity. And she was not so desperate as to accept half-hearted, merciful pecks on the cheek, offered to make her feel as if she was part of the festivities.

He was staring at her again, as if listening to her

thoughts. 'It is a frivolous waste of time,' she said, not wanting to admit the truth.

'Perhaps it is,' he agreed. 'But it is the season for frivolity. And no one is looking. This decoration is hung conveniently out of the main rooms. No one will see if you allow yourself a moment of foolishness.' He leaned back against the door frame, arms folded, waiting.

Her heart pounded as she looked at him, which was ridiculous. He was right in that it was just a moment's fun. But this was not the time for it. His pockets were full of stolen jewellery and people were searching the house. If anyone guessed what he was doing for her, he would be as deep in scandal as she was.

'If you are worried that I mean to take advantage, you needn't be,' he said with a gentle smile. 'I am not the sort of fellow who will demand more than you are willing to give because we share a secret.'

Surprisingly, blackmail had not occurred to her. There was a trace of delicious wickedness in the idea that he might seize her and force passionate kisses upon her, and she did not think she would want to resist should he do so. But it was highly unlikely that it would happen. She was simply not the sort of woman to drive men to act rashly.

More likely, she would give him a peck on the cheek and perhaps receive a similar peck in return. Then, perhaps, she would convince him to treat the matter at hand with the seriousness it deserved.

But she had hoped for so much more, from life and from him. Still, if this was to be the only memory she was to have of the season, it would be foolish not to grasp it. Far better to have something real to dream of than to have to make it all up out of her imagination.

'Miss Bingham,' he said sternly, 'are you coming or not? We do not have all day.'

She hesitated a moment more, then wiped her damp palms on her skirt before striding towards him. She was standing beside him now, noticing how tall he was up close. She swallowed once to hide her nerves, closed her eyes and craned her neck to reach his cheek.

But it was not stubble she felt when she touched him, it was the softness of his lips on hers. Her eyes flew open to find that he had turned his head. She could feel him smiling against her.

She gasped, and her mouth opened, which was the biggest mistake yet, since he took it as an invitation to kiss her as she had never been kissed before. His tongue slipped between her parted lips, to offer a slow lick against her own.

She should pull away. It was exactly what she would have told any other girl, caught under the mistletoe. One kiss only.

But what a kiss it was. His hand cupped the back of her neck, holding her close as he explored her mouth. His other hand circled her waist, drawing her body near to his. In response, she gripped his shoulders, letting him support her as she sagged against him, closing her eyes again.

And then he swept her off her feet.

Up until the moment it happened, she had thought the phrase nothing more than an expression. But he gripped her firmly at waist and shoulders and made the swift quarter turn of a natural dancer, bending her back in his arms until one of her feet was waving in the air and the other balancing on tiptoe. The kiss had already been dizzying, but now it swept over and through her like a storm-tossed wave, wiping away any reservations she had about the future. The man holding her was capable of working miracles. She could feel it in his kiss.

Then it was over, and he was setting her gently back on her feet. 'There, now. That wasn't so bad, was it?'

She should lecture him about the liberties he had taken and demand an apology. But she could not find the words. Nor could she seem to stop grinning.

He stepped out from under the kissing bough, plucking a berry and dropping it into her hand. Then he gave her a rakish smile, patted the pocket that held the jewellery, and walked away.

She stood there, dumbstuck, before remembering to step out of the doorway herself before someone saw her and gave her another kiss and spoiled everything. Anything else would pale in comparison to what had just happened.

Charles walked down the hall away from the library, revisiting the urge to whistle. A woman who looked like Daphne Bingham should not be so surprised by a simple kiss. She should be showered with them daily.

The fact that he had been the one to shock her made the kiss doubly sweet. He could not help but think of other pleasures that she had not yet experienced and the possibility that she might be persuadable.

But first, he needed to fulfil his part of the bargain and see that the missing items got back to where they belonged. He climbed the stairs and ambled after the distraught Dowager and her daughter, tut-tutting and displaying the proper and useless curiosity of a nosey gentleman as they were shown bedrooms of footmen and chambermaids, and even the private sitting room of a quietly irate housekeeper, and it was proven to them that the servants had nothing to do with the losses.

The Duchess offered an apologetic shake of her head to make sure the housekeeper continued in her silence, and then shot Charles a desperate look and announced that the items were likely gone for good.

Charles cleared his throat. 'Are you sure that you have searched your own rooms?'

'Are we sure?' barked the Dowager, glaring at him. 'We would not have the household in an uproar if we were not sure that the things were gone.'

'For the sake of thoroughness, it might be wise to look one more time,' he said mildly. 'I am particularly good at hide-and-seek. Perhaps the talent extends…'

The Dowager looked ready to explode, but the Duchess laid a soothing hand on her shoulder and they returned to the first floor and the guest rooms. Once inside the Dowager's room, he touched his finger to his chin for a moment, then opened the wardrobe and thrust himself, head and shoulders, inside it, coming back out a moment later with a diamond eardrop in his hand.

The Dowager gasped, one part gratitude and one part embarrassment. 'How did you…?'

'It was hooked in one of the lace ruffles of the gown you wore,' he said, smiling. 'I could see how you might not have noticed it when you got ready for bed.'

'Well,' the Dowager replied.

'Well, indeed,' he said, then looked at the Duchess. 'What else has been reported missing?'

It was suggested that he find Lady Priscilla's pearls next. He questioned her about her movements when last she had seen them, then produced those from a floral arrangement in the ballroom. Then, a ring and a bracelet were found folded amongst the sheets used for tableau costumes, and the Feltons declared their daughters most foolish for the loss of them.

To prevent the gentlemen from becoming too smug at the ladies' foolishness, he discovered a gold earring in the boot of one of them, and another's missing stickpin in a vest pocket.

The one room he made sure was totally empty belonged to Miss Bingham, who, as far as he knew, was still in the library, afraid to move.

Once his pockets were empty and everything was restored to its rightful owner, the audience that had gathered around him declared it the best entertainment of the day, and suggestions were made for a rousing game of hunt the slipper in the parlour.

He wished them well, declaring himself exhausted and ready for a glass of brandy and a nap. Then he retired to his room to contemplate Miss Daphne Bingham's future. If she hadn't had the dubious help of her loving family, she would have been married ages ago.

It was time that someone corrected that mistake. He had not come to this house with matrimony on his mind, but after the kiss in the library he could not seem to stop thinking about it. And what better way to stop this supposed thief than to take her permanently into his custody and take her from the house with him?

Chapter Six

That night at dinner, the Duke offered a toast to Mr Pallister, the gentleman who had so miraculously solved all the mysterious disappearances.

If Daphne noticed the Duke staring at her in disapproval, she was the only one who saw. All the same, the fact made her feel uneasy for the conversation that awaited her after Twelfth Night when the guests would be gone and she would be forced to account for herself.

There would be no Cousin Charles to protect her when that happened. In a few days, he would be gone from here and she would never see him again. The fact should not have mattered at all to her. Their interaction had been pleasant enough, but there was no reason to read any hidden meaning into a dance, a few conversations and a kiss.

But just the thought of what they had shared so far made her body tremble with excitement. When she had been alone in her room, she had imagined what it might be like to have him lying beside her, his arms reaching to hold her and his lips on her skin.

She must not think of such things at the dinner table. To cool her blood, she concentrated on his departure. But it left her feeling panicked, as if an opportunity was slipping away before she even knew what it was. Why would she want to see more of the man who had pried into her business and badgered her relentlessly this afternoon on the subject of her happiness?

But that same man, when presented with her most dangerous problem, had solved it in a way that had made everyone happy. And the only thing he had expected from her in return was a kiss.

What a kiss it had been. No matter how she tried to forget, her mind replayed the moment, over and over. What she'd experienced was more intimate than anything she'd put a stop to when guarding the young ladies and gentlemen giggling under the mistletoe. When it was over, she had felt as if she was awakening from a long sleep. Tonight, everything around her was magical. The colours seemed brighter, the laughter more infectious and the food more delicious.

'More wine?' he said from beside her, topping up her glass before the footman had even noticed her lack.

'Thank you,' she said, embarrassed by the breathiness in her voice and the flush on her cheeks.

'Will you be dancing this evening, Daphne?' The question was presented innocently enough, but there was something in his smile that hinted at a future in his arms.

'I think I might, Mr Pallister,' she said, wishing she had the nerve to call him Charles.

'Then you must promise me two dances, at least. And I wish to reserve the waltz now, before anyone steps in front of me.'

The ridiculous suggestion that he had rivals would have annoyed her this afternoon. But tonight, she could almost believe it might be true. 'You know that no one else is clamouring for that opportunity,' she said, smiling down into her plate.

'Only because none of the other gentlemen have realised what a superb dancer you are,' he replied. 'We will waltz. And perhaps later I shall see you in the library. I have been meaning to investigate the collection. This house is really full of the most delightful entertainments, wouldn't you say?'

She coughed into her wine before composing herself and taking a long, slow sip. Had he just suggested a liaison in the library? No one had ever been so forward with her before. In truth, no one had ever been interested enough to try.

Years of careful training told her to distrust men who wanted the advantages of marriage without having to make a binding offer. If it had been Honoria who had received such an offer, Daphne would have reminded her that virtue was a pearl to be cherished. Once lost, it could never be regained.

But that had never done *her* a bit of good.

She took another deep sip of wine and remarked, 'The library here is particularly good, Mr Pallister. It is a favourite room of mine for needlework. And other diversions.' Was she actually flirting back with him? She could hardly believe her own voice.

If he was surprised, he gave no indication of it. Instead, he replied, 'I will take you at your word on that. But not until after the waltz, for I would not want to miss that.'

'Neither would I,' she agreed, and went back to her dinner.

After eating, the party retired to the ballroom, and for a time she lost sight of Charles, who moved easily through the crowd, laughing and talking, as if he had been a close member of the family for years. But, as promised, he stood up with her for the Sir Roger de Coverley, and again for the waltz.

They danced in comfortable silence tonight, and she focused on the feel of his hand at her waist, guiding her around the room as if they belonged together. When the music ended, he smiled and stared into her eyes, and it was as if they'd held a conversation, though no words had passed between them. Then he excused himself and left the room.

She would wait a few minutes and follow, for it would not do for them to be seen leaving together. But before she could reach the door, she saw the Duchess waving a handkerchief to get her attention. 'Daffy!'

She flinched at the sound of a name that had never bothered her before this week. Then she pasted a smile on her face and walked across the room to speak to the Duchess. 'Was there something you wanted, Your Grace?'

'Miss Stanhope is missing a cameo brooch,' the Duchess said.

'How unfortunate,' Daphne replied, wary.

'I thought you might know where to look,' she said with a significant glance.

She resisted the urge to check her pockets. Even if she had taken it, she would find nothing there. She never did. But her mind raced over the events of the last few hours and she could not remember being within six feet of Miss Stanhope, much less stealing her brooch. 'I have no idea,' she said and received a sceptical look from the Duchess in response.

'Perhaps you could search the house for it,' the Duch-

ess said, and raised an eyebrow in something very like
accusation.

Daphne wanted to snap that, if it was so important,
perhaps Miss Stanhope could search for it herself. It was
not as if she was responsible for every mislaid glove
and lost trinket in the house. But she had been held responsible for so many of them that it was hard for her to
mount a defence.

Instead, she decided to make use of the opportunity
presented to her. 'I will go and look,' she said with a
smile and a curtsey. Then she headed out of the ballroom to the library.

Charles paced the empty library, more nervous than
he had ever been in his life. How did one announce that
one had fallen in love with a woman that one had known
for less than three days? And yet, when he looked at her,
it felt as if it had been much longer than that.

It would not be terribly flattering to tell her that just
the thought of her made him hard. Spinsters were not
necessarily naïve, but neither were they used to being
courted in such crass terms. But surely there should be
something in his speech about physical desire. He just
could not lead with it.

It might be better to assure her that he felt she deserved more than the cold comfort she got from Twinden and his wife. The sight of her jumping each time she
was called left him simmering with anger. His life might
be more humble than she was used to, but if she would
come away from here, he might make her a queen in her
own kingdom, and not some lowly serf for the Duchess.

Or perhaps he should simply tell her that the kiss
they'd shared was everything he had hoped it would be,

and he was eager to have as many more like it as she would allow. And that there were things even better than kissing that could be shared, if she was willing to trust him.

The idea of a future with her made him smile. Was it more correct, he wondered, to address his suit to her or to the Duke, who was technically the head of her family? To her, he decided. He did not want to give the Duke a chance to refuse during something that he had meant as nothing more than a courtesy. At seven and twenty, she was more than old enough to know her own mind.

The accusations her family had weighed against her were a bit awkward, of course. But he had met many thieves in his line of work and she was the nicest one so far. If she was guilty at all, which he was strongly beginning to doubt, he suspected that it had more to do with the way she was treated here than any deep-seated criminal tendencies. If she had a man who adored her, she would have no need to steal.

And perhaps he might have no more reason to chase thieves.

He'd had no reason to question his career up until now. But returning the stolen items to their owners had been the most fun he'd had in ages and far preferable to persecuting Daphne over the loss of them. And, while he refused to think of himself as old, this time spent relaxing indoors was much more enjoyable than traipsing through the English countryside after people who did not want to be found.

His reverie was cut short as she appeared in the doorway, the light from the hall forming a nimbus around her hair that made her look even more like an angel than he already thought her.

He smiled. 'Daphne, my darling.'

She flustered. It was the only way to describe the little shake of her head and shoulders, followed by a step forward, towards him. It was as if she tried to shake off the unexpected endearment like water off feathers, while yearning to hear it again. 'Charles?' she said in a hopeful tone. But nothing followed the single word.

'Come in and shut the door behind you,' he suggested, smiling.

She glanced worriedly at the door, her hand on the knob, trying to decide if the impropriety of being alone with him in a closed room was worth the risk.

'Surely you are a capable chaperone of your own behaviour,' he said.

'I do not think it works like that,' she replied, but she smiled as she said it and shut the door.

He was across the room to her in an instant, taking her hands and pulling her after him, towards the couch by the fireplace.

Once there, she swayed forward, her eyes closed and her lips set in a half-smile as if primed for another kiss.

His plan had been to talk to her before the kissing started. She deserved some sort of gentlemanly assurance that he was not taking advantage. But the temptation was too great to resist. He took her by the shoulders, touched his lips to hers, and they sank into bliss.

This time, there was no surprise on her part as he opened her mouth and deepened the kiss. She tasted of punch and sugarplums, like Christmas itself. Her hands were feathering through his hair, her thumbs stroking his temples and tracing the planes of his face.

He could imagine coming home each night to such sweetness, and more. He allowed his hands to stray from her shoulders, down to cup the sides of her breasts, which were high and firm beneath the fabric of her gown. In response, she gave a purr of contentment and pressed herself forward, into his palms, offering herself to him.

Then they parted on a happy sigh and he whispered, 'When I was hired to come here, I had no idea that it would be such a delightful assignment.'

She pulled away, a shocked look on her face. 'You were hired?'

He could feel the smile on his own face freezing, as he became aware of the magnitude of his mistake. 'I thought you understood.'

But that was a lie.

She'd known his job. But she had known nothing about his true purpose here, and he had not wanted to spoil things by explaining it to her. He had planned to suggest marriage without telling her why he was there in the first place. He had not even told her he was from London.

'Understood what?' she said, and she could see the suspicion on her face as she slid out of his arms and further down the sofa.

He reached for her hand, trying to tug her gently back to his side. 'Before this goes any further and I say what I truly want to, there is something I must tell you.' He took another deep breath.

She took one as well, then she nodded, to give him permission to speak.

'My name is Charles Pallister, just as I told you, and it is the truth that I am a thief taker. But I am not a distant cousin or related to the family in any way.'

'Then who are you and what are you doing here?' she asked. Her smile had turned to an incredulous grimace.

'I live in London and advertise in *The Times*,' he said.

'That is likely how the Duke and Duchess found me. They brought me here to see that you did not steal from the guests.'

It was probably good that she was sitting down, for he felt her hand go limp in his as the shock hit her. 'At Christmas?' she said in a strained whisper.

He squeezed her hand, rubbing the warmth back into her fingers. 'I have found that people steal at all times of the year. And with so many people here, there was ample opportunity. But that does not mean that I believe...'

'In my innocence?' she snapped. 'Or in my guilt? Even I do not understand what is happening here, so how am I expected to stop it? I do not remember taking the things that I found in my room. Perhaps I have not done it at all and they are trying to drive me mad.' She was shaking her head in disbelief. 'Why would the only family I have ever known treat me in such a way? If they wish me gone, why do they not just tell me so?'

Because it was too handy having her at their beck and call. They wanted her terrified, not gone. 'Do not think about them,' he said, patting her hand. 'And by all means, do not worry about the future.' He would take care of everything if she would just let him.

She laughed bitterly. 'Why would I worry? I have been living an elaborate lie and have...'

She had been about to say something, but she stopped before the words were out of her mouth and pulled her hand away from his. 'And now you are patting my hand like I am some sort of pathetic spinster who needs the charity of your affection.'

'It is not that at all,' he said, reaching for her again.

She lurched away from him, backing towards the door. 'It is even worse than that,' she said, shaking her head.

'I have let you kiss me and kissed you back, and now I find that you have been hired by the people I thought I could trust, to spy on me. Even knowing that, I cannot trust my own mind when it comes to other people's possessions. What could I possibly worry about?'

He stood and took a step towards her, arms out to comfort. 'I know things do not look good right now. But I have a solution to all your problems.'

'Then perhaps you should have told me about it before you kissed me.' She wiped at her mouth as if she could scrub away the touch of his lips. 'I do not need the help of a man so despicable as to take advantage in that way. Now, if you will excuse me, Mr Pallister,' she said, walking towards the door. 'It is late and I am sure your services will not be needed. Even the Duchess allows her servants some rest.' Then she was out of the door and running for her room.

Chapter Seven

Daphne retired early and slept fitfully, dreaming of a kiss and the crushing disappointment that followed it. Charles had assured her that it would be all right, and that he had a solution to her problems, but she could not think what it would be. She had to leave this house, for she did not think she could face the Duke and Duchess after their betrayal. But that meant work, for she had little money of her own saved.

She would require references if she was to take a position as a governess in another house. And if the Duke and Duchess stooped to hiring a watchdog for her, she doubted that they could be trusted to write a kind review of her behaviour, should she wish to leave. Without realising it, she had become trapped here and had no idea how to free herself.

The next morning, she breakfasted alone in her room, too ashamed to see or be seen by the guests, and too angry to see the Duchess. Most of all, she did not want to see Charles. He had been so sweet to her when they were alone. But how much of that was honest feeling and how much was an attempt to keep her too busy to cause trouble? She could not tell any more.

There was a knock on the bedroom door and, before she could offer permission to enter, Lady Honoria came bustling in and sat on the end of her bed, moving the black and white cat that was sitting there onto the floor. Then she said without preamble, 'Have you seen my emerald hairpins?'

'Good morning to you as well, Honoria,' Daphne replied, trying not to be any more annoyed than she already was.

'Because one of them is missing,' Honoria continued.

'Then I should search my dressing table, if I were you,' she said, with a tight smile.

Honoria stared across the room to the vanity.

'*Your* dressing table,' Daphne said more firmly. 'I have no idea what happened to your pins. You were wearing them last night when I went to bed, and I have not been out of my room since.' It was embarrassing that she even needed a defence when, for once, she was sure she had done nothing wrong. Then she added, 'And why do you need them now? They are not suitable for daytime.'

Honoria shrugged. 'I thought one or two might be appropriate, since the day may be special,' she said, with a secretive smile.

'And what would be special about today?' Daphne asked, counting the days until Twelfth Night on her fingers.

'Mr Pallister was speaking with my father again,' she said, still smiling.

Daphne's heart sank. Such a meeting could only mean one thing. They were talking about her. She had hoped they would forgive her for the missing items at the beginning of the party. But now there was a brooch gone, and Honoria's pins, and lord knew what else. Perhaps they were talking about sending her away. It would be even more embarrassing now to have Charles lead her off to wherever the bad women went.

Honoria laughed. 'Do not look so dire, Daffy. I will miss you, of course. But it is not as if anyone is going to die.'

'Not die?' She had not even wanted to consider hanging. But perhaps Honoria knew the plan already.

'When I marry, I will leave the house. But I will still write to you,' Honoria said, making things even more confusing.

'You are getting married?' she said.

'To Mr Pallister,' Honoria said, triumphantly. 'Why else would he be spending so much time in Father's office? They are probably making arrangements as we speak.'

'To Charles?' Daphne said, feeling more like a Daffy by the minute.

'I do not know him very well, of course. We have danced a few times,' Honoria said, with a softer smile that sucked all the joy out of the brightest spots in Daphne's week.

'I thought you were fond of Lord Beverly,' she said, feeling a flush of jealousy.

'But if Father prefers another…' she said with a shrug and another smile. 'And Mr Pallister is very handsome, don't you think? Quite distinguished. Even if he's not titled. And he's very well spoken.'

'I agree,' she said with a frown. She must remember that Lady Honoria was like a sister to her. A little sister at that. But until today she had never wanted to push her little sister face down in the washbasin.

'How else do we explain his sudden appearance at the party, and the secrecy about his past?'

'I am sure there is a perfectly logical explanation for everything,' Daphne said with a sigh, wishing that she was still ignorant of it.

'Then what is it?' Honoria looked at her, blinking her big blue eyes in a way that would melt the heart of any gentleman in the room, including Charles Pallister, should she use them on him.

Daphne felt her heart sinking again. 'I would have no idea,' she lied. 'But I know that not everything is about you. Now, run along and look for your pins. And do not put them in your hair until dinner.'

Lady Honoria stood with a huff of surprise and walked towards the door. 'You do not have to be nasty about it,' she tossed over her shoulder. 'And you had best stop dawdling and go downstairs. Mother has been looking for you all morning.' Then she left, leaving the door open a crack so the cat could follow her out.

'I thought you had matters in hand. And now more items are gone.' The Duke glowered over his desk as if he expected Charles to produce the missing things from his pockets as easily as he had the last time. But after last night he doubted that Daphne would even speak to him, much less come to him for help.

'I will see to it that they are found and returned,' he said with more optimism than he felt. 'But this case is proving more challenging than I thought.'

'Perhaps you are spending too much time on the dance floor to accomplish what I have hired you to do,' the peer snapped.

'Only so that I might be in the same room with Miss

Bingham,' he said. And so far, it had done him no good. He had been with Daphne almost every moment from supper until she'd retired for the night. And, since he had requested a room across the hall from hers and slept with his door open, he was sure that she had not crept out in the night to rifle through jewellery boxes. He had not seen anything more interesting than a cat walking the halls at night. 'And, though I have been looking, I have yet to see Daphne Bingham take anything.'

'But you do not need to see her do it. We all know she is at fault,' said the Duke.

'Do we really?' Charles said, increasingly suspicious.

'Of course we do,' the Duke replied. 'That is why we hired you. If you have a problem with it, then clearly you are not as good at your job as you claim to be.'

'If you think I am not doing the job correctly, then...'

He stopped himself before offering the Duke an invitation to go ahead and sack him. He could not leave here until he solved the mystery that was Daphne Bingham. And when he left, if he had any worth as a man, she would be going with him.

'Then I had best go back to work and prove you wrong,' he finished with a subservient smile. He rose and bowed. 'If you will excuse me, Your Grace?'

The Duke bade him go with a single, curt nod.

He stepped into the hall, shutting the door quietly behind him, and cursed under his breath. It would serve the fellow right if he collected Daphne and left today. It would require another apology, or perhaps two. But there had to be something he could say to her that would render her as pleasantly eager as she had been moments before everything had gone wrong. He was passing the library now, a place that had become his favourite room in the house, even though he had yet to pick up a book.

But Daphne was not standing in the doorway this morning. Instead, he saw Lady Honoria.

She beamed at him, then glanced up to the mistletoe above her, and then back to him again. 'Good morning, Mr Pallister.'

'Good morning, Lady Honoria,' he answered, not slowing his step.

She reached out and caught his sleeve as he passed. 'Do you not want to wish me a Merry Christmas?'

'Christmas is two days' past,' he reminded her.

'But the celebration continues for nine more days,' she reminded him, looking up again.

Short of insulting her, there was no other way out of this situation. 'Very well, then,' he said with a polite smile, and took her by the shoulders. 'Merry Christmas, Lady Honoria.' Then he gave her a perfunctory kiss on the cheek.

Behind him, he heard a gasp.

He turned to see Daphne, halfway down the stairs behind him, one hand clutching the banister, the other pressed against her chest as though she'd just been struck to the heart.

When he turned back to Lady Honoria, hoping she would come to his defence, he saw the feline smile on her face, and the look of triumph in her eyes. He was not sure what had just happened, but a part of him wondered if it had anything to do with him at all.

Like love, anger was a new experience for Daphne. So was jealousy. Perhaps, when the novelty had worn off, she would thank Charles Pallister for expanding her horizons. But for the moment she was incapable of speech, much less gratitude.

She swept down the stairs and past the couple under the mistletoe and continued on through the house towards the kitchen, where she checked on the menus for the day, and the refreshments for evening. When that was done, she checked the supply of sheet music on the pianoforte for ladies who might not have a prepared piece for the evening's musicale, and practised a few simple accompaniments for those who might wish to sing.

From there, she returned to the library, which was now empty, and pulled down the kissing bough, stuffing it into the fireplace and jabbing it repeatedly with the poker to make sure that the fire consumed every last berry. When she was done with it, there was nothing left but a few shrivelled leaves and a charred scrap of wire.

Someone would ask about it later, she was sure. When they did, she would tell them she had no idea what had happened to it. For a pleasant change, those words would be a lie, and she did not care a bit if they were. The thing had caused enough mischief and she was done being bothered with it.

'Are you cold?' Charles asked from the doorway. 'If you like, I will build up the fire for you.'

'I am quite warm enough without your help,' she said, not bothering to look at him.

'What you witnessed earlier was none of my doing,' he said, as if that were the only problem she had with him.

'You were an unwilling participant, then?' she said, still refusing to meet his eyes.

He stepped closer until she could see the toes of his boots less than a foot away. 'I was not the instigator, nor would I have wished to be.'

'You could have refused,' she reminded him.

'Perhaps. But I thought the situation would be over more quickly if I did not. And I cannot afford to have Lady Honoria working against us, just yet.'

'Against you, you mean,' she said, finally braving a look upwards. He seemed even taller when she was crouched at his feet, but his face was not unwelcoming.

He offered his hand to help her up. 'I meant against us. I am not your enemy, Daphne. I want so much more for us than that.'

'For us?' she said, doubtfully. 'I do not even know who you are.'

He looked guilty for a moment, then gave her a hopeful smile. 'There is not much to know about me, really, but you are welcome to all of it. Where shall I start?'

'I have heard that some in your profession are little better than the men they chase,' she said, staring at the hand he offered until it dropped to his side.

'My family is not so good as that of your mythical cousin Charles.' Then he added, 'Despite what I told you, my brother still lives in England, as do my parents. They are all in London, where I live as well. And I assure you, they would box my ears if I were any less honest than I claimed to be.'

For a moment she smiled, in spite of herself. Then she reminded herself of his reason for being here. 'And once you have caught the thieves, what do you do with them?'

'It depends on what my client wishes for them,' he said, his expression serious. 'Sometimes it is nothing more than to have the missing items returned.'

She stood without his help, wiping her hands on her skirts to hide her nerves. 'And what did the Duke want you to do with me? Your first responsibility is to him, after all.'

'He hired me to stop you from stealing,' he said, smiling again as if he knew something she did not. 'He was none too specific about what would happen once I did. But I have no reason to believe that he wanted you removed from the house.'

'And you took the job not caring what would happen to me,' she reminded him, and saw him wince. 'You will be gone soon, and I will still be here. Have you thought for a moment what will happen to me if the next man they hire is not so understanding?'

'I have no intention of leaving you here, at the mercy of the Duke,' he said firmly. 'When I go, you must leave with me. I will take you to a place where, I am sorry to say, there is very little worth stealing.'

'Prison?' she said, shocked. 'Or will it be an asylum?'

He laughed, surprised. 'Neither. We will go to my home in London.' He reached into his pocket and pulled out his watch and chain, then pressed it into her hand, holding it there with his. 'This is all that I have in the way of jewellery, but it is yours if you want it.'

'Your home?' she said, confused. 'And what would I do there?'

'I am trying to ask you to be my wife,' he said, softly. 'You must know how I feel about you by now, Daphne. The kisses I gave you, and the way it feels when we dance… It is all real and not some game I am playing to please Twinden. You are a jewel amongst dross here. I cannot abide the thought of you toiling for the Duchess like an unpaid servant when you could have a house, a husband and servants of your own.'

It was what she wanted, in her heart of hearts. But

it made no sense that the offer would come now, of all times. 'It is your job to punish me,' she reminded him.

'I don't care if it is,' he said. 'I cannot bring myself to blame you for something that, one way or another, is the fault of the horrible people in this horrible house.'

'You were kissing one of them just a few moments ago,' she reminded him.

'That meant nothing,' he replied.

'Then why should I believe that the kisses you gave me meant any more than that?'

He opened his mouth and closed it again, at that moment lost for words. And then he said, with a vague flailing of his arms, 'Did you not feel what I did when we kissed? It was not the same as the peck I gave Honoria, I swear to you.'

'Less than a week ago, you'd have sworn to me that you were from Gloucestershire and not London.'

'That was just a story I told so as to fit in with the guests,' he said with a shrug.

'It was a lie,' she corrected. 'You must call it as it is.'

'All right,' he said. 'It was a lie. But it was a small one.'

'So was your reason for being here. And how many others might there be?' she said. It was why, no matter how much she might wish to, she did not dare to marry him. How could she trust him enough to go away with him when she had no way of knowing if his latest story was true?

'Daphne,' he said urgently, 'I swear, from this point on, there will be nothing but truth between us.'

'I am sorry,' she said, staring down at the smouldering remains of the mistletoe. 'But from this point on, there will be nothing at all between us. There will be no more dances, no more kisses, and no more private conversations. If you must take me away as the thief I am, so be it. But I will not marry you simply to prevent the justice that I deserve.'

And without looking back she walked past him and out of the room.

Chapter Eight

He had not expected rejection.

Perhaps no man did. But Charles in particular had not
been prepared for it. When one got the person one was
looking for, clapped hands on them and said, 'You'll be
coming along with me now,' they damn well had better
come along if they knew what was good for them.

And that, he suspected, was the problem. As gently
as he had put it, she still saw his profession and not the
sincere offer of his heart. Though he had serious doubts
that she was the thief everyone claimed her to be, she
saw herself as quarry, with him in pursuit.

And when did the fox ever run up to the hunter and
expect to be rescued from the hounds?

Since departing from the library, he had not been able
to get a moment alone with her to apologise, not that he
could think of a word to say that might make a difference. At dinner, she had been so obviously frightened that
he had behaved like the churl she probably thought he
was and offered only the most superficial conversation.

And now he was trapped at the evening musicale,
listening to Lady Honoria's off-key singing. As usual,

Daphne played a subordinate role, dutifully accompanying her and any other talentless lady that wanted a moment's attention. Having never heard it, he could not be sure. But, knowing how everything else in the house went, he would bet she had a lovely voice and never sang.

His fingers drummed on his folded arms, keeping time with his thoughts and not the music. If he could not find some token to offer beyond his heart and watch, there was no point in offering again. What could he give her that would change her mind? Not jewellery, surely. She deserved a wedding ring. But, despite what Twinden seemed to think, there was no sign that she coveted gold or diamonds.

Nor could he sway her with happiness. She clearly did not trust it, for she was willing to stay miserable where she was rather than coming away with him. He mused, why did one stay where one was not happy?

For safety. If she remained here, her life might not be pleasant, but she was confident that there would be no surprises in the future.

If he was to win her over, he must find a way to offer her the same security that she had here. A thought occurred to him, something that would satisfy her needs as well as his own. He had but to find a way to get her alone so he could explain it to her.

It had been the most difficult night of Daphne's life.

When she was refusing his proposal she had not thought that she would be sitting at dinner with him just a few hours later. And tonight, instead of calling her away in the middle of the meal, the Duchess had allowed her to choke down every last bite. The normally delicious roast beef had tasted like sand in her mouth, and the trifle like lead.

And through it all, she had been forced to make small talk with Charles, commenting on the weather and receiving monosyllabic replies. It had been a temporary respite when the time had come to speak to the gentleman on her left. But even without looking, she could feel him on her other side, as if the unspoken thoughts between them were a dark cloud.

After dinner, the party adjourned to the music room to showcase the talents of the guests. There, Daphne was left to accompany a besotted Honoria, who sang 'Drink to Me Only with Thine Eyes' to Charles, who sat stoically at the back of the room, arms folded and glaring at the pair of them.

And through it all came the call for Daffy.

Daffy, do this.

Daffy, do that.

Daffy, can you help me...?

The name had never bothered her before the arrival of Charles Pallister. But now, each time she heard it she felt a little smaller, a little more worthless.

Now that she was in her room, she stood with her back to the panel of her bedroom door, as if it were possible to keep out all the ugly truths along with the man she had been foolish enough to love. When he had told her the truth about himself, she had come close to blurting her feelings out to him and revealing her stupidity.

She had been wrong to trust him, and the Duke and Duchess as well. No matter what they might claim to her face, she was an embarrassment to them.

For the first time in as long as she could remember, there were tears in her eyes. It was just another troublesome emotion that had arrived along with Charles Pallister, like the laughter and the anger and the sudden thumping of her heart whenever he walked into a room.

And jealousy. In all the years she had watched Honoria get the things she had wanted for herself, she had taken it as a natural fact of life. But the idea that she wanted Charles was just too much.

She sat down on the bed, and the black and white cat that had been sleeping on her pillow marched onto her lap, trying to dry her cheeks with rough kisses and a swipe of a fluffy black tail.

She gave the cat a brief hug and set her on the floor. It was all Charles's fault. Before he had come, she had not thought further than one moment ahead. And because of that, she had been content. Now she had hopes. And when one hoped, there was always the risk that those dreams would be dashed as hers had been.

She stared at the watch he had given her, which was sitting on her night table. She had not meant to storm out of the room with it. But now here it was, in her room, like so many other valuables had been before. It was some consolation that, this time, she could remember taking it.

Suddenly the door of her room opened and Charles stepped in, closing it quickly behind him.

'Get out,' she said, wiping her face with the back of her hand and pointing a shaky finger at him.

'Daphne,' he said, holding up his hands, palms to face her. 'I know you are angry...'

'I am not angry,' she said, trying to control her breathing again.

'Really?' he replied. 'Because most women in your situation would be.'

'You have no idea what it is like to be a woman in my

situation,' she snapped, completely undoing any hope
that he would believe what she had just said about the
state of her mind.

'I know that if anyone finds me in your room, you
will be ruined,' he said quietly. 'But I had to talk to you
again and I could not manage to get you alone when we
were downstairs. It is probably for the best that you do
not raise your voice, no matter how much I deserve to be
shouted at. Please let me speak my mind.'

For a moment, the horror of the thought was more than
enough to silence her. 'You cannot be here,' she said.

He gave a sad shrug of his shoulders and leaned back
against the door as if showing her that he meant to block
the way, should she try to run. 'And yet, I cannot be anywhere else. I cannot leave things as they were when we
parted this afternoon.'

'You mean, you cannot take no for an answer,' she
said hurriedly, trying to ignore the hurt that was still
fresh in her heart.

'You said my lies were what upset you. But the truth
upset you more,' he corrected her, walking slowly towards her. 'I love you. And I think you might love me,
as well.'

'Well, you are wrong,' she said with another shake
of her head, wishing this could be over quickly before
she began to cry again. 'It is not your fault that you were
hired to watch me, nor can you be blamed for misunder-
standing my feelings. I...' She swallowed. 'I led you on.'

He laughed, then came and sat on the bed beside her.
'When you know me better, you will find that it is very
hard to lead me where I do not want to go.'

He was close to her now, and it felt like every inch of
her had come alive. 'I will not have the opportunity to

know you better because you will be gone from here in a few days.' And she would be left dead inside, just as she was before.

'I suspect I will be gone sooner than that,' he said, still smiling. 'Likely by noon tomorrow.'

'You are leaving,' she said.

'I will be put out, more likely,' he said. 'The first thing tomorrow, I mean to tell the Duke that I can no longer work for him.'

'Why would you do that?' she whispered, both hopeful and afraid for the answer.

'Because I want to remove the barrier between us,' he said, holding his hands out to her again. 'No matter what you might say to me, I am not going to spend another moment of our acquaintance hounding you over things that do not matter to me.'

'You would do that for me,' she said, surprised.

'That and more. When I get back to London, I will go to my brother and ask for a position in his law firm.' He gave her another encouraging smile. 'I have no interest in traipsing about the country and profiting off the misery of others. Perhaps it is time that I used my talents to help the accused rather than catch them.'

For a moment her words stuck in her throat. Then she stammered, 'You would d-do all this for me?'

'For both of us,' he said firmly. 'No matter what, I cannot bear to be the person you fear. When I leave tomorrow, come with me.' He reached for her hand. Then he raised her knuckles to his lips and kissed them, one at a time. 'Give me a lifetime and I will see that you never regret it.'

It was too much. Even if he was telling the truth about his plans and his feelings for her, and even if she could trust her own, how could she go off with a man she had just met and leave everything she'd ever known?

But how could she let him go after only a few kisses? Her hand was still resting against his lips, which moved gently over her skin as if whispering secrets with each light kiss. She felt the heat of those kisses inside her, warming her heart and somewhere deep and untouched.

'I will give you tonight,' she said in a shuddering sigh. 'And we will see what tomorrow brings.' And surprisingly, she did not regret the words. Now that they were said she knew them to be more true than any she had spoken so far.

He leaned into her, capturing her lips with his own, and the glow inside her blazed into fire.

And suddenly, the cat forced her way between them with an annoyed meow.

He gave her another quick kiss, then scooped the cat up in his arms and carried her across the room, putting her out in the hall and closing the door. 'If you are serious in your offer,' he said, 'we must have no chaperone.' Then he stripped out of coat and vest and pulled his shirt over his head, tossing it aside.

What had she done? There was a moment of pure terror at the sight of his bare chest, all sculpted muscles and curling hair. Then the fear was gone and she was hungry for more.

He sat beside her again, taking her hand and placing it over his heart. 'It beats for you,' he said, closing his eyes and waiting.

Carefully she stroked his skin, trembling as she followed the curves and angles of his body, trailing her fingertips towards his waist.

He gasped and she felt his stomach, rock-hard against

her palm. 'Woman, you are driving me mad,' he said, reaching behind her to search for the closures of her gown.

She reached to drop the front of her bodice, revealing the laced panel underneath. 'It is easier, when one does not have a lady's maid,' she said, blushing.

'Miss Bingham, you are a most sensible woman,' he said with a growl, undoing the lacings and pushing her bodice down until she was bare, except for her shift.

She took a steadying breath then stood and let her gown fall to the floor, kicking it away. Then she came back into his arms.

He groaned and took her mouth with a kiss that was full of raw need. Hungry and hard, his tongue filled her with a single thrust. His hands found her breasts, first over the shift, then pushing the fabric aside and pinching her nipples between thumb and forefinger, making them hard and needy for more. He broke their kiss and took them into his mouth, with kisses that were both soothing and arousing. With his hands free, he reached for the buttons of his breeches, stripping them down his legs and kicking out of shoes and stockings until he was naked beside her.

The sight of him gave her another moment of panic. She had not reached the age of twenty-seven without some understanding of what was to happen. But how was it even possible? She must trust that he understood. And that if she did not like it, it would be over quickly.

He kissed her again and she could feel the smile on his lips, as if he knew something she did not. Then she felt his hand slide under the hem of her shift, glide along her stocking until it reached the bare thigh above the garter, and then…

She clutched his biceps and her back arched in shock. Instead of trying to escape the invasion, she leaned into his hand. He was playing with the folds of her body, finding the most sensitive places. And…oh, dear lord, thrusting inside her.

Her fear was forgotten, replaced by an urgent need to be filled by him. This was what she was born for, and what she had wanted without knowing. She was begging now. 'Love me, please.' Her voice was an urgent whisper.

'Soon,' he whispered against her temple. 'Soon.'

And then she understood. A night was not enough. She wanted to live this moment over and over, even if the pleasure undid her, as she feared it might.

Soon he was on her and inside her and the magic of it changed and grew as she felt the pleasure seizing him as it had her. He moved slowly at first, his hips barely rocking against hers, sliding deep into her body and withdrawing until she had almost lost him. Then he returned, even deeper than before.

As his speed increased, so did her ardour and the desire to hold him, keeping him buried inside her for ever. She wrapped her silk-clad legs around his waist and met his thrusts with moves of her own, pushing him to the limits of his control.

He spent on a groan and the rush of it sent her to another pinnacle of joy. They floated back to earth in each other's arms while he whispered, 'I love you… I love you…' over and over again.

How could she have doubted him? 'I love you, too,' she whispered back, kissing his face and tasting tears of relief.

They lay there entwined for a time, without speaking. Then he raised his head to stare into her eyes. 'Please tell me that this is for more than one night. Now that I have found you, I cannot stand to lose you.'

'Nor I you,' she said with a sigh. 'I do not know how we can be together if I cannot trust my own mind. But I do not know how I will live without you.'

As he rolled to kiss her again, there was a soft, persistent scratching on the door to the hall.

'Go, let Domino back in,' she said, pushing him gently towards the edge of the bed. 'If you do not open the door for her, she will meow until everyone in the wing is awake, and give us no peace at all.'

'I suspect she will give us no peace if she is inside either,' he said. But he did as she requested and opened the door a crack to admit the cat.

He stared down in surprise. 'What the devil?' Then he smiled back at Daphne and said, 'Your cat has brought you a present.'

Daphne pulled the blankets over her head and shuddered. 'She is not my cat. And please, tell me it is not a mouse. She is always so proud when she catches one, she brings it to my pillow to show me.'

'Not exactly,' he replied, making a grab for the cat, who dodged out of the way.

'Do not say it is a rat,' she said, poking her nose out from under the covers. 'I have never seen one of them come closer than the stables.'

'Not a rat either,' he said, making another grab for the cat. 'Come here, you little demon.' Then he lifted her in the air and plucked something from her mouth, tossing it on the pillow beside Daphne.

She sat bolt upright and scooted away from the pillow, which held something far more dangerous than a wounded rodent. 'The Duchess's emerald eardrop.'

Domino let out a hiss of disappointment and swiped at the hand that held her.

'Dammit,' he said, clutching his wounded hand as the cat bounded to the floor and disappeared under the dressing table. When she reappeared a moment later she walked head held high and proud, with the end of a strand of amber beads clasped firmly in her jaws.

'She has excellent taste,' Charles said drily. Then he grabbed a candle and got down on his hands and knees to inspect her hiding place. A moment later he rose, holding an onyx stud, a gold earring and Honoria's emerald hairpin. 'She has quite a collection here. I think she is building a nest of sorts. Does she have access to all the bedrooms?'

Daphne nodded. 'And the main rooms and retiring rooms as well. She is very generous with her affection if she gets her way, and unbearably loud when she does not.'

'Then I think we have discovered why you had no recollection of stealing anything,' he said. 'You had nothing to do with the thefts at all. I wondered why I could not catch you at it, no matter how closely I watched. I had come to suspect it was the Duke playing tricks on you. But sometimes the truth is stranger than one can imagine.'

'That a cat has been the one responsible for all the trouble?'

'And that the Duke and Duchess are holding you responsible for something that you had no part in,' he said with a serious look. 'And have done so for so long that you no longer believed in yourself.'

Daphne stared at the cat, who rolled onto her back, balancing the beads between her paws as if admiring them. Then she righted herself and began the laborious process of dragging them onto the bed for Daphne to find. 'I did not think I was such a bad person,' she said, and slowly, like melting ice, the tight feeling that she got in her chest whenever she thought of jewellery began to dissipate.

'They were wrong about you,' he said. 'And they were wrong to treat you like you were less than their own daughter. And to make you think you were some sort of plain, unmarriageable spinster. They were especially wrong to call you Daffy, for there is nothing the least bit silly about you.'

She looked at him, still surprised at the earnest love in his eyes as he stared back at her, and her hand crept to her chest to cover her own rapidly beating heart. For the first time in as long as she could remember, she felt young. Not just young, but also complete. It was as if some part of her had been hidden and Charles had found it and given it back to her.

'Come away with me, Daphne,' he said, his hand in that same coaxing gesture he had given on the first night, when asking her to dance. 'Be with me. Always. As my wife.'

'Yes,' she said. And it was as if the last pieces of her life fell into place and she was the girl she'd always hoped to be, with a life full of dancing and laughter and love. 'I cannot wait to tell the Duchess. And Honoria, of course.'

He rushed forward again, pushing an indignant cat onto the floor and taking her in his arms again. 'We will talk with them in an hour or so. For now? I have other plans for you.'

A short time later she packed a carpet bag and allowed Charles to lead her down the stairs and into the breakfast room, where the Duke and Duchess were gathered with several of their guests. Once there, he dumped the jewellery they had found on the centre of the table. Then he reached into the carpet bag and produced the cat, dropping her onto the middle of the table, with the jewels.

'What is the meaning of this?' the Duke demanded, pushing back from the table as his guests gasped in horror.

'I have found all the missing items and captured the thief as well.'

'It was not me,' Daphne said, and felt a rush of triumph that she had not felt in all the years living at Twinden House. 'It was never me.'

'The cat has been hiding jewellery in her room,' Charles said. 'I saw it with my own eyes.'

'What were you doing in Daffy's room?' the Duchess demanded in a shrill voice.

This was the moment when Daphne should have been shamed into silence. Instead, she said, 'I would prefer to be called Daphne. It is my name, after all.'

'It has never bothered you before,' the Duchess insisted.

'Just as it did not bother me that you accused me of theft and hired a thief taker to punish me,' she replied, surprised at how calm her voice sounded.

'We did not want him to hurt you,' the Duchess said hurriedly. 'Only to make you stop.'

'But I wasn't doing anything,' Daphne reminded her. 'All the times I told you I did not remember taking things, it was because I had not done anything wrong.'

'And now you are trying to tell us that the cat is at fault?' the Duke said sarcastically.

As if to prove the point, the cat, who was still on the

table, batted the cameo brooch into the bacon plate and seized a shirt stud in her teeth, then leapt for the door.

Before she could escape, Charles seized her again and pried the stud from her mouth. He prepared a plate of eggs and kippers and presented it to the cat, who forgot the jewellery in favour of breakfast. Then he said, 'I think you owe Daphne an apology.'

'We do not owe the chit anything,' the Duke barked. 'If anything, she owes us. We did not have to take her in.'

'I should think decades of free labour would be reason enough to keep her,' Charles said with a cool smile. 'But that is at an end now. I am taking her from your house, just as you wished.'

'That was not what we wanted at all,' the Duchess insisted.

'But it is what you deserve,' Charles said, his smile widening. 'It is my job to catch the guilty, not to harass the innocent. And I certainly will not leave the woman I love in this household to be treated like a servant and accused of theft every time a spoon goes missing.'

'You love Daffy?' the Duke said, staring at the two of them in disbelief.

'Daphne,' Charles repeated, his eyes hardening to a steely glint. 'You can use her correct name when you wish her farewell.'

Daphne could not decide which she enjoyed more, Charles's declaration, or the incredulous looks on her family's faces as he swept her up into his arms as if she weighed nothing at all and carried her through the breakfast room door.

'What are you doing?' she said breathlessly, kicking her feet and wishing half-heartedly for the ground.

'I am carrying you across the threshold,' he said, walking through the front hall, calling for his horse and signalling a grinning footman to open the door for them.

'I do not think this is the way it is done,' she said, staring at the fast-approaching exit and letting the cries of protest from the family fall away like so much unwanted chatter.

He kissed her before stepping through and setting her on the ground again, taking the cloak that the footman handed to him and wrapping it about her shoulders. 'The ceremony is meant to make sure you start your new life on the right foot. And your life begins as of this moment, Daphne. The whole world is yours. If you want it, I will give it to you.'

Before she could answer, she felt the familiar brush of fur against her skirts and the black and white cat at her feet chirped expectantly.

She sighed in resignation and smiled to her lover. 'I do not need the whole world. But perhaps a little part of it. Is there room in your saddlebag for Domino?'

Charles smiled back at her. 'Until we get back to London, I am a thief taker. It would be remiss to leave her behind. We will send for the rest of your things after we arrive at my home.'

He mounted his horse, and she handed him the cat, who was stowed snugly in a pouch behind him.

Then he reached for her and swung her up to sit in front of him with his arms wrapped firmly about her waist. 'We will rent a proper carriage when we get to the inn, and I will take you to Gretna Green,' he said with a smile.

'I cannot think of a better Christmas present than that,' she said, and settled into the custody of his arms.

'How about a wedding ring?' he suggested.

She laughed. 'As long as it does not come from the cat.'

* * * * *

ONE NIGHT
WITH THE EARL

Sophia James

This one is for you, my little Beau,
and also for my baby Question Mark who is
yet to be born. I hope you will always be
the very best of friends and have many
happy Christmases together.

Dear Reader,

Christmas is a wonderful time of the year. My husband
and I always spend the celebration with our large
family, and this year we will have welcomed two
more little babies into the world to join the four lovely
grandchildren we already have. So I imagine it will be
busy, with cricket and soccer and dough and painting
and drawing and six little people very excited with the
presents and food. It's hot at Christmas in New Zealand
so we will have a lot of swims, as well.

Alexander and Elizabeth's story begins with a note
from a child who desperately wants a happy Christmas.
On thinking about what would make it perfect I knew I
needed other children, a large noisy family and a man
who would be there for a woman who has always
struggled alone.

I hope you enjoy this story. When I wrote it our first
little baby grandson had just been born. His name is
Beau, and so I used his name in the epilogue and I
smile each time I read it.

Have a fun, happy and peaceful Christmas.

Much love,

Sophia

Prologue

Somerset, November 1815

Elizabeth Martin stood alone at the top of the hill and screamed, as loud as she could and as long, the muscles in her throat tightening in fury as she finished. It was over, the tumult, the deceit and the sadness. She would be safe here.

The clouds of night rose from the western hills, rain chasing on icy heels as she raised her arms to receive the moisture. A baptism of sorts, she ruminated, for in desperation there also dwelt possibility, the possibility of a new life, different, better. Her own.

She felt insignificant amongst the movement around her, in the trees and in the sky, the West Country raw and beautiful and big, and there was comfort in such a thought. She was home. She recognised the call of a robin and then a lapwing, birds she had known as a child in Wales and had not heard for twelve long years. She loved it here, cocooned in the welcoming cold of winter, sealed off from London and from people. The smells and sounds and colours and plants were familiar, as was the language.

Guy, her husband, would have said to her that she never took a risk and that the known was always disappointing, but Elizabeth could no longer think of him.

She needed to believe in the direction she was taking her small family, away from the anger and the lies, away from the jeopardy. This was a new life and if she dwelt on the goodness of being here she was certain they could flourish. She still had some money left and if she was careful they could survive until the summer, when she could take in sewing for the ladies of the big houses standing on the outskirts of the village to supplement their income.

She smiled. Guy had forbidden her the company of many others, but the servants from their house in the hills above the port of Bilbao had formed a group around her and shown her things she would otherwise have had no chance of learning. Sewing. Cooking. Gardening. The art of mending clothes, adding up accounts and building a fire.

Useful life skills, daily routine tasks, her upbringing with her grandmother precluding all but the reading of the Bible and endless meditation upon its teachings.

She looked up to the heavens and knew that many of the verses she had loved in the Holy Book had helped her too, but now it was time to find a way to live and hope again, and Christmas was not long away.

In the cold Elizabeth felt a rebirth, a quickening, and as she turned for the Grange she thanked the Lord for providing her with a place to call their own.

Alexander Grey watched the woman walk across the path on the top of the hill, her dress blowing in the wind.

She was thin, her long, dark hair falling to her waist un-bound, whipping against her back, curling in the breeze.

Like a wood sprite or a faerie.

He'd heard the scream and had come to investigate, but it was easy to see that it was not help she required. He waited as she began to move down the path towards the Grange, the last of the day's light reflecting on the small windows.

She hurried now, head bent, arms wound tightly around herself. Running for shelter and warmth.

Mrs Martin. It must be her, for he had heard whispers in the village of her arrival. From the north coast of Spain, no less. He hoped that she would be welcomed here and that in the quiet of Somerset she might find her place. Find her peace. There was gossip around that spoke of harder times and desperate loss, but then, he'd dealt with rumours before, too, when his father had died, and so few of them had been true.

She was gone now, disappeared into the gloom. Perhaps the Grange would prove to be a sanctuary, for there was something in the soil and the water hereabouts that nurtured one back to happiness. He hoped it would be so for her.

Chapter One

December 17th 1815

> *Please, please, please, let Mama have a happy*
> *Christmas this year.*
> *Thank you.*
> *Jenny*

Lord Alexander Grey found the note tied to a small hawthorn bush by the river, a series of colourful ribbons trailing near it. The handwriting was careful and well formed, all the consistent and connecting strokes sitting faultlessly on an invisible line.

The missive had been there for a few days by the looks of the tangle of ribbon and paper, and there was no sign of footprints in the loamy sand beneath.

He frowned. A hawthorn bush. Perhaps the girl who had placed it knew of its association with the fairy folk and wished to invoke their magical powers?

Jenny? He could not think of a child by that name who lived around here but the word *'Mama'* had him guessing she must be one of the children newly come to the

Grange. He wondered why the previous Christmases she wrote of by implication had not been happy. With care he disengaged the piece of paper and put it in his pocket, berating himself for the bother even as he did so.

It was the three pleases that had done it, he thought, as he walked, for they denoted desperation. Perhaps he should pen a reply in case the author of the note returned. That brought a smile to his face. He was thirty-eight and owned all the land for as far as his eyes could see. He was a busy man and the flighty notes of young girls were something that should not concern him.

The weather was closing in and cloud bands were forming on the ranges, the wind telling him that snow was in the air. Eight days until Christmas and already the preparations had begun in earnest.

His sister and her family would be at Goldings to-morrow, her brood of unruly children filling the house. His mother would come, too, with her constant questions and her unwanted advice. The family dogs undoubtedly would follow, pampered, ridiculous and coddled things who chased the children and barked incessantly. His mother's twin sister would be part of it as well, her husband, Dickie, having passed away in the year that had been, and they would all stay until well into January before they returned to London. He knew his aunt was bringing two guests with her for a few days and reason told him they would be feminine. His family had after all not given up on their quest to have him married off, and in most years there were young women paraded from good lineages and with unblemished reputations, especially at Christmastime.

Trying to distract himself, Alexander looked at the smaller pines in the far clearing, his mind trying to decide which green bough would be the one they could cut and bring into the house to decorate on Christmas Eve. Sarah, his sister, would no doubt pick the largest.

Despite it all he liked this time of year, for these weeks were full of a life that eluded him for the rest of it. He was too busy making money and seeing that everything did not simply fall over into a big pile of problems, too busy with the careful investments of the estate, investments that would make sure that the future of Goldings remained safe.

A noise stopped him and he tilted his head, listening. There it was again, the sound of fighting. Striding through the undergrowth with intent, he broke into a clearing where three youths were beating up a much smaller boy.

The lad between them had a bleeding nose and a swollen eye and seemed to be just standing there taking it.

'What the hell are you doing?' Alex made sure his voice was loud and threatening, and movement stopped for a split second before the three perpetrators simply ran for it, leaving the younger boy leaning against a tree.

'You all right?' He checked the boy over with a glance, determining that he'd look the worse for wear come morning, but nothing seemed broken.

'I did not need your help.'

Sneering anger was all over his young face.

'You'd have preferred to be beaten alive for your pride, perhaps?'

Alex made no attempt at doling out pity, knowing if he'd been in the same position he would not have wanted it at that age.

'I can fight. Just didn't want to.'

The lad's voice was unusual, tinged with the cadence of another land, though his English was cultured.

'Show me, then. Raise your fists and fight me.'

The boy did that, his thumbs tucked in and his elbows skewed.

'Your arm will break if you hit someone hard that way. Bring your elbows in against your sides and turn a little. And make sure you keep your thumbs out.'

As he moved to show him an arm shot out. Alex easily dodged the blow.

'Catching people by surprise has more of an effect.'

The boy lashed out again.

'Better.' He could not help a half-smile, which was the wrong reaction altogether.

'I could kill you if I wanted to.'

'With words?'

'No. With a sword.'

Now, that was interesting. The boy had dark hair and green eyes and was at that stage of boyhood where everything was mismatched and gangly. But underneath in the bones of the lad Alex saw something he recognised.

'You are Guy Martin's son?'

Anger changed to fear.

'From the Grange?'

He took off without another word, running like the devil from the clearing, his breath leaving white smudges on the cold air. Reaching down, Alex lifted up the coat left behind and tucked it beneath his arm. Mrs Martin's offspring? It made sense, for he had her colour of hair, while Guy had been blond.

God, the family had only taken up residence here for a month or more and already the local boys were fed up with him? Perhaps he was difficult, like his father?

The rain had begun properly, running in sheets across the sky, chased hard by the northerly wind behind it. Another freezing night with the promise of snow. His eye caught a circle of jet-black beads as he turned, a rosary with an ornate crucifix hung on a gold chain, and encrusted with rubies.

Was it the boy's? He could not imagine the lad would own such an expensive or feminine piece. Was it his mother's?

Lord, had he arrived slap-bang in the middle of some family problem that would now be his to solve if he was not careful? Could he just leave the things here and hope the lad returned for them? He was torn between duty, the oncoming snow and memories of his own youth, which had sometimes been difficult.

Guy Martin was a man few had much liked. He'd been here only seldom from London but every time he came he had managed to raise the local ire. Then he had left for the north of Spain and a life as a wine merchant with a new wife in tow whom nobody had even seen, let alone met. The Grange was boarded up and abandoned, the house on its five acres of land left only to the weeds and the weather. He'd kept an eye on it in the interim just to make sure that broken windows were fixed and that the locks were secure.

Then the widow Martin had returned with the express purpose of living there.

It was at least a twenty-minute walk to the Grange, and in this weather he did not wish to chance it. No, he would go home and saddle up his horse and then pay the family a visit.

He supposed that, given he was the nearest neighbour, it was the least that he could do. Besides, he wanted to make sure that Guy's son had arrived home safely, as the boy had looked anxious in a way Alexander could not quite understand, and the weather was worsening.

His mind counted back the years since Guy had left, and determined it to be about twelve. Was theirs a wedding that was hurried up by a pregnancy? There was another child too, he thought, a twin, it was said, though no one had seen much of the family since they had arrived.

He remembered back to the dark-haired woman he'd encountered a few weeks before screaming at the sky. Gossip had it that Guy had died in an accident, a fight, if he remembered rightly, and there was some scandal attached.

Angry man, angry son, angry wife.

He should consign the coat and rosary into the hands of one of his servants and have them deliver the lost property to the Grange. But even as he thought of this he knew that he wouldn't. The rosary was too valuable and the weather too inclement. If the child got lost and wandered in the wrong direction the cold might kill him without the protection of a warm coat, and besides, he was new to this area.

The Grange. It had never been a happy place or one that was tended with care, the gardens overrun and the stonework compromised. In this weather it would be draughty, and he doubted the roof would allow water-tightness for very much longer without a tidy sum spent upon it.

Luis had been hurt again. This was the fourth time in as many weeks he had come home and gone straight to his room. She would not see him till the morrow, by which time he would have conjured up another unlikely accident that had befallen him and his fury over their move would have grown.

Jennifer was out of sorts, too, this new land being cold and grey, and the shyness her daughter had been afflicted with in Bilbao seemed to be worsening.

Perhaps they should have stayed in Spain? Elizabeth shook away that thought quickly because the sojourn there had been entirely Guy's idea, whereas all she wanted was to be home in the countryside of Britain, the greens of the trees, hills and fields comforting, a landscape that allowed her to regain a tenuous balance.

She would leave Luis alone just now, for experience had shown her the futility of knocking at his door and trying to communicate from one side of a thick wooden portal. Sometimes she wondered if he hated her. She knew he blamed her for Guy's long absences away from them, but he was a child still and any explanation of why his father had left them for years on end and rarely visited was hardly wise.

The doorbell sounded as she was standing in the small salon off the front hall and, knowing the downstairs maid to be in the kitchen and busy with the evening meal, she answered it.

The man who stood there, windblown and dark, was beautiful. So beautiful her mouth fell wide open, allowing no words at all to come. In the dusk he reminded her of one of the gods from the underworld, the dangerous strength about him beguiling.

'Are you Mrs Martin?'

Even his voice was beautiful.

'I am. Sir.' She added this as an afterthought.

'Do you have a son of about twelve? A dark-haired boy with green eyes?'

She nodded. Oh, God, what had Luis done now? Had he stolen something from this man? Had he been caught doing it?

One hand came forward bearing Luis's winter coat and her rosary. The rubies at the base of the cross glinted in the last light of day and her heart sank lower. He was stealing from her now, too, for she had missed the crucifix yesterday when she had looked for it before her nightly prayers. The horror must have shown on her face, for he began to speak again.

'I met your son in the woods and he ran off, leaving these behind. He has the look of his father about him, for I used to know Guy once, so I thought to bring the items back.'

As if remembering he had not supplied his name, he suddenly smiled. 'I am Lord Alexander Grey. From Goldings. Your nearest neighbour.'

The huge house just over the hill? She had found a view of it on a walk the second day she had come to the Grange and had often gone back just to look again.

Lord Grey. Master of Goldings. Was he here to understand if they were a threat to him or not? She needed to be careful.

'Thank you for returning the items. I shall give my son his coat when he comes down, my lord. The crucifix is mine.' She felt the warmth of him on the ancient gold even as she said it.

'Comes down?'

'He often sleeps in the afternoon, my lord. A Spanish habit, you see. A way to join up the hours of the early mornings with those of the late nights and, as we are all just readjusting to the shock of my husband's death, there are many of those.'

She swallowed, wishing she could take those words back because she could see in his expression the same distaste she had seen on all the faces around here. They did not quite fit in. Still, he had those unparalleled manners that were the inbuilt default setting of the English aristocracy.

'I offer you my sincere condolences, Mrs Martin. It cannot have been easy to lose a husband.'

'Indeed, my lord, it was not.' That sentence at least held a great dollop of genuine feeling, though he would never know the true interpretation of the words as he stepped back.

'Perhaps your son might welcome a tutor in the art of boxing? He seems to have a need for more competence.'

These new words astonished her. When she failed to speak he began again.

'There was a skirmish I observed in the woods between him and a few of the local lads and he appeared to be wanting in his ability to defend himself. I would be more than happy to give him a few tips should he wish for them with his father not around...' He let that sentiment settle.

'I am not sure. Luis is rather shy in company.'

He nodded and bowed. 'Of course. Then I shall be on my way.'

Suddenly she wanted to stop him going, wanted to have him here to talk to, a man who may know what to do with a difficult, withdrawn boy of eleven.

'But if you could find some time in the next few days to visit us again I may be able to persuade him.'

It was such an impossible ask, she knew it was. Lord Grey was a man who would have every second of his time filled up with the demands of his huge tracts of land. The onus of visiting again to perhaps persuade Luis to cooperate would be of no interest to him whatsoever.

Surprisingly he nodded. 'I shall come by tomorrow in the afternoon, then,' he said quietly, the blue in his eyes startling against his smile. 'Around two.'

Beautiful.

She bit down on such foolishness and smiled back.

'Thank you, my lord.'

Then he was gone, walking down the steps into the wind, a hat jammed over his deep brown hair, his coat-tails moving in the breeze.

'Who was that, Mama?'

Jenny crept up behind her, her face creased in concern.

'Our neighbour, my dear. He has offered us his friend-ship, for he knew your father.'

Jenny, unlike her son, seldom spoke of her father and she saw anger cross into her daughter's green eyes. It was an unwanted topic of conversation and so she changed it.

'Luis's face is bleeding again, Mama, and one of his eyes is swollen. He is hiding in his room and won't come out.'

'He will feel better in the morning, I promise it. Now let's go and see what is for dinner and perhaps if we find something delicious we can persuade your brother to join us.'

When her daughter's fingers crept into her own Eliz-abeth noticed ink all over them. She had been writing again. She hoped with all her might that Lord Alexander Grey had not found any of her heartfelt notes.

Elizabeth Martin was hiding things, Alex thought as he crossed over into the copse of trees that shielded the Grange from Goldings. The boy had been listening to what they had said, for he had seen the crack of light glimmer in an upstairs doorway and there had been a girl of about the same age sitting immobile halfway up the staircase, staring at him.

Jenny perhaps? The twin?

He felt for the note in his pocket.

From the look of the Grange there would not be much joy there over the Yuletide, the furniture threadbare and the place needing more than a slight repair.

Why had he not heard of how this family was faring on the grapevine of communal gossip? Perhaps because the new inhabitants had seldom strayed from their lair and the youths who were beating Luis Martin were hardly going to confess openly to such a cowardly thing.

She was Catholic. If the crucifix had not told him so then he would have seen it in the few paintings that had been hung on the wall behind her. She was also far younger than he had guessed her to be.

A child bride. His memory worked backwards. There had been some gossip of Guy visiting a convent in Wales and coming away with a novice whom he'd married before the week was up. Surely that was just hearsay?

But there was an innocence in the face of his unexpected neighbour that pointed to the fact that such a chance meeting might not have been quite so impossible, and Mrs Martin had taken the rosary into her grasp in the way of someone long used to reciting the many and complex mysteries. Why had the son brought something so precious with him into the woods and taken so little care with it?

A puzzle with parts that did not make any sense. One thing that did make sense though was the fact that Mrs Martin was unlike any other woman he had ever met.

Fragile. Beautiful. Secretive. Sad. She had eyes the colour of river plants just beneath the surface in shallow
water, running fast on a summer's day. A mosaic of light
and dark, the pure green of them startling.

He could imagine her as a novice in a white veil and
grey robes, the simple clothes of some obscure Welsh
order showing up her beauty in a way that would catch
the attention of all who would meet her. As it had caught
Guy's.

He shook his head. Hard.

She had not flirted with him in the way every other
woman usually did. She had given him no reason to think
she may have been interested in friendship either, the invitation extended to him to visit furnished only for the
sake of her son.

Alex had enjoyed the company of many females, but
business had always come first, and after the disastrous
investments of his father's, when they had nearly lost the
lot, he had had to knuckle down further.

He liked his own space. He'd never truly understood
children. The visits from his mother and sister lasted
longer than he wanted them to and the peace and quiet
afterwards always made him grateful.

He was building a future for his family, a future to
see them all safe and taken care of and to see the estate
of Goldings stride in good shape into the next century.
It was enough.

Case Thornton, his farm manager and a friend since
childhood, met him as he gained the final hill before
home.

'You're out in poor weather, Alex. A storm is coming,
I am thinking, and it won't be pretty.'

'Which is why I am heading back.'

Case frowned. 'Have you met Guy Martin's widow yet?'

He'd noted his direction, then. 'Just now. The son dropped his coat down by the river and I took it over.'

'A surly child, by all accounts, and one who boasts constantly. I doubt the children hereabouts like him any more than we liked Guy.'

'Some of the youths have been beating him up. I caught three of them doing it. The Martin boy hared off home with a face that looked worse for wear.'

'I'll have a word with Timothy, then, and see what he says. Don't think it would be my son doing the fighting but he might know something.'

'Ask after the sister, too, while you are at it. Her name is Jenny.'

'You sound interested in them?'

'Interested in the way a neighbour is. Interested in quelling any problems, too.'

'You think he is one? This boy?'

'He looks lost, and Guy certainly did not teach him to use his fists.'

'Yet he used his all the time at that age. Remember how fast we'd run past the Grange just to make sure he did not see us whenever he was there in the holidays.'

'We were good at making friends though and Guy was not. This lad doesn't seem to be, either.'

'I should tell you there's a rumour going round Mrs Martin is running short of money. My wife said Molly Alpin, a kitchen hand at the Grange, told her that the mistress of the house will take in sewing come the New Year, so perhaps they won't be staying, after all.'

After bidding Case goodbye Alex tried to think back to what Mrs Martin had been wearing when he met her. A plain dark blue gown without much decoration on it. If she thought to make money from her stitchery she might have to come up with something more striking. But his understanding of the widow was growing and he was not surprised at all by the idea that Guy had made no provision for his family after his death. He was a man who had lived in the moment and if that moment was about him then all the better.

He wondered how she had coped with such a husband. Perhaps she had been damaged by Guy's selfishness and had come to Somerset to take stock of things. That was the only explanation that made any sense, and the note the daughter had written indicated a family under duress.

Goldings was coming into view now and he could see shadows of people against the curtains of the main front salon. His Christmas guests had arrived early. The constant barking of the dogs made him grimace, and if he listened further he could hear the crying of one of the children. Was Gerard here with them this year? Alex hoped not, for his sister's husband was difficult company. His mother would already have disappeared upstairs, the travel from London exhausting her, and she would not be down until the morrow. He knew Sarah had brought two governesses and two maids as help, for he had seen the list she had sent a few months back so that sleeping arrangements could be organised.

Sarah was similar to him in that way, for he liked things in order. The Martin woman had surprised him and this was part of the problem, the colour of her eyes so startling he kept returning to the memory. The boy worried him too, because he'd held the shadows of a lad who could so easily go astray, and though he did not owe Martin anything at all he also knew if the tables had been turned he would have liked Guy to reach out a hand in help.

Just in principle.

The door opened as he put his foot on the last step up to the front door, the light and warmth flooding across him as his sister flung herself into his arms.

'I told Mama you would be here soon, and I was just wondering where on earth you could be, for no one here had seen you in a while, and the weather is worsening.'

This flood of words came as she banged shut the door behind him and lifted up a small child for him to observe.

'Matilda is two tomorrow, Alexander, and hopes you have remembered her birthday.'

The little girl hid her face in her mother's shoulder and refused to look at him.

'Christopher is somewhere in the house, probably endeavouring to find some space away from us all, and John and Anthony have gone up with their governess. Mama has taken Caroline with her for an hour or so and I have only Mattie. Silence is golden, as they say.'

Privately Alex wondered at her reasoning, for the child had only just stopped crying as he had walked in. He'd heard the yowl from a good distance away. Still, the topsy-turvy chaos his sister brought with her had a sort of energy that always made him smile.

'I take it that Gerard is not here with you?'

'My husband relishes the moments he can sleep in and not be disturbed, Alexander. Surely you know that about him by now, and in all honesty a break from each other is sometimes a good thing. Marriage is not as easy as you might think.'

'But you are happy?'

'I am and I wish you would be, too. Aunt Mary and

her guests are not due to arrive until the morrow, but she has spoken highly about the daughters of her friend, Mrs Fry, every time I have visited her in London. The two oldest girls sound sensible and well-educated.'

Here it was again. It had taken her no longer than a few minutes to bring up his unmarried state, which had to be some sort of a record. He went to say something, but she stopped him.

'If you can't come to the society balls, then the eligible young ladies must be brought to you, for it was most unfair of Papa to make all those awful investments which ruined Goldings and then expect you to take over and make everything right again. It gives you so little time to socialise, to find a woman you could lose your heart to and…'

He stopped her by laughing.

'I can assure you that I have not been completely without female company.'

This banter between them began every time they'd been apart for a few months, as only a year stood between them, and with no other siblings they had always been close.

'I know that, of course, for every female in London is besotted by you, but you never reciprocate, Alexander. You never get lost in love.'

'Like you do with Gerard?'

'Well, no.'

'Then let's say no more. How old is Christopher now?'

'Almost twelve. Why?'

'Guy Martin's widow has come back to the Grange and has a son of the same age, a troubled boy, I think, who could use a friend.'

'Chris is rather shy and not at all urbane…'

'All the better for it. Perhaps I could borrow him for an hour tomorrow, for I have promised Mrs Martin that I would teach her son how to fight with his fists and protect himself.'

'Of course you can take him, for he would love to spend some time with you. What does she look like, this widow?'

'Dark. Sad. I've only met her once.'

The expression on his sister's face was suddenly hard to read.

'Perhaps you could also ask them all over here for a Christmas drink? They are our nearest neighbours, after all?'

'Sarah...'

'You need to be free again, Alex, to live your life. Free not to worry about Goldings and all it entails.'

'I am fine.'

He left her then and bounded up the stairs to find his mother.

Elizabeth stood before her full-length mirror that evening and looked at herself. She was being worn down by anxiety and worry and it showed. She could barely remember a time when she had last laughed or done something entirely for fun. Even breathing was hard these days, with every problem sitting so heavily on her shoulders.

Luis had not come out of his room since he had returned from the woods, and the plate of food left at his door had not been touched. The bullying had been going on for some time now and she couldn't find a way to stop it, but she was glad that her son was, at least for this moment, safe.

Lord Alexander Grey. She had heard his name mentioned often in the English community in Bilbao. An earl who was trying to save the family finances from ruin and who was doing a spectacular job.

Guy had hated him and every time his name came up he had made sure to say something uncomplimentary to whoever was listening. Elizabeth thought it was jealousy that made him so sour, for, while the Greys' star rose into the heavens without pause, theirs had dulled with each successive year.

When her husband had died from wounds suffered in a duel she had simply buried him there and packed up and left, relieved to be free of both his anger and his bitterness and glad that there was a house in Somerset to use for shelter.

The Grange. It was a sanctuary. Guy had given her the keys a few days before his death, perhaps in some ghastly premonition as to what might happen to him. One last act of honour in a marriage where there had been very little of it.

Today when she had opened her door and found Lord Alexander Grey there it was as if God might have finally answered her desperate pleas for help. He was solid and honest and honourable. She had heard that about him always and he wanted to teach her son how to defend himself, how to stand up to bullies and survive. It was a miracle, a redemption and a way to find the path back to normality and hope.

If the Earl was on Luis's side they might just manage it, this shift, this place, this need to feel secure. Taking up her rosary, Elizabeth closed her eyes while saying the Fourth Luminous Mystery: the Transfiguration, with all the feeling she could muster.

When she had finished she attached her own prayer. 'Please let Lord Grey come tomorrow. Please let him keep his word. Please don't let him forget.'

For a moment she had the uncanny feeling that she was starting to emulate her daughter with the heartfelt notes she wrote and left anywhere and everywhere. Please, please, please. But she still held enough honesty to admit she was struggling and that any aid might ease the load. Her grandmother's constant admonitions about the power of prayer had left their mark, too, and if the Lord above was at this moment listening she begged he might allow her just a small respite. To catch her breath and make a plan, to find some peace. A Christmas wish that held at least a little hope.

Crossing to her wardrobe, she sorted through the four dresses she owned and chose her best gold-velvet gown to wear tomorrow. She needed confidence and this one gave it to her. She thought then that it had been a long time since she had last worried about what she wore.

The sound of crying had her placing the dress down on her bed and hurrying along the hallway to Luis's room. When she knocked quietly and waited he opened the door and fell into her arms, an eleven-year-old who needed his mother. Holding him to her, she rocked him as she had when he was younger and the world was unkind. She whispered her love as well, all the things from her heart that she felt for him, this child who had always found life so very difficult.

Finally, he quietened and raised his head. She was shocked by the swollen eye and the cut lip, the bruising already coming out in whorls of purple, yellow and red. No wonder Jenny had reported his injuries to her with such worry, for this was the worst beating yet.

'I heard what he said. Lord Grey. I heard him say he would teach me to fight and I want him to, Mama, because he looks like a man who would know how to do it properly.'

She nodded and he went on. 'He found me being beaten up by the river and he frightened the other boys away. They were scared of him, I could tell. He knew Papa, too. He told me that he did.'

'Which is the reason he has offered his help, my darling. I am sure he will keep to his word.'

'I am sorry I took your rosary. I would have brought it back but in the rush of getting away I left it there along with my coat.'

'Why did you take it?'

'I thought of all the prayers you have said across the years and how none of them has ever been answered and I wanted them to stop because nothing ever seems to change.'

'Well, we are here now and England is a big change, and, while it might take time to understand the ways of the Lord, this part of Somerset is a place your father always loved.'

'I hate it so far.'

'I know you do but if you give it a chance you might not.'

'Jenny hates it here, too. She hates Christmas because it never turns out how she hopes that it will.'

Elizabeth's heart sank but she took his hand.

'We'll go down to the kitchen and find you something to eat. Life always looks a lot more hopeful on a full stomach.'

'Papa would have taught me how to fight. He would have shown me everything and they'd be scared of me.

No one would have dared hurt me because I'd be the winner like he was. He could beat anyone. You know that he could.'

'Sometimes, Luis, it is a better idea to explain the problem and try to find a solution...'

It was the wrong thing to say, she knew it as she felt him stiffen.

'You are not always right. Papa said you were wrong so many times.'

'He is not here any more, Luis, but I am, and anger is not an easy companion, no matter what stage of life you are in.'

He stepped back at that and hurled more words at her.

'You don't know what it's like to be me. You only think of yourself. You dragged us here to England against our will and just expect us to like it. Well, I do not. I hate it here.'

Then he was gone again, the door to his room slamming in a resounding crash just as the clock in the corner of the hall struck eight.

Sorrow consumed Elizabeth. This had been the pattern of their relationship ever since Guy had died six months ago. One step forward and then two back, her son's anger overriding everything else. Even as a child he had not been easy, using his loud voice and fury like a weapon. When Guy had made one of his infrequent appearances he always distanced himself from his son after a few hours. As if those minutes were all he could stand, and that fact had not been lost on Luis.

But he had never been as morose as he was now, the weather and the house and their isolation bringing forth another aspect of him that she despaired of. He'd barely interacted with anyone in weeks and he slept a lot of the time.

Once back in her room she sat on the bed and laid her face in her hands, taking deep breaths as she did so. The hope she had in wearing the golden gown beside her was ridiculous, and she admonished herself for the vanity. She was twenty-seven, soon to be twenty-eight. A widow at her age did not prance around in finery and imagine that a handsome earl would find her attractive.

She needed to concentrate on her children and try to smooth out all the rough edges that Guy had left them with. Herself included.

Chapter Two

Lord Grey came just after midday and he was accompanied by another child. A boy about Luis's age who had the look of the Greys about him, with his dark hair and blue eyes.

Luis was unhappy about this unexpected visitor, but Elizabeth held him there and waited as they joined them.

Alexander Grey's glance went to her son's face.

'This is Christopher, my nephew, and he wants to learn the art of boxing as well. It will be easier with the two of you because you are much the same height and weight. Chris, this is Luis Martin and his mother, Mrs Martin.' His quick notice of her as he said this was negligible.

The boys sized each other up, but the newcomer held a temperament that seemed easy and relaxed and for that Elizabeth was grateful. Not a boy to make a fuss.

'We brought some gloves over for you to protect your hands, Luis,' Lord Grey said. 'They were mine when I was about your age.'

She saw her son nod, and after putting them on and showing him how to tie the straps and make them comfortable, Lord Grey got Luis to stand before him.

'Right, put your hands up to protect your face. Feel the leather there. Good. Now, when you box it's not a straight punch. It's a diagonal movement left to right, right to left.'

Lord Grey raised his own hands, which were gloved now, too, and her son did as he asked, punching into the leather, left right, right left, and then changing both the tempo and the number of punches. Within a very short time he seemed to have mastered the way of it. When it was Christopher's turn he did much the same.

'Now, I want you both to practise what I have shown you. One of you call the shots and the other deliver them. Understand. If you hurt each other we will stop. It's a practice, not a battle, so no accidents.'

The Earl watched as they got down to it and Elizabeth saw something in Luis that she had not seen in a very long while.

Concentration.

She stood beside Lord Grey, her heart brimming with joy, watching as he unlaced the boxing gloves he wore.

'I cannot believe Luis could be so good so quickly.'

The man's laughter was welcome.

'It's just the start, Mrs Martin. There is a lot to still show him.'

'Elizabeth,' she answered and turned towards him, and in that moment a feeling she had never before felt passed through her, a breathless knowledge of attraction that sent butterflies into her stomach and her heart beating far too fast.

'Elizabeth.' His voice was deep. 'You have a daughter too, do you not?'

'Yes. A twin to Luis. Her name is Jennifer but she is always known as Jenny.'

'I know. I found one of her notes by the river. She wishes for you to have a very happy Christmas.'

The blood ran into her cheeks and she swallowed. 'It is because we have not had very many and she has read of those families who never falter in the Yuletide season.'

'Few and far between, I think. My own has descended upon me and already there are arguments.'

But he was laughing as he said it, laughing as if he understood the true meaning of family in all of its shades. A man who was at home with honesty and was not one to be chivvied into trying to live up to the expectations of others.

So very different from Guy.

And so attractive.

She looked away because to be even thinking such things was foolish and irrational.

No, it was his help with her son that she must concentrate on because if Luis did not become less angry soon she was sure he would grow up like his father and die like him, too.

The boys were yelling now as they sparred, playing at ridiculous caricatures of boxers, and such silliness warmed her. Her son could still be a child in the moments between anger, and that had to mean something.

'Do you have children yourself, Lord Grey?'

'Call me Alex,' he said as he turned, his eyes the blue of a wintry sky. 'And, no, I've never married.'

Why not? She almost asked this and swallowed twice to stop herself.

'I've been busy with Goldings and the land here, trying to piece things together after my father tore it apart.' He hesitated and then continued. 'You are shocked at such honesty, but it is no secret, and my father is long gone.

He's buried in the chapel grounds of the estate and sometimes I sit on his headstone and tell him of all the ways I am rebuilding what was lost. Like a circle. It's what life truly is, I expect, the good and the bad.'

'You think it is always a circle?' From her point of view she could find no goodness in all that had been taken from her, no way of joining loss with gain, and yet the very thought that she might retrieve the person she had once been was beguiling.

'I do, although there were years when I wondered. How did your husband die?'

The question came from nowhere but she wanted to answer it.

'In a duel. He had an affair with someone's wife and the man killed him. It was not the first time he had...dallied, and neither was it the first duel. He had something of a reputation...' She stopped herself from continuing, for she'd never told anyone this before and wondered why she was telling this man now, but it was so good to be honest.

'Did you know Guy well?' Suddenly she wanted to know.

He shook his head. 'He was barely here. His parents died early on and he spent most of his time in London with an uncle and aunt. What I do know is that he was good with his fists but he lacked finesse with people. As a boy I simply made a point of running away when he came near me. As a man I seldom saw him.'

'Yet he spoke of you, often. I think he envied you.'

He did not take her observation further but instead asked a question of his own.

'How did you meet him?'

'I was brought up in the church under the guidance of a strict grandmother. I was a novice in a convent when

I first met Guy, for my own parents passed away early, too, and it was a pathway my mother hoped I might take.'

'And instead you ran away with Guy?'

'I did.'

She looked at him then, straight into the dark blue of his eyes, shame no doubt written on her face. But if he was to be a help to Luis she needed him to see a truth, a sincerity that could not be questioned. This was her only chance of finding a way out of the lies she had been surrounded with, and she had promised herself even before she had left Spain that she would never again be immured in deceit.

Alex wanted to reach over and touch her, reassure her, make certain that in all the turmoil of her world she knew that he was here. But he didn't, because she would not want it probably and the boys were close by.

Elizabeth Martin did something to him with her innocence and beauty and with that strange mix of hope and fear. He had never talked to another woman as he did to her, with such honesty and frankness. The green in the dress she wore today brought out the colour of her eyes and the dark of her hair. It also showed off her curves.

He needed to find a way forward between them that would keep her in his orbit so that he might discover more about her, and he suddenly thought of one.

'Tomorrow the rain will be heavy.' He looked at the clouds gathering. 'If you brought Luis over for practice at Goldings it might work better. Jenny would be most welcome to come, too, if she would like.'

'Will your family mind?'

'Having guests?'

'I don't think my husband was very popular around here. I hear the servants talk.'

He didn't let her finish.

'All those years back should not matter. It's what comes now that does, and Christmas is a good time to take stock of what has happened in the past year and work out what you wish changed for the next one.'

'Do you do that?'

He saw humour in her eyes, and liked it.

'To be honest I have never changed that much, though every year I promise I won't work as hard.'

The boys seemed to have finished their bouts of boxing and were looking over at him in anticipation of what should come next. He'd get them to put down their gloves and start doing some training. He remembered his own training in London when he'd been sent to the city, a young green boy without much muscle and whose only true knowledge of the sport had been running away as fast as he could from the aggressive and older Guy Martin.

'Why did you learn to box?'

Elizabeth's question made him smile because here he was, all these years later, teaching this gangly young son of hers the rudiments of it.

'It was your husband's proficiency in the sport that made me want to.'

She did not answer that but looked away, worry on her brow.

'I'd like Luis to be able to defend himself, Lord Grey. As you know, it seems he is at odds here with some of the other boys and I hope it will not get worse. Perhaps if he had enough aptitude to scare them off...'

She left the question there.

'Then I had better give them some more exercises to get them going.'

After setting up a series of things he wanted the boys to do he returned to stand beside her. The girl, Jenny, had come out now. She was thinner and taller than Luis, but her demeanour held the same wariness.

'Good afternoon.'

She looked shocked that he had spoken to her.

'I found a note in the bushes with ribbons on it from someone who signed her name as Jenny. The words were hopeful of a lovely Christmas. Would that be you?'

The girl nodded and looked at him directly for the first time, her eyes the exact shade of her mother's.

'If you and your mother would like it I could cut a pine bough and bring it over to the Grange to decorate on Christmas Eve? We will be finding one for Goldings, so it won't be a bother.'

Jenny pulled back and watched him with interest as she waited for her mother to answer.

'That is very kind of you, Lord Grey, and we would be most appreciative.'

Elizabeth saw the desperate hope of a wonderful Christmas in Jennifer's expression. She knew exactly what would have been written in that note he had spoken of because she had been finding similar versions of the same thing all over the Grange.

She was grateful for the invitation to join the Greys at Goldings, though she hoped the family he mentioned would not be averse to strangers inveigling themselves into their celebrations and that her children would be on their very best behaviour.

She hoped, too, that she might be interesting enough

to make such a kind offer worthwhile and that they would not see the sadness in her that had grown and grown in each successive year after her marriage.

She also thanked God that Jenny had not burst into tears when Lord Grey had asked her his question, because their family was on the edge of disintegrating, of melting into the chaos of confusion and bitterness and fear. It would only take a very little thing to allow others to see that she could crumple, too, and right now pity was the very last thing that she needed.

Luis came over to stand beside them.

'Can I take Chris up to my room for a moment, Lord Grey? He wants to see my collection of flags.'

'Of course you can. You've probably done enough exercise for today and both of you managed the practice very well. I will have you boxing proficiently in no time at all.'

Elizabeth saw pride in her son's eyes. 'Jenny can come too if she wants, Mama. She likes flags.'

Unexpectedly Jennifer pulled away from her mother to follow the two boys, leaving Elizabeth standing there watching them all disappear.

'I am glad my son can still be kind sometimes.' She said these words without thinking.

'Eleven is a difficult age for anyone.' Alexander Grey did not sound at all perturbed. 'Being caught between childhood and what comes next takes courage, and yet most of us come out all right in the end.'

Sage and sensible advice. The voice of reason that she had long lost hold of in her isolated and lonely world. She swallowed to try and find some equilibrium.

'Thank you for today, my lord. I have appreciated it more than you can know.'

'You are welcome.' He looked around, his glance falling on the hedges at one edge of the garden. 'Is there still a maze in the corner?'

'I don't know. I have not ventured out here at all.'

'Let's find out, then.'

She followed him and was surprised when he slipped through a small entrance and she could no longer see him. But, taking the chance of following him, she squeezed through the dishevelled branches and came up beside him.

Inside it was worse.

'My friends and I used to play here when the family was not in residence, and as they were seldom in Somerset that was often. But the gardener kept the lines clipped then, and it was easy to find the way.'

'The way to where?'

'The centre. The rose bush in the middle was said to come from the fields of some far-off war, and its blooms were blood-red in the winter when everything else was dormant.'

Her own interest surfaced. 'Can you find it again?'

'Of course.'

Leaning over, he took her arm in a solid, warm grasp and he used his other arm to spread the leaves and rid the way of spiders and their webs.

It was like an adventure from a book, the wind above them circling in a darkening sky and the smell of the pine hedge close. Here it was still as he led her through one walkway and then many more, finding the gaps with ease and finally coming into the middle.

Nothing was there save for emptiness.

'I think plants as fragile as a rose bush need a more careful tending than this one got.' His words held humour.

An old dead trunk was clearly visible as he kicked away the weeds, a cloud of small insects surprising him.

'Not bees at least, for they all die in the winter,' he said as he turned to stop the flying cloud from reaching her.

Such closeness inside the centre of the maze took away Elizabeth's breath, the world far from them, nothing here except silence and solitude. And them.

'A maze is a path or collection of paths, from an entrance to a goal.' His voice was softer now, yet more immediate for it. 'A metaphor for life if you like, with all the wrong turnings before a final destination.'

'A life like mine?' She could not help but say it.

His hand came up, one finger brushing across her cheek in a single sensuous line.

'Don't look back, Elizabeth, for the world here will help your family if you will allow it to.'

He wanted to kiss her. He wanted to pull her down to the long grass beneath them and know her scent and her softness. He wanted to understand her sorrow and try in some way to temper it, to fill up the lost pieces of her beauty and make her whole again.

He wanted things he had never desired in any woman before her, a knowledge of her body and her mind, a joining, a fusion, a connection that might stop them both from spinning into loneliness.

God.

He almost swore as her hand covered his, the warmth of her skin, the honesty.

'Thank you, my lord. For this. For bringing me here. For showing me a place that I would not have found otherwise. For believing that life can become better. For helping Luis. For bringing your nephew over as a friend. For being kind to Jenny and not laughing at her notes.'

'That is a long list of thank-yous.'

She smiled and he clamped down on his control as he stepped away, letting his hand fall and understanding that in reserve there was also safety. For them both.

Never once in all of his life had he felt like this. Breathless. Unsure. He did not like the feeling at all, but even at a distance, in the rain and the wind when he had first seen Elizabeth Martin screaming at the sky, he had felt the same thing.

He knew her and he understood her.

'We should go back.'

His words, sliding between alarm. If they did not go soon he would say things he shouldn't.

'Of course.' She looked around. 'But which way is back?'

He strode through the first opening, glad when he felt her behind him.

Elizabeth hurried to keep up; the rain had now started as a drizzle, the darkening sky threatening to open.

Alexander Grey had not liked her touch and she was furious at herself for reaching out when he had only tried to offer kindness and friendship.

Had he seen she would have liked more?

She pushed that thought away and walked faster, anger gathering, for where did she go from here and what must he think of her? A foolish old widow with a thousand worries and the temerity to imagine that she might mean something. To him.

It was the maze, she thought, and the fact of being at the centre of a place of such solitude. The end of a journey, an arrival, a destination. When he'd sheltered her from the insects arising from the dead trunk of the ancient rose bush she knew a heat that had been long lost in the frozen wasteland of her unwise marriage. As his body had come against her own, solid, warm and real, it had shifted reason in a way that she had not expected.

She felt the burn of it all the way to the centre of her heart and in other places too. And that was the problem. A forbidden hope. An unwise infatuation.

Coming out of the maze, they found the children searching for them, full of words and energy. As if a magic spell had been cast across the whole of the Grange and its inhabitants. To make them quicken and live again.

She must do nothing to curb Alexander Grey's help and she looked away as she saw him watching her, jamming her hands into her pockets, the chatter of the children emphasising the great divide between them, the heights of his exalted existence compared with the troughs of her own.

Running away with Guy had been a disaster almost from the very first day, and within a month they had actively disliked one another. He had sought out the company of women who gave him the sort of adulation that he required to survive, and she had turned inwards.

The twins had been her salvation, though as they had grown Guy had tainted even that relationship with his rare visits that always ended in tears.

Now she needed to gather her thoughts, to become stronger in her own right. She needed to find goodness and honesty again and use these things to build her family up, to reframe morality, to foster integrity. To live by all those teachings that had been so much a part of her early life.

She knew she could not weather another disastrous relationship, and to imagine that the wealthy and powerful Lord Alexander Grey might hold an interest in her was pure foolishness.

But he could help her with her children, and right now this had to be her focus.

'Tomorrow when you bring Luis and Jenny perhaps you could stay on for a glass of punch. We have a few guests at Goldings, and my sister, my mother and aunt are in residence.'

'A lot of people, then?' Already she felt nervous.

'It's just a Christmas drink.'

'Of course.'

'And a chance to show you Goldings.'

She looked up at that. Did he want to show it to her in a personal way or was he just asking as the lord of the house and as a neighbour? She could not deduce quite what he meant, so she stuck to the second option.

'I have heard much about the house and have seen it on my walks since arriving here.'

'Then we were remiss not to have you come and visit earlier. Neighbours are always valued in the country.'

The second option, then.

She plastered a smile across her face and turned to Christopher.

'Thank you for coming and visiting my son. You would be welcome to return to the Grange any time you like.'

Luis added to her words with his own. 'We are coming to see you tomorrow for some more boxing practice, too.'

Alexander Grey interjected.

'Bring the gloves, then, Luis. I will be able to slip away

from company for an hour or so to show you a few more
things, and then you can practise together.'

'I can keep these gloves here?'

'They are yours now.'

The delight Luis showed at this gift had Elizabeth
swallowing and she thanked Lord Grey profusely. Even
Jenny looked happier.

On the way home Chris chatted nonstop about the
morning, about the flag collection Luis had amassed and
about how beautiful Mrs Martin was.

'She looks like someone from a painting, doesn't she,
Uncle Alex, a beautiful painting done by one of the old
masters? Papa has books on them. She doesn't seem old
enough to have a boy the age of Luis but sometimes she
does look sad. Perhaps we should find them some furniture that isn't used at Goldings? Their house was very
bare.'

'I'll see what we can do,' Alex said, thinking privately
that Elizabeth Martin might be horrified at receiving such
overt charity. He also hoped that Christopher would not
tell his mother what he had just told him, for his sister
would use the information about her appearance with
relish.

The house was busy when they returned, his Aunt
Mary and her two guests all in the downstairs parlour
with his mother and Sarah.

Chris used the busy chatter as a way to disappear,
and Alex wished that he could have done the same, but
there was no way without rudeness to simply turn around
and leave.

'Alexander.' His sister's voice held that certain delight

in it, the tone she used when introducing the next suitor she thought might be just right for him.

'You must meet Aunt Mary's friends.'

Aunt Mary herself was now kissing him on the cheek and telling him that it had been far too long since he had been up to London. Then with a deftness that was surprising she brought the first girl forward.

'This is Miss Arabella Fry. Arabella, this is my nephew, Lord Grey; and here is her younger sister, Miss Abigail. There is only a year separating them.'

'Indeed,' he answered as the other girl came across, for the blonde curls and blue eyes were identical.

'Their father is the nephew of Lord Drummond and he has made a veritable fortune in the new railways.'

A further feather in their caps, he thought, at least in the eyes of his aunt. Rich and beautiful. And with good manners, he added privately as Miss Arabella impressed her sincere thanks for this invitation upon him.

'We will not stay for Christmas, of course, but having us for a few days is very generous of you, as it has been many years since we have been in Somerset.'

'You reside in London, then?'

'We do, my lord. In Grosvenor Square. My mother and your aunt are friends.'

'I see.' He said these words and then struggled to find more.

His sister, sensing awkwardness, quickly dived in. 'Arabella sings.'

'She does?'

'Yes, beautifully.'

Arabella shook her head and smiled.

'I believe I sing much the same as other women who are brought out into Society.'

'She has been admiring our garden, too.'

'You enjoy plants?'

'Flowers, Lord Grey. I particularly like the scent of roses in the summertime. We have two unmatched specimens in our townhouse garden that are spectacular.'

'Quite.' His vocabulary seemed to have shrunk into platitudes and pointless rejoinders that added nothing to the conversation. He wished Elizabeth Martin were standing before him with her honesty and her difference, a woman who had forged her own way in life despite numerous difficulties. How long had the Misses Fry said they were staying? A few days. The time ground out before him in an endless length of hours.

'Perhaps you might like to hear us sing, my lord?'

He looked up and saw Sarah watching. Aunt Mary also had her eyes upon him, a small smile playing around her mouth.

'Of course. I shall look forward to a recital.'

Alexander hated this sort of exchange, with no true discourse in it. Taking a glass of wine from the tray that was being offered around, he wondered for a second how Mrs Martin might find such a stifling social occasion. She would be here for drinks tomorrow and, as it would be all the same company, he imagined her pleading her need to return home as soon as she could. She did not seem like a woman who might suffer the extreme manners of silly young girls for long.

That thought had him reaching for another glass, this time one filled with strong brandy.

There was still supper to get through and then a recital. Chancing a look at the clock, he saw that it was only just before five, and he took a large swallow of his drink.

* * *

Elizabeth sorted through all her bills after the children had gone to bed and made two piles: those that had to be paid immediately, and those that could wait for at least a few weeks.

Unfortunately, the former pile was far bigger than the latter one, and her ready cash could not even wholly cover all the accounts owing.

She could sell three portraits, the ones that had been left to her as a child after her parents had died. She knew they were valuable because she had shown a broker in London on her way here and he was very interested. She had kept his address so she could write to him if she needed to. She could still afford a coach ticket to London and back, and Emmeline, one of the maids at the Grange, could watch over Luis and Jenny while she was gone.

But it was getting harder, this constant worry about money, and she had no true hope of gaining more.

She looked around the room she sat in. The furniture was sparse and the sofa in the far corner was threadbare. Even the colourful Spanish fabric draped across it which she had brought with them from Bilbao failed to hide the wear and tear.

She could only imagine what Goldings must look like inside. Opulent and lavish were two words that came to mind, with no doubt a great deal of furniture as magnificent and prosperous as its owner.

The invitation to drinks worried her. She had heard from a maid that guests had arrived at Goldings earlier this evening and that the carriage they had come in was liveried.

Another set of titled people to have to carefully tread

around, and undoubtedly ones who would have some knowledge of her sordid marital history with Guy.

In London she had visited the townhouse of his only living relatives when she returned, an ancient aunt and uncle who wanted absolutely nothing to do with her or the children. They were most emphatic over the lack of duty they now felt, the old man setting it out baldly.

'Our nephew made bad decisions and now he's paid for it. He bled us dry of resources with his schemes that came to nothing, and we can no longer condone any of it. His death, of course, at such a young age has come as a shock but he must have known that his decisions could cost him his life if he insisted on fighting the duels he did.'

To give them their due they had pressed a hundred pounds into her hands.

'For the children,' they had said pointedly before asking a servant to show them all out.

For so long she had been the wife of a husband whose life had lurched from bad to worse and who gave no care for her wants or fears. Guy had made it eminently clear that he would never agree to a divorce, and when he did visit the children any dialogue between them was negligible.

He never stayed long.

Thus when Lord Grey had held her in a way that had protected her from the insects in the middle of the old maze it was the first time a man had ever made sure that she was unharmed and safe.

She wished she were back in that moment, in the magic of it, and not sitting here in the semi-dark at the Grange, up to her neck in bills.

What was he doing now, she wondered, in his magnificent mansion over the hill? If she did not have Luis and Jenny she might have left the estate to creep across in the darkness to watch the lights of Goldings. Shadows on the curtains always told one thing, and with a carriage full of new arrivals there would be music, no doubt, and laughter.

The clock ticked in the corner, marking out the silence. Almost nine o'clock. She stood and walked to the window, pulling back the heavy velvet. The rain had stopped and the moon was out, clouds scudding in the wind across the brightness of its face, lightening the land and then just as quickly darkening it.

Did Lord Alexander Grey stand at his window at this moment and see the very same sky and land that she did? It was a connection that felt both flimsy and important.

If she thought of him, could he be thinking of her?

What was it he had said? Life was a circle. The circle of her thoughts. The circle of gold that still sat upon the fourth finger on her left hand proclaiming to the world the eternity of matrimony.

She wore it for the children and for those adults who had an inclination for harsh judgement. She wore it because it was hard enough to be a young widow but especially difficult when you were a grateful one.

When Guy had died she had thanked the Lord and she still thanked him. For her freedom. For her escape. For all the dread that she could let out now that she was never again going to see him.

Salvation.

If it were just her in the world she would have tugged the thin gold marriage band away from her flesh and thrown it as far into the distance as she could. To be lost for ever.

Lost to an empty place. A place as empty as her heart.

Not long until Christmas. She clenched her teeth together and wished the whole pretence of the season gone. But it wasn't just her. She had the children to consider now as well as her social standing. One more mistake could ruin them.

Luis had been so much happier tonight, full of chatter about boxing and Christopher and Lord Grey. It was as if the Earl had cast an enchantment across her son, allowing him to see things with more clarity.

She knew her children would enjoy their afternoon tomorrow at Goldings. She only wished she were looking forward to it with as much fervour.

Chapter Three

Alex saw them from the window of the drawing room, for he had been watching out for their arrival.

They came on foot.

He should have sent the carriage to collect them, but he hadn't thought that they would not have the use of one.

Miss Annabelle Fry was standing next to him and did not hold back from expressing her surprise at the small group coming in such a way, which brought the rest of the party over to the window, too.

'I cannot imagine walking to an engagement as they are doing, but I suppose in the country one does things differently from in the city?'

'The Grange is only close, Miss Fry. Many a time we have walked the very same journey.'

Even if it were not true, he had the urge to protect Elizabeth, and Sarah, overhearing, looked over at him quickly and continued the charade.

'We have always held close ties with our neighbours and, although it might be unusual in the city to walk from place to place, here it is a far more normal thing.'

Privately Alex could not remember one time when

the inhabitants of the Grange had held close ties with Goldings, or indeed walked over for any social occasion, but the explanation seemed to have doused the criticism, which was just as Sarah had intended.

Excusing himself to go to the front door to greet the little group personally, he did not care what the new guests thought of such a thing.

Elizabeth Martin wore a hat which shaded her face, and her hair was pinned back at her neck so that the wood sprite was transformed into a tighter version, her dress underlining the change.

The lighter gold she wore suited her, the darker colours he had only ever seen her in gone.

Her smile was sincere, though he got the impression that she was nervous. Both children held gifts wrapped in a colourful fabric.

'For your mother and your sister,' she said as she saw him looking. 'In a way of thanks for having us here today. I am sorry I have nothing for you, as you were the one who asked us, but the gifts are feminine and I make them by hand, so…'

She stopped and looked at him aghast as if she had spoken too much, as if the whole visit was going to be a disaster, as if she was out of place and knew it.

'They will be most grateful.'

Taking the gifts, he placed them on the table in the front hall. 'Perhaps it might be better if they were to be opened later in private as we have other guests today as well.'

'Of course,' she returned, the green of her eyes shaded, any smile gone as the social occasion dawned upon her. He knew exactly how she felt.

'Christopher is waiting for Luis and Jenny,' he said,

gesturing to one of the governesses standing near a door. Both children looked about as fearful as their mother. 'Mrs Wilson will take you both upstairs, for there is lots planned to entertain you.'

He watched as they left and saw that Jenny's hair was plaited and threaded with fabric flowers. A Spanish influence, he supposed, and realised then that of course the children had spent their entire lives in the far-off country, and England must appear strange to them.

Not for the first time he imagined this invitation to be unwise. The Fry sisters were from that particular segment of society in London that favoured a great dollop of manners and convention, and Elizabeth with her vibrant raw beauty and her outdated clothes might not please them.

When she removed her hat he noticed she had plaited her own hair and tied the same fabric flowers into the twists as were in her daughter's.

An unmatched and natural beauty and a woman who did not follow the fashion of the time.

Every other woman in the room looked overdone in style as he brought her forward to meet them. She was taller than both the Fry girls but much thinner.

'Mama, I would like to introduce Mrs Elizabeth Martin from the Grange. Elizabeth, this is my mother, Lady Grey, and my sister, Lady Herbert.'

His mother looked over carefully as his sister grasped Elizabeth's hand and held it in her own.

'It is lovely to have you here, Mrs Martin, and especially as it is so close to Christmas. I have heard much about your son, Luis, from my eldest boy.'

'Thank you for allowing Christopher to come to the Grange, Lady Herbert. They had a boxing lesson from the Earl and made so much progress.'

The Fry girls were less ebullient. They observed Elizabeth with varying shades of displeasure as he made the introductions.

'We have heard of your husband, of course,' the eldest Miss Fry said. 'It seems he was quite the adventurer?'

'He was.'

'Oh, we were most sorry to hear of his death, and it must have been so hard to lose him under difficult circumstances. His demise was the talk of London town, for it was a sad end to a man with much promise, and I am sure you must miss him with all of your heart.'

Elizabeth took a large sip from the glass of wine she had taken, and then another one, and did not answer.

Alexander moved in closer.

He wanted to take her hand and hold it in his, signalling to the Misses Fry that he was here to safeguard her, to shield her from everything. From their questions and from their disapproval.

But Arabella Fry was speaking to him now, of the London balls, the exalted guests and the joy of the season. She was speaking of all the things that Elizabeth Martin probably had no notion of at all.

Miss Arabella Fry was flirting with Alexander Grey and she was using her eyes, her fan and her voice to do it. She was beautiful, as was her sister, beautiful in the way fair and wealthy women could be, the blue in their eyes the shade of a gentle summer sky, no storms at all evident.

Innocent. Virtuous. Untouched.

All the things that she was not.

They were staking out their ground against her and

with Lord Grey. Keep away, the undertone suggested; you have had your chance and now it is ours.

The world Miss Arabella Fry described was one Elizabeth hadn't known. She had never been brought out or enjoyed any time in London. Wales had been a closeted and quiet existence and her grandmother whilst well born had also been a woman of moderate income. Thus, the dazzling wealth of the *ton* and all the things the girl in front of her described were as far from her own understanding as the moon.

These were the sort of females men such as Lord Grey would choose as a bride. They'd probably been invited here for that specific reason, to be dangled in front of the eligible lord of the house in the way young women had been for centuries.

Taking another sip of her wine, Elizabeth thought that she must not drink any more, for the world was spinning a little, and she needed all of her wits to survive this.

Alexander's sister, Lady Herbert, had come over to talk to her now, her smile warmer than the other guests'.

'My brother mentioned he noticed some splendid portraits on his visit to your house. If it is art you are interested in perhaps you might ask him to show you the Grey relatives' portraits along the walls leading to the library. I am sure he could make the time.'

She looked over at Lord Grey, who was in conversation with Arabella Fry, and he was laughing at something she said. All she wanted to be was home, away from Goldings and its beauty, away from the hopes and dreams that lay untethered inside her, spilling out across anticipation; stupid, useless wishes that would never, ever come to pass.

As if noticing where she looked, Lady Herbert added

a further remark. 'My brother has been chased by such women for years, Mrs Martin, and has never once been caught by them. There is an unwritten understanding in our family that Alexander will choose a wife when he wants to and he will choose the wife that he wants without a care for all the expectations of others.'

Elizabeth did not quite know how to answer such a statement. Was Lord Grey's sister implying she might have a chance? Surely not. Perhaps she only meant to relay a truth so that she might know how the cards would fall. To save any disappointment. To soften the blow.

'I am sure he will find a most appropriate bride. He deserves to be happy because he is a good man, my lady.'

'But it does not always work that way, does it? Sometimes men with character find women who never appreciate the fact.'

'It can work the other way around, too.'

The returning frown made Elizabeth stiffen, for Lord Grey's sister's explanation was nothing like what she'd expected.

'It's easy to look back and see turnings that you wish you had never made, Mrs Martin, but let me assure you almost everyone does it. It's only luck to end up in a place where everything is perfect and I am most wary of those who insist it to be otherwise.'

'Thank you. I appreciate your honesty.'

'I am Sarah to my friends. I hope you will be one too, now that you are come to the Grange.'

Lord Grey had left the side of the vivacious Miss Fry and walked across to them. Elizabeth felt his presence with a sort of aching dread because she could not stop the beating of her heart and the raised hopes inside her.

'Mrs Martin was expressing an interest in the old family portraits, Alexander. Perhaps this might be a good time to show her?'

The blaze of humour in his glance was striking as he looked at her, the dark blue suddenly lighter. She knew the Fry girls had heard his sister ask her question and hoped with all her heart that they might not be invited, though when Lady Herbert moved across into their circle and began to talk they were given no chance to even make the suggestion.

God, Sarah was lethal. She had organised him into this tour of the paintings alone with Elizabeth Martin and extracted him from the company of the Misses Fry all in one breath. And now she was waylaying them with a long monologue on the wonders of Goldings and barely giving them a chance to break in with their own questions.

He was free at least for the next half an hour, free to take Elizabeth on a tour of the house without interruption.

He could not believe his luck.

She, however, looked tentative as laughter echoed after them.

'It is a rule that some ladies follow, I think. If one laughs loud enough and long enough, Mrs Martin, one might make an impression. I sadly fear it is the wrong one.'

At this she did smile. 'I suppose they are young, my lord?'

'And you, on the other hand, are ancient?'

She stopped at that and looked at him.

'Sometimes I feel it. Sometimes I even wonder if I was ever that young in the first place, that happy, that mindless, that carefree.'

'I know what you mean. As the heir to Goldings, I have a lot of responsibility.'

'The title, you mean—being an earl?'

'And an only son.'

'When did your father die?'

'When I was twenty-three. If there is such a thing as dying of a broken heart I think it would apply to him.'

'He was remorseful?'

'Very, for my last conversations with him were all apologies and regret.'

'At least you have that to remember him by, my lord, which must be a comfort. My late husband, on the other hand, apologised for nothing at all.'

Elizabeth coloured and felt the blush of anger rise into her face as she turned away. She was still allowing Guy to ruin things for her and it was a bitterness that was hardly flattering. She wished she could have taken the words back in order to return the day to one more conducive to light and airy musings and the shallow topics permissible in the social setting. Lord Grey did not appear to be displeased though.

'If it's any consolation, Guy was always selfish, right from the start. Every boy around here knew to keep their distance from his anger and his arrogance and the proficiency of his fists.'

'An unhappy truth, I think.'

'He did not much care for the thoughts of others. It was why he was so lonely, I suspect.'

They were in a corridor now that held the pictures his sister had spoken of, but he did not pause. Rather he led her through to a door at one end, and then they were standing in a library, books stacked on high shelves around every wall.

A man's room, decorated sparsely. There were papers

on the top of a large desk, with a variety of quills and smaller books also there.

When Alexander Grey shut the door she knew a moment of uncertainty.

'Was your marriage a happy one, Elizabeth?'

His query came so out of the blue she was momentarily silenced.

'If you'd rather not answer that...'

But she shook her head. 'My husband was a liar and a cheat. But the worst of it was that he believed he was not.'

'Yet you didn't return to England and leave him.'

'With what? I had no personal income or the hope of it. I had two young children and very few friends, save for the servants. No. I did what women have done through the ages—I hid the truth and put a smile on my face in order to survive. When Guy died the Grange came to us and finally there was a place that was ours.' She breathed out heavily and thought he could not want to be hearing this, days before Christmas and minutes away from the uncomplicated and flirtatious laughter of the Frys.

People had been avoiding her for years, so it was nothing new, but the hurt of it here, with him, was unbearably sad.

'I should leave.' Her words came quietly, apology within them, but he caught her hand and shook his head.

'There are things I do not understand about your life, Mrs Martin, and God knows you must have questions about mine, but I don't want you to go.'

Shock ran through her, like a tuning fork she'd once seen in the Welsh convent, its pronged forks vibrating at the sounds emitted from the chapel organ.

Could he feel it, too?

The answer was in his eyes, all distance submerged

in passion, the high-born lord replaced by a flesh-and-blood man, his mouth coming down upon her own, tipped up to receive him.

Not a gentle kiss or a timid one. Not a tentative exploration either. No, he took her offering and turned it into a gift with the heat of him and the strength, and for this moment she was someone else entirely. Not an aging widow full of regret. Not a mother coping badly with the anxiety of her children. Not even a woman balancing on penury and homelessness.

This was different because in his embrace she found courage and an appetite for life and for living. But mostly she found joy, an emotion so foreign and wonderful that she could barely take in a breath.

'Kiss me back, Elizabeth.'

Soft words, underscored in hunger, and when she did as he asked a storm of excitement overtook her and carried her to a place that was all fervency and delight. His hands brought her closer as he shifted his angle, her breath lost in his, only them, only now, only here.

He kissed her mouth and her neck, nuzzling the soft skin, and when one hand loosened the laces of her bodice she allowed it, the feel of his fingers around the heaviness of her breast and the growing ache inside her astounding.

So long since a man had touched her. So long since she had wanted one to. When his free hand came against the column of her throat and he brought his mouth around her nipple and sucked hard, she pulled him in.

Other feelings rose as the thin pain of yearning blossomed. He took her acquiescence with fervour, wrenching her bodice down so that the cold of the day was contrasted against the fire on her skin, gold velvet sagging against the whiteness.

The desk was behind her and she had a vision of herself lying down upon it, her legs open, her skirts raised up, available to his needs and to hers. No rules, no limits.

Perfect until the clock in the corner boomed out the hour, drawing them back, and he stopped, holding her still against him, his breath fast, his heartbeat faster, the day outside returned, the thin winter sun marking the windows.

The Frys. His family. Her children. All here and close. Any moment someone could come and find them, alone and compromised.

Horrified, she stood there, unable to look at him and ashamed at how easily she had let this happen. But mostly shocked by her willingness to abandon everything for pleasure. Her dress hung away from her breasts, exposed in the daylight. As if she were a whore. Did he think her that?

'This is not right.' Her voice shook as she said it.

Her laces were in her fingers and she retied them, smoothing down the creases in the fabric. She was shaking so much it was hard to manage.

Then she was at the door and Lord Alexander Grey made no move whatsoever to stop her.

Hell. What had just happened?

Alex stood and listened to her footsteps retreating down the corridor, hurrying to join the others, moving to safety. If the clock had not brought him back to sanity, could he have stopped, would he have stopped?

He'd always been so careful around women, circumspect, controlled. But with Elizabeth Martin lust ruled him as well as longing. Ever since that first moment of

seeing her screaming at the sky with the rain on her face
he had known a connection and a yearning.

This is not right.

Her words burnt shame into him, though the hunger was not slaked. If the clock had not made its sound,
would he have brought her down to the floor and lifted
her golden dress and simply had her? Just like that? Without words? Without preamble? She was hot and ready,
her nipples hard buds of need, her legs opening around
his, her hips beckoning.

God, surely he would have had some control had she
asked him to cease. He liked to think that he would.

But she was correct when she said it wasn't right. He
should never have escorted her here alone into this room
and kissed her as he had. He should have chaperoned
her to see the portraits within the sight of others, within
convention, within the age-old customs of guardianship.

His hand came down hard on the polished surface of
his oaken desk and he looked around.

A man's room. Like a lair.

The smell of her remained. Lavender and lemon. Soft
smells devoid of all the harsher scents women now favoured. Lifting his head, he drank her in because his
body had not understood yet what his mind did, and the
desperate want hurt.

He couldn't go back to the salon with all the others.
Not yet. He couldn't stand there in a room of laughter
and Christmas drinks when what he felt was so very far
from it, any social nicety demolished by what had just
happened here.

His fingers curled around the edge of the desk, for
balance.

* * *

Lord Alexander Grey had still not returned to the blue salon with all of its colour and chatter.

The eldest Fry girl was now singing a tune, attended by her sister on the pianoforte. A song of love and happiness, the light and gentle lyrics grating on Elizabeth after what had just happened.

'Did you enjoy the paintings, Mrs Martin?'

Lord Grey's sister had come to join her, her smile genuine.

'I did.' She was glad her voice sounded so normal. 'Your house is very beautiful.'

'Goldings is my brother's house now. I live mostly in London.'

'Of course.'

'Where is my brother, by the way? I thought he would have returned when you did?'

Elizabeth tried to appear puzzled but knew she had failed when Lady Herbert looked at her strangely.

'Work rules him and that is the trouble. He barely has an hour for any social discourse and to get him to even attend any sort of gentile gathering of suitable and available women is completely impossible. He is a good man and an honourable one. He used to be more…relaxed, but Goldings and all its associated problems has tempered that.'

Miss Fry had finished her song now and she had come over to join them.

'Mama says that Lord Grey's endeavours with his holdings have been remarkable. She says that if every other lord of the realm did half the work he did England would be in much better shape altogether.'

'An interesting opinion.' Lady Herbert said this with feeling.

'Well, Mama is one of those women who seldom stumbles in life.' This was said with a direct look at Elizabeth.

'She sounds a saint, then, for in truth most of us do have a few falls.' From Lady Herbert the words sounded like a rebuke, and uncertainty crossed the young Miss Fry's face as she excused herself and moved away.

'She is young...' Elizabeth began.

'And silly,' the older woman returned. 'Sometimes I think London makes those new to Society foolish. How old are you, by the way, Mrs Martin?'

'Twenty-seven.'

'Young but not foolish, then. It is a relief.'

She wondered what Alexander's sister might have thought of her behaviour a few moments ago in the room at the end of the corridor. She had caught sight of herself in a mirror placed just outside this room and was astonished to find that she looked just as she usually did. Not bright red, not swollen with feeling, not marked by the passion that had consumed her.

She was simply astounded that the outside could reflect a person so very different from the person on the inside.

It was not until a good hour later that Lord Alexander reappeared, and when his eyes met her own they were distant and civil. Only that.

She should have expected such, of course, her lapse in sense and wisdom in the library exacting some sort of rebuke. But he had made mistakes, too, and again, all she wanted to be was home.

She glanced at the clock and realised that she had

spent a sufficient amount of time at Goldings. It would not now be rude to return to the Grange.

When the children were brought downstairs with a maid she was pleased to see them both thank their hosts. The surly boy of a day or so ago seemed reborn in this friendlier, kinder version of Luis, and Jenny too was emerging from her shell with surprising ease.

Be thankful for this, she thought, and made her own goodbyes, though Alexander Grey left the room as she came nearer and she did not speak with him again.

Chapter Four

His sister had told him repeatedly about how much she'd enjoyed the company of Elizabeth Martin.

'She is sensible and beautiful, and when Chris told me the same after meeting her at the Grange I was sure it could not have been true. But it is. My God, how did she fall in love with Guy Martin, I wonder, and not go mad? Perhaps she is a saint? She wears a cross about her neck. Did you notice?'

He had. It had fallen over his hand as he had unlaced her bodice, the fragile gold against the fair of her skin. He had held it then between his fingers and smiled and she had smiled back, a moment sandwiched between lust, a small interlude of sanity.

Sitting up against the headboard of his bed, he rearranged the pillows, his eyes straying to the clock on the mantel. Just after ten-thirty. He did not feel like sleeping but nor did he relish the regrets of the day in a recumbent, wakeful state.

His body ached for her, for her softness and her curves.
This is not right.

Her words echoed as he thought back across the years after his father's death.

He'd made love to a good number of eager women but never to those in Society, never to a woman whose whole reputation might be lost on an error, an error of misinterpretation such as a forbidden tryst in the library.

But Elizabeth Martin had kissed him back and held him to her. He had felt the sharp run of her nails on his neck and knew as he had taken her nipple in his mouth her hands had wrapped into his hair. Not all one-sided, then, and not completely his fault.

Outside the night was clear and cold, the snow holding off and the winds quiet.

After Elizabeth had left the library he'd spent the next hour tutoring Luis and Christopher in the art of boxing and enjoying the release of tension that that brought. Jenny had asked to be shown the upstairs library, and when he had looked in she had a large selection of books spread out all around her. He knew she had enjoyed some time with the small children as well, for the governess had been more than impressed by her kindness.

After the Martin family had left and the Frys had retired until dinner, his sister had devoted the late afternoon to cutting out coloured paper with her children and making small decorations for his house. Sarah had brought in pine cones, too, and the many and varying Christmas offerings were now on all the empty surfaces of the blue salon downstairs, a vivid reminder of the season.

Perhaps he might take Jennifer a sack of the extra cones and some of the coloured paper tomorrow, and on Christmas Eve he would cut the green bough of pungent pine that he had promised her. He imagined the family decorating their more austere house with some joy. But would Elizabeth want to see him?

Sarah and his mother had opened their presents after the Fry girls and his aunt had gone upstairs, and there had been the same colourful flowers inside that Elizabeth and her daughter had tied in their hair. Both women in his family had been delighted by the gifts.

Elizabeth.

Elizabeth.

Elizabeth.

She was all he could think of.

Alexander was restless and uneasy and so, rising from his bed, he found his warmest coat and hat and left the house.

Elizabeth sat in the room downstairs in the darkness, a single candle burning.

Everyone was asleep, as she had dismissed her maid hours ago.

It was cold tonight but very beautiful; a crisp, clear, nearly Christmas night like the sort she had known as a young girl and loved. Bringing her shawl around her shoulders, she was pleased for the warmth of it.

She should have simply gone to bed, for she'd donned her nightclothes hours ago, but she felt agitated and sad and incomplete in a way that she never had before.

Alexander Grey. It was all because of him. His touch. His kiss. His caresses. Her hand cupped the breast he had suckled and she moved slowly, the rhythm of lust strong, wanting what she would never have, needing a completion to all that had been started.

She had never felt like this before, like a licentious woman with a mounting hunger that was foreign. The urge for him had her tipping back her head and simply feeling, there in the darkness with the sky cloud-blown outside and the land laid bare in a darkened curve. It was in shock that she understood everything sensual inside her was not dead, and that the fire Alexander Grey had begun in the library was unquenchable.

And then he was there through the glass, watching her, like a shadow soul, but real because of the whiteness of his breath.

Here?

She moved, unlatching the window, and, dropping her shawl to the floor, watched as he stepped inside.

No words were spoken as he reached out and gathered her in, warm against the cold, male against female. Her hair moved all around them, dark against the white of her nightclothes, falling across his arms.

Unbound. Undressed and ready.

He knew it, too, as he removed his coat and hat and his mouth claimed her own. He kissed her as he had done in the library at Goldings, no small, timid thing but bursting with need. And then he blew the candle out and took her to the floor, the rug there bathed in spotted moonlight.

Her bodice fell open, the ties already loosened, the thin white lawn of the gown exposing bareness.

'God, help me.' The first words he'd spoken, and rough with emotion. 'If you don't want this, Elizabeth…'

She stopped him by raising one finger to his lips and opening her legs. She did not wish for the arguments of sense. She did not want to be careful any more. All she wanted was him, showing her the things she had never known and finding in a joining the truth of a different life.

Lifting her, he undid his front in one movement and then he was hard against her.

'You are sure?'

She was and he came inside, filling her, making the ache deepen, the wet of want unmistakable, the joy of it making her cry out. The budding lust, the building storm, the release of tension as the waves broke, hot against the coldness of night, taking them both to a realm that was disconnected and apart from ordinary life.

They lay still afterwards, not daring to move. She wanted him never to leave her and the morning never to come. He pulled her shawl across them then, in a bid for some privacy, she supposed, or for warmth. His heart beat so hard against her chest it was like a drum.

Their silence. Their solitude before the day broke and the world came back, for the consequences of what they had done here were distant, unthought-of, banned to another moment.

She had never climaxed like this with Guy, never felt the thrill of her body closing around bliss. Sexual intercourse had been mundane and ordinary in those first few months of marriage and then it had stopped altogether, and she had been glad of it because she'd hated him by then. Hated a husband who was immoral and greedy and coarse.

But this…

This was something she had not even imagined, and her body quickened as he brought his fingers to the place he had just left.

Wet. So wet. She could hear the sound of it as he moved faster and higher, the tension in her heightening into stiffness. Then he found another point, his thumb rolling a nub until she shattered into pieces, her breath caught and released, his mouth on hers capturing the ecstasy.

Pleasure had its own rhythm of delight, she decided then, and time stood still because of it.

'Thank you.' It was all she could think of to say.

She felt him breathe out and relax and felt her own tension dissipate too, because no one would ever be able to take these moments away from her no matter what happened next, and she had recognised the glory of a paradise lost and now found.

Her glory and his.

He brought her in for comfort because she was crying, tears spilling down her cheeks in a new liberation and relief.

'Where is your bedroom?'

He lifted her as he mounted the stairs and closed the door behind them. Sitting then against the bedhead, he rocked her in his arms until the world fell away into sleep.

Elizabeth woke with the sun streaming in through the windows, the curtains open. And he was gone. She looked over to see if the bed had been rumpled on the other side but it had not. It was as if those stolen midnight moments had only been a dream, but she knew full well that they were real, from the soreness between her legs, and from the wetness that was still there.

She was glad Jenny and Luis were late risers and that the maid would not come till well after this hour. She had time to wash and dress and put herself together, to contain the passion, to hide the truth.

Would he return again tonight? That thought came next and she smiled because she hoped he would. She hoped he would come every night until the end of her life. Or until he married some suitable young girl who could give him heirs and bring in a rich dowry for Goldings, because, despite what his sister had said, Elizabeth knew that this was how things worked, titles married titles and wealthy families sought out their well-endowed counterparts.

Her delight withered a little, but then, she had never expected permanency. Lust was not love, and Alexander Grey did not know her well enough to hold an exact opinion of who she was. He did not know of her many problems and limitations.

'Oh, God,' she whispered and brought her face into opened hands. If he came again she would not refuse him, not even if she heard he was to be married to one of the very available Misses Fry, and what did that make her?

A woman who was exactly the same as those Guy had slept with. Marriage breakers and homewreckers. Making the descent from righteousness to immorality. As bad as her husband had been. Living only for the sins of the flesh.

She shook her head, hard, because she always did this. She overthought things and it was her greatest fault. She imagined horrors that might never come to pass, dreadful possibilities that denied reason.

The Earl was thirty-eight and he had not married yet, but she knew there would be plenty of other young hopefuls with their beauty and their determination.

Lord Grey had spent part of his afternoon during the social gathering tutoring Luis and Christopher again in the art of boxing, and both Luis and Jenny had been asked back to Goldings today. That meant she would have to take them over, at least.

What would it be like to meet Alexander Grey in the light of day and in genteel company after the night that they had shared? Would the need for each other be seen in their eyes and on their faces, their bodies drawing together like iron filings to a magnet, a true north and unstoppable.

Perpetual.

Unmistakable.

She pushed back the covers and stood catching her reflection in the mirror as she walked to the washbasin.

Ripe, full and happy. A change that had her taking in a breath and holding it.

'Please help me,' she said aloud but to no one in particular because to beseech the help of the Lord above after such a sin seemed wicked.

Alex returned home and went straight to sleep on the bed counterpane and in his clothes and boots. He slept like the devil too until his valet wakened him by pulling the curtains back at the usual hour of seven.

Bright sunlight streamed in as if it was a reflection of his mood. He couldn't believe what had happened last night between him and Elizabeth, and almost without words.

Sensual, heated and incredible. He wondered if he had dreamt the lot but when he looked in the mirror and saw her scratches on his neck he smiled.

She was the most beautiful woman he had ever seen clothed or unclothed, but she was also an enigma. He knew so little about her, her family, her history with Guy, her time in the convent, the journey she had made back to England after Spain.

The currency of communication between them had been in flesh and not words, and he needed to right the balance enough for her to trust him. This morning Luis and Jennifer were returning to Goldings, for Chris had asked them both back. Alex imagined Elizabeth would bring them but after yesterday he doubted she would want to stay.

Therefore, he would need to visit the Grange again and try and understand what this was between them.

The Frys unfortunately were still here, though his mother had told him last evening that they would be departing on the morrow with his aunt. For that at least he was grateful.

Sarah had smiled at him all of last evening, too, in that infuriating way of hers. He knew she wanted to ask him about Elizabeth but refused to be drawn in and did everything he could to not be alone with her. When Matilda had vomited just after dinner it had helped him immensely, for he had not sighted his sister since.

He would take over the bag of pine cones to the Grange with the special coloured paper and some drawing things. He doubted Elizabeth had much in the way of extras for the children and knew they would be well received. At the very least it was an excuse to visit her and try to make sense of their attraction.

And at worst…

His cock rose. To have her beneath him in the garden under winter sunshine and alone… A further thought followed that one: to see her swell with his child and know that such a connection was for ever. To keep her here at Goldings safe and protected, the world held at bay and the years falling by.

He was thirty-eight and he needed to settle down with a wife and children to secure the estate of Goldings, an estate he had worked so very hard to save. All those years for this. Life suddenly made sense and the toil and hardship which had taken a toll felt far more worthwhile.

Almost an apprenticeship for this moment. A place for Elizabeth and her children to be safe.

Elizabeth walked over to Goldings with some trepidation, wanting to see Alexander and not wanting to see him equally and at the very same time. When the servant at the front door said that he would take the children up she nodded and then left as quickly as she could, not looking back once. She strode with the sun on her face and the wind in her hair and she thought such freedom was like an offering from nature. She remembered the feeling from girlhood, unrestrained and unreserved. Wonderful. It was a feeling she had not known in a very long time.

Alexander Grey was waiting for her at the fork of the path that led down to the Grange and he carried a bag. At first she thought he had been hunting but when he tipped his hat and opened the sack for her to see what was inside, the pine cones astonished her.

'For Jenny,' he explained. 'My sister made Christmas decorations last night and I thought you might like the chance to do the same with your children.'

'It is perfect,' she replied, her hands reaching for the papers of gold and silver and red. There was paint there, too, and brushes and two pairs of scissors wrapped carefully in red-and-green cloth.

'I also came to explain about last night.'

'Explain?' Sudden fear flared.

'You don't know much about me and I hoped you would like to. I thought perhaps we could talk?'

The grove behind them was out of the wind and she saw he had laid a blanket down near the base of a tree

over a bed of pine needles. The same desperation began
to gather; the exact heat that had been there every single
time they had met.

She kissed him first this time, her body plastered
against his own, greedy for him, for more, for a repeat
of last night here in the daytime.

'I want to talk, my lord, but I want this more.'

He had her skirts up even as he took her down, no
time given to a gentle courting, and the shock of his entry
made her groan. Not quietly either, not muffled, the full-
throated relief and longing loud amongst the whispers of
leaves in the wind.

He watched her as he moved in and out, watched
her desire and her breathlessness, watched the way she
arched her hips and took him inside.

And when he began to stiffen she held him still and
felt the pulse of him deep, the spillage of his seed, the
way her flesh swelled around his with wild delight, tethered by nothing.

'Marry me, Elizabeth.'

Three words that spoiled everything.

'I can't.' She pulled away from him, replacing her
skirts, and surprise was stamped into the dark blue of
his eyes.

'Why not?'

'You need a younger wife. After the twins the phy-
sician said I would not have another baby...' Sorrow
scoured out hope as she sat. 'And with Goldings you
will need one.'

He did not answer, and she knew the second she had
lost him, the master of all the lands she could see before
her, the Earl who had worked so hard to save what his
father had ruined.

* * *

The dream Alexander had held this morning shattered with a sudden certainty. Family. A home. A bevy of small Greys to take the name down into history. A son to stop the title being passed to the next male heir, his cousin George with his shallow arrogance and his expensive tastes. Goldings would be ruined all over again.

'You are sure about…?' He could not finish what he began to ask.

'I am.'

She stood then, slowly, one arm heavy against the trunk of the tree.

'It is this or nothing, my lord.'

He could not understand what it was she was saying.

'This?'

'We could be lovers.'

But Alexander knew that if he said yes to such a thing he would ruin her, a mistress who would have no place in the world, a lady of gentle breeding whom one man had already failed, and failed badly.

'I can't.'

This or nothing, she had said, but the choice was not his to make. His family depended on him and Goldings needed an heir even if it would break his heart to provide one, with another woman, a different woman, a woman who was not Elizabeth. He wished she had not told him this truth of hers, he wished she had kept quiet and he had married her and then the die would have been cast, the sanctity of marriage an unbreakable bond.

But she was too honourable for that deceit.

Sadness overwhelmed him. 'Guy was a fool not to treasure you and hold you safe, Elizabeth.'

Her smile came nowhere near her eyes.

Chapter Five

Please, please, please, let Lord Grey be a friend to Mama. She smiles more when she is with him and she is happier.

This is my Christmas wish.
Love
Jenny

Alex found the note in exactly the same place he had found the last one.

This time several pine cones decorated in gold, silver and red were scattered around the hawthorn bush, the paper catching the sun and glinting in the light.

He knew the girl would have wanted him to find it, and that thought made him smile. As with the first note, he carefully untied it and placed it in his pocket, but this time he decided to write back.

Dear Jenny
I would like to be a friend to your mother.
Perhaps you might like to invite me over to show me the other decorations you have made?

Sincerely yours,
Lord Grey

With care he attached the letter to a band of ribbon, pink this time and frayed by weather, knotting the end to make sure it did not blow away.

Elizabeth had spent the past two days at the Grange and her children had not visited Goldings. When his sister had sent a note over inviting them back, a careful refusal had been returned.

Sarah was furious, blaming him for frightening her off, for not seeing a beautiful woman when she was placed right before him and for being a man who had no notion of the concept of luck. He could say nothing of the reasons that kept her away and so he remained silent.

The Fry sisters and his aunt had departed on time and there were to be no new candidates paraded before him, which was a decided relief.

He had not made any return nocturnal visits to the Grange, the shock of Elizabeth's confession at being barren and the guilt at his own unparalleled behaviour creating a barrier to any pathway that might have led to a resolution.

He had friends who had married for convenience and kept a lover on the side but he had never thought to countenance such a deception. Until now. Until need drove shards of real pain into his body and made him shake with the thought of never seeing her again, never loving her.

Loving her.

She imagined their connection to be only in lust, a shallow thing of the flesh. But it wasn't.

He hoped that the note he had left for Jenny might allow a conversation at least.

It was Christmas Eve and Elizabeth looked at the small note her daughter had found on the hawthorn tree and felt sick. She knew that Alexander and she needed to talk about what had happened between them but she just could not quite face up to an ending. For ever.

At this point there was still a chance that he might take up her offer to be his mistress, for she could not recant such a proposition even though she knew it was morally wrong. She had no one to tell her what to do, no husband to be faithful to, no parents to disappoint. This would be her own decision, played out in secrecy and far from any societal pressure.

But she did not want her children involved in any of it, for a friendship between Alexander Grey and their little family could only lead to their disappointment. They liked him. They liked his substance and his solidness. Their father had been shallow and selfish, and it was only when Alexander Grey had come into their lives to show them what honour and principle really was that they had been able to recognise the difference.

Luis slept with the boxing gloves beside him in his bed, and Jenny's face on showing her the note had been full of an unmitigated delight.

They wanted the Earl here at the Grange in any form that they could get him, and her refusal to listen to their pleading was becoming wearisome, to say the least.

A Christmas wish.

That notion made her very heart sink.

Every night since she had last seen Alexander Grey she had sat near the window of her bedroom, looking out over the lands before her, and she had hoped. Hoped he would come. But he had not, and out of self-preservation she had rebuffed any invitations sent to the Grange from Goldings because she did not want to stand before Lord Grey and pretend.

Even now, looking around the house, there were constant reminders of all that she had lost. The decorations, the boxing gloves, Jenny's note, the fabric flowers that sat at her mirrored armoire beside her brush, ones she had not worn again.

The Grange had always been a silent house since she had come here to England after Spain, but now it was a lonely one as well. She was pleased when Jenny came into the room because it took her mind from such maudlin thoughts.

'Mama.' The tone of her daughter's voice was urgent. 'Luis has left the Grange and taken a saw from the stables to meet Christopher. I think he has gone to find you a green branch of pine like the one Lord Grey mentioned because he said the best time to cut the bough was on Christmas Eve and that's today.'

This ploy sounded dangerous and she hurried to find out more.

'When did he leave?'

'An hour ago. He asked me not to say anything to you but...'

'You were right to. Come, we will find our coats and go and search for him. Did he give you any idea as to where he had gone?'

'He said the trees near the old red barn on the way to Goldings looked like a good place to start.'

Elizabeth remembered those trees, for they were huge

and old, many of the branches dead wood and brittle. 'Did you see the saw he took?'

'Yes. It was this big.' Both her arms stretched out on either side of her. 'And it was a bit rusty.'

She swore under her breath but clung to her composure so as not to alarm her daughter. Luis had never climbed a tree in his life and she only hoped that Christopher Herbert had some sort of expertise in the area.

Case Thornton arrived at Goldings just after lunch. He'd brought the figures with him for the new yearling calves standing in the lower fields, and they were impressive. Another year and production would be up again, the year-on-year return of the Goldings stock notable by any measure.

'I saw the Martin boy and your sister's son disappearing into the trees behind the red barn a little while back. From the looks of it they were finding a bough to cut, though I am not sure of the sharpness of the saw they had.'

'Saw?' Alexander asked with concern in his voice.

'An old, rusty, bent one but of a good width. It didn't look like something Goldings would have left lying around, so I presume it came from the Grange.'

'Was Mrs Martin with them?'

'No, they were alone and running for their lives when they saw me coming round the corner.'

'They didn't want to be seen?'

'They certainly did not.'

'God. Christopher has been raised mostly in London. I am not sure his tree-climbing skills would be up to much, and I can almost guarantee that the Martin boy's won't be either. I think I might go and take a look, if you don't mind. We don't need broken bones just before Christmas and an old rusty saw is another worry.'

Thirty minutes later he found them perched high above the land on an old brown bough that hung across a small stream. The saw was on the ground beneath them, dropped there, he supposed, and by mistake.

'Stay there and hold on tight,' he instructed them just as Elizabeth and her daughter came into sight. 'I am coming up to get you.'

There was a rope on the horse, for he always carried it, a precaution that had long since held him in good stead. Unravelling it, he threw the end coil up over the branch near the fork they held on to.

'Feed it down to me, Chris,' he instructed, 'with each end of the rope on different sides of the bough.' He waited as his nephew did just that.

Elizabeth was beside him now, her expression tight.

'Can you get them down safely?'

'Yes.' It was better to keep the tone light in cases like this, as any panic always made things more difficult.

Her hand came out then to lie across his arm. 'Please be careful.'

He felt her touch like a flame.

'I will.'

Then he had the rope in his hand and, using the trunk as a way of climbing up, he had soon joined Christopher and Luis on their high branch.

If the Earl had not come just then Elizabeth was not sure what might have happened, for the panic on both boys' faces was noticeable and the wind had started to rise, the limb upon which they sat moving markedly up and down with the force of it.

Alexander Grey had had a lot of practice with rope, she thought next, for the knots he made around Luis's middle were complicated ones, and she ran over with Jenny to help her son gain his footing as he was lowered to the ground.

But Alexander Grey was not finished with Luis's help yet, as he barked out further orders. 'Throw up the rope again, Luis, and make your aim good.'

Such an instruction had her son turning and he did exactly as was asked, the rope coiling through the air with force and straight back up.

'Good throw. Now stay there to help Chris. Move back, Elizabeth.'

In another moment the next child had landed safely on the earth and Luis untied the knot, the responsibility of Alexander's instructions sitting easily on his shoulders.

Looking up then, Elizabeth saw the Earl feed the end of the rope around himself in a looser way. Within a moment he had swung down too, running the length through his hands as he descended, his expertise astonishing.

Was there anything this man could not do and do well?

'Thank you.' She looked straight at him and said it from her heart because Alexander deserved her absolute gratitude. He was about to answer when his sister came rushing into the clearing, a manservant behind her.

'Case Thornton said my son might be here. Christopher, what have you done?' Her voice scaled up a few octaves as she grabbed him, the rope in her brother's hand and the sagging bough above probably telling her just what had happened.

'We wanted to cut a Christmas Eve bough for Mrs Martin, Mother, because Jenny loves Christmas and it would mean a happy one at the Grange.'

Sarah Herbert's mouth flew open.

'Did you know of this, Mrs Martin?'

'I didn't. Jenny told me of it about half an hour ago and I arrived here to find your brother rescuing both boys from that bough.'

Alexander's sister glanced up.

'How on earth did you even get up there?'

'We climbed, but the smaller branches broke as we got further up and we couldn't get down, and then we dropped the saw.'

'Well, thank goodness it was not either of you who dropped down, for your Christmas would have been completely spoiled. McDonald.' The servant came forward. 'Would you escort the children back to the carriage, please, for I want to have a word with the Earl?'

'Yes, my lady.'

The three children went quickly with barely a backwards glance, and after a moment or so there was silence in the glade.

'I will take the three of them back to Goldings,' said Sarah, 'and make certain they are bathed and fed. I will leave you both here to talk, for I think you need to.'

'We do.'

The Earl said this and his sister nodded.

'Take your time, then, and thank you, Alex, for rescuing my son.'

Then she too was gone, the late afternoon gathering in with the dusk, and the cold of the season more noticeable.

'Do you want to talk here or at the Grange, Elizabeth?'

He gave her the choice.

'At my house.' Already the shock of the escapade was making her shake.

'I have my horse. I will take you back, then.'

Calling his steed, he placed her up on the saddle and told her to hold on to the reins. Then he came up behind, his warmth welcome.

They rode without speaking until they came to the house and he stopped at the stables, an old, dilapidated building with doors that creaked as he moved them.

'Demeter will be fine in here. There is water and feed.'

Taking off the saddle, he brushed his mount down briskly with handfuls of hay and then tethered him in one of the old stalls.

'The place has lasted surprisingly well,' he said, 'and I am glad because I always liked this barn.'

'Did you come here often?'

'I did, but never with Guy.'

Then came an awkward silence as all the grooming was finished, the words between them stalling into the truth of their situation.

'We need to talk, Elizabeth. I need to put my cards on the table and so do you. I think we at least owe this to each other. Do you agree?'

'Yes.'

'Good.'

His smile was beautiful, and she was taken back to the first time she had seen him at her door.

'Shall I start?'

She nodded.

'I told you I was twenty-three when my father died. I did not tell you that he shot himself and that he was not successful in dying immediately. Very few people know this. As he died he asked me to save Goldings, as he had been negligent with it, and he made me promise that above everything else I would protect it. I gave him that promise.'

'I see…'

'No. You do not. I gave that promise before I met you and I have worked for the last fifteen years to make certain that I honoured my father's memory. When you told me you could not have children I imagined things that I now realise were wrong. If Goldings is lost when I die then so be it. I have enough money to protect the family, and we have years and years before us. Here in Somerset.'

'We.'

'You and I. I can't live without you, Elizabeth. The past days have been…' He stopped as she finished the sentence off for him.

'Desolate. Bleak. Unfathomable. Lonely.'

Smiling, he nodded.

'But we need to tell each other honestly who we have been in order to become who we want to be in the future.'

He was pleased as she began to speak. 'I met Guy Martin in the last week of June after he passed through the small village where the convent I had just begun at was situated. He saw me in the orchard with another novice and arrived there with an offer of marriage. I agreed. He was handsome and seemed kind, and I longed to escape the fetters of the place. Within a month I was pregnant and within two months he was gone. Into the arms of women who were more worldly, more interesting and more sensual than me. Those were his words. When I had the twins in a tiny house alone eight months later in the north of Spain I thought that if I died along with the babies it all might be simpler. When I did not die I decided I needed to live as a mother instead of a wife, and I have for all these years until…'

She stopped.

'Until you met me?'

'Yes.'

'Marry me, Elizabeth.'

A repeat of his words the first night they had lain together.

'Marry me and live with me for all the years of our lives.'

'But what of heirs and the march of history?'

'If it were a choice between Goldings and you, I would choose you.'

Elizabeth began to cry, huge tears welling from nowhere. She couldn't even remember the last time she had cried twice in a few days, her staunchness the only thing that had allowed her to carry on.

This was no lightly given marriage proposal as Guy's had been and based upon nothing. This offer was given with all of his heart. He would lose much to gain her hand and he did not seem perturbed by the exchange.

'I love you, Alexander.'

There, she had said it, and she watched as his eyes lit up his face.

'I love you too, Elizabeth. Above everything, though I like your children, too.'

'What would your family think if I said yes to your proposal?'

'I imagine my sister would stop berating me for making you unhappy and my mother would be delighted. They have almost given up on expecting a bride.'

'But the Misses Fry…?'

'Are their attempts to bring me happiness.'

'Or remind you of your duties.'

He caught her hand as she said this and kissed the back of it. Twice.

'Will you marry me, Elizabeth?' The plea in his words broke her heart.

'I will.'

'When? Tomorrow?'

She laughed and then saw he was serious. 'We could get married that quickly?'

'In the Grey chapel at Goldings with the Reverend Elliott officiating.' He delved into his pocket. 'I purchased an Ordinary Licence yesterday.'

'After you told me you could not be my lover?'

His arms were around her fully now as he brought her closer.

'I want this to be for ever, Elizabeth, and I do not wish for us to be hidden.'

'I love you, Alexander, and it is like a Christmas setting here, with the manger, and even the stars are coming out. With Guy I can't remember a moment that was beautiful. I wanted to return to the convent even by the time we got to the coast to find a ship, but he said I was ruined and there would be no chance for anything better. Then I found out I was pregnant.'

He kissed her again, a soft and gentle kiss that bespoke much care.

'Let me cherish you, Elizabeth, and treasure you. Let me show you that we could have a life here that is good and honourable and full.'

'But what of children?'

'We have Luis and Jenny and they are enough.'

'Are you sure?'

'I am as certain as I have ever been about anything and I cannot wait to give everyone our wonderful news. I think my sister has a notion of my thoughts already

and is probably at a window this very moment watching
for us to arrive.'

'Will they be pleased, do you think?'

'They will love you. They have been hoping I would
find a bride for years and now I have found the most
beautiful one in all the world.'

She took his face between her hands and looked directly into his dark blue eyes.

'I will always be by your side, Alexander.'

'Do you promise?'

His face was solemn as he took her hand and drew
her in. When he kissed her she forgot to think altogether.

Their wedding was small and beautiful, the chapel at
Goldings decorated with Christmas roses and daphne.
Fabric flowers were hung on the pews along the aisle,
the colours of yellow, red, cobalt blue and magenta making the place look festive in a Christmassy sort of way.

Elizabeth had chosen daphne sprigs for her hair, too,
and her dress was of a pale pink.

Luis and Jenny had sat with Chris and Sarah, his
mother on the other side with Case Thornton and his wife.

A small party but a joyful one, a day of new beginnings and different directions, and as the sun broke out
through the clouds and the music from the small organ
filled the room Alex was imbued with a gratitude and a
pleasure that he had not felt before.

Elizabeth was perfect. A wife he would protect, treasure and cherish until their dying days.

It was much later now and she was asleep, the moon
still high in the sky, a crescent-shaped slice of light in
the darkness.

As if she could tell he was thinking about her, her eye-lids fluttered and then she was looking at him.

'I was remembering everything about our wedding,' he said, 'and thinking what a perfect wife I have.'

Her dimples showed.

'Did you remember what happened when you finally brought me up to this room, Alexander?'

'And we were alone for the first time in a proper bed?'

'To undress in the moonlight without interruption?'

'To take off your wedding gown bit by bit until only skin was left?'

'And my garters. You liked those.'

'I liked nothing on you better.'

She pushed back the sheets and arched against them. 'Like this?'

'And like this.'

With care he sat astride her, positioning her hips to find her centre and entering slowly. She was wet from their lovemaking and when she breathed in hard he knew he was in paradise. Here, with her, at Goldings, the freshly fallen winter snow making everything hushed and cocooned.

With care he pulled her up to him so that their bodies touched, the heat that had always been between them surging. Then the age-old dance of love began in earnest, the give and the take, the finding and the losing, reaching up for what was just beyond them and dissolving with the pursuit.

It began slowly, the final beauty, a small, thin knowledge merging into a wider one and then taking every bit of both of them in a wrenching joy, the glory and the splendour unmatched as the storm possessed them.

Afterwards they were quiet in an echo of the tempest, peace after tumult, the calm a way of readjusting.

'Promise me that it will always be like this between us, Alexander, and that you will not tire of me or be disappointed.'

'With my heart and my soul, I promise it, Elizabeth.'

Epilogue

Christmas 1816

Goldings looked beautiful.

Alexander had cut a bough of pungent pine from the same tree that the boys had tried to saw one from last year. This year he had made sure that they helped him to do it and in safety. Jenny, Luis and Chris had then decorated the downstairs salons in silver paper moons and golden paper stars, as well as the ever-present pine cones painted in red and green.

There were candles everywhere, too, a scent of lavender permeating the room, which was at the moment full of family and friends, all enjoying the companionship of the season.

'Penny for your thoughts?' he asked Elizabeth as she came to stand beside him, looking contemplative.

'I was thinking of how far we have come in a year. How many things have happened and how they have all been wonderful.'

'At least Jenny and Luis enjoyed the first term at their new schools. I think they both felt happy with the fact we allowed them to choose where they wanted to go, and having my sister in London to keep an eye on them has been a boon.'

'She looks happy, doesn't she? Sarah?'

'Gerard is here and her children are older. She's probably getting a lot more sleep than we are.'

His wife began to laugh as she took his hand and held it. It was one of the things that he revelled in, this sense of constant touch between them.

'Beau is teething. It isn't for ever.'

'I am not complaining, my love.'

Alexander looked at his little four-month-old son cradled in the arms of his mother, both their faces ones of pure contentment.

'He is a gift as much as Jenny and Luis are gifts.' His sentiment was straightforward.

'A gift we were not expecting?'

'Love moves in ways that are sometimes hard to explain, Elizabeth, and Beau is the proof of that.' She could hear gratitude in his words.

A second chance. A new beginning. A way of mitigating the past and travelling into the future. They had named their son Beaufort Alexander, after his father and after him, and it was a healing thing, the whole family pulling together with the arrival of the new heir to Goldings.

A whole assortment of young children sat around his mother and Beau, singing and laughing. Sarah and Gerard's brood.

Case Thornton and his wife, Sally, were there, too, for their son Timothy had become as thick as thieves with Luis and Christopher. A small gang of friends and allies roaming the estate every holiday, just as he himself had done with his own friends all those years before.

Jenny was plaiting her cousin Caroline's hair, the little girl idolising her older relative. Clementine Thornton sat next to them, a quiet, thoughtful child a year younger than Jenny who was often here at Goldings in the holidays, writing stories, performing plays and doing all the things that she and Jenny most enjoyed.

To one side of Elizabeth, Guy Martin's old and frail uncle and aunt sat. They had been pulled into the family circle and every day became more and more a part of the tapestry of life here, residing in a cottage in the village that they had made their new home after losing the last one. Alexander liked them both.

A disparate lot, he thought then, made up of people who had found each other through adversity and bravery and honour.

The dog that he had brought home for Jenny and Luis lay sprawled out on the hearth in front of the fire, snoring loudly. They had called him Chance.

A good year. A fruitful year. A year of firsts and new beginnings. A year, too, where work had taken second place and where he had relished family life.

Beau's sudden cry had Elizabeth going over to collect him, and she brought him across to lay him in his arms, a dark-haired child with eyes the same colour as hers. He was glad for it.

Loneliness was now in the distant past, for with all the comings and goings and the busyness of a new baby there was no time for excessive self-reflection.

Aunt Mary, on the other side of the room, caught his eye and she smiled.

This year, at least, it was only family and good friends,

though he groaned as Sarah went over to the pianoforte and began to sing. She had a poor voice but a joyous delivery, and he grimaced.

'This has been by far the happiest Christmas of my life, Alexander, and I have you to thank for that.' Elizabeth spoke quietly so as not to interrupt the music.

'It has been easy to love you all.'

Alex looked over at the table beside him. Jenny had made him a Christmas Wish Tree, with myriad notes and ribbons attached to it, and every one held a story about the things she loved about being at Goldings. He'd always keep it, he thought, just as he would always keep Luis's awards from school in mathematics and in boxing.

The ring Elizabeth had had made for him glinted on his finger, the words 'for ever' engraved inside.

She'd given him children, love and laughter. She'd given him hope, too, and a future, his beautiful and kind-spirited wood sprite so full of joy.

'I love you,' he whispered and felt her squeeze his hand as Beau nuzzled into his neck.

This was paradise and Elizabeth was his angel.

Shutting his eyes for a second, he listened to the laughter and music all around, the lights glowing and the fire warm.

'May there be many more Christmases like this one before us,' he added, and as she leaned across to check on Beau he kissed her, ignoring the groans of the boys near by.

Love should be visible, he thought, and smiled as she kissed him back.

* * * * *

A MOST SCANDALOUS CHRISTMAS

Marguerite Kaye

Chapter One

Saturday 3rd December 1825,
Darlington, Yorkshire

'Lady Merton? I thought I recognised you. I'm Ellis Wyn-Jones,' the stranger clarified in response to Silvia's blank look. 'We met at a dinner hosted by the Thornhills about four years ago.'

'Did we?' The man who had greeted her in the crowded reception area of the posting house was tall, with tousled black hair, craggy brows, liquid brown eyes and absurdly long lashes. But it was his smile, tentative and rather charming, that sparked her memory.

'I remember now; you are the inventor,' Silvia said, smiling back. 'We talked about the machine you were developing to cut metal shapes. You explained it so well that I was persuaded I understood how it worked.' And at the other end of the table, Edward had been blatantly flirting with his current mistress, she remembered. Mr Wyn-Jones had deliberately shifted in his seat to shield her from the unedifying spectacle.

He shifted again now, this time to protect her from

being buffeted by the stampede of new arrivals at the inn, all demanding service. 'Are you waiting on your carriage?'

'I have a hired a post-chaise. I'm waiting on a change of horses. They said it would be an hour at most. I did enquire about a private room, but was told they were all taken. That leaves the tap room, but...'

'Good heavens, no!'

'No, on reflection, perhaps not,' Silvia agreed. 'I do like a pint or two of ale with my breakfast, but I prefer to sup it in private.'

His eyes lit up with laughter. 'I have a parlour to myself. Why not join me? You can have a pint of gin or a quart of ale or even a cup of coffee in comfort.'

It was a tempting offer, for not only was the prospect of respite from the hustle and bustle appealing, so too was Mr Wyn-Jones. He had made no attempt, that evening four years ago, to hide either his contempt for her husband or his attraction to her, and both had been a balm to her miserable state of mind. 'Thank you,' Silvia said regretfully. 'I know your offer is kindly meant, but you are clearly unaware of my change in circumstances.'

His mouth firmed. 'If you are referring to your divorce from Lord Merton, I am aware of it. It would have been difficult not to be, given the press coverage. If you'll excuse me for being blunt, I reckon congratulations rather than commiserations are in order.'

Silvia was startled into a laugh. 'Thank you. You are the first person to say so, and in actual fact I couldn't agree more.'

'I am glad to hear it, Lady—Miss—Madam? How should I address you?'

'I am Mrs Armitage now, for I have reverted to my maiden name, but Silvia will suffice.'

He sketched a bow. 'Then Ellis it must be, at your service.'

There was just a hint of flirtatiousness in his smile and for the first time in a very, very long time she felt the stirrings of attraction. 'Ellis. Is that Welsh?'

He rolled his eyes. 'From the Hebrew, Elijah. A sacred name for the second son who was expected to take holy orders. But my true vocation is mechanical innovation, thus making me a permanent disappointment to my genteel family.'

'Not, I fear, as much of a disappointment as I am to mine,' Silvia retorted. 'If your offer still stands, I would very much appreciate a cup of coffee provided you don't mind sharing it with a scandalous divorcee.'

'It was your husband's behaviour that was scandalous, in my opinion. I'll let the landlord know where to find you when your transport is ready. Are you sure you wouldn't prefer beer?'

'No, thank you,' Silvia said, getting to her feet, 'I'm trying to cut down. Coffee will do nicely.'

The door closed behind the waiter, and Ellis sat down opposite his unexpected guest, nodding when she offered to pour the coffee. Silvia had taken off her gloves and travelling cloak, but kept on the bonnet which covered her silver-blonde hair. He remembered her very well from that dinner, the almond-shaped green eyes, the perfectly arched brows, the high cheekbones and the generous mouth, which made her so arrestingly beautiful. She had been rigid with repressed fury when they first took their seats, anger glinting in her eyes each time her glance strayed to her husband at the other end of the table. He had launched into a description of his steam-powered lathe merely to distract her, but she had surprised him by showing an interest, and he had set himself the task of first making her smile and then laugh. For a delightful hour the pair of them had forgotten their surroundings, but when their hostess rose, and Silvia was forced to withdraw from the table along with her husband's mistress, her light-hearted mood had given way to a chilly reserve.

There was no trace of that in the woman who sat opposite him now, who made him think rather fancifully of cool, fresh breezes and hot kisses. 'Divorce suits you,' Ellis said impulsively.

'Thank you. Once again, you are the first to say so, and I am happy to agree. I suspect I looked far from my best the night we met. I had a great deal preying on my mind.'

'Fragile, is how I would have described you. But look at you now—you are clearly thriving.'

'Like a botanical specimen replanted in fresh soil?'

'A wild orchid,' Ellis said promptly. 'Delicately beautiful to look at but deceptively hardy.'

Silvia laughed. 'That is the oddest compliment I have ever been paid.'

'I pride myself on my ingenuity,' Ellis said. 'It's how I earn my corn, after all.'

'And judging from this parlour, which is clearly one of the best the inn has to offer, you are reaping a healthy crop.'

'I am now, thanks to my steam lathe. When we last met, I was beginning to wonder if I would ever manage to make a living from my inventions.'

'So you are a success,' Silvia said, smiling broadly.

'Congratulations. Of course, I knew from the moment you described it to me that your lathe would be much in demand.'

Ellis laughed, but then shook his head. 'I've fulfilled a lifetime's ambition. I've come up with something that has proved to be revolutionary and is a huge commercial success.'

'Why do you sound less than thrilled?' Silvia asked.

'I just hadn't bargained for all the tedious business dealings that go along with it. Now I am so busy travelling the length and breadth of the country installing and modifying the machine, and attending endless meetings with factory owners, I barely have time to think about inventing anything new, far less get down to the practical business of testing it out, which is the part I enjoy most.'

'Can't you employ someone else to oversee the commercial side of things?'

'There are two problems with that. The first is that I'm the type of person who never trusts anyone but themselves to do a proper job, and the second is that my customers think pretty much the same thing.' Ellis grimaced. 'It sounds dashed ungrateful of me, I know, for I've succeeded beyond my wildest dreams, but the simple truth of the matter is, I'm not cut out to be a successful, respectable businessman. Frankly, I'm getting bored.'

'Perhaps it's time to take stock, then? Or to take a holiday, at the very least, and work on your next invention.'

'My brother thinks what I need is a wife and family. I'm thirty-eight years old, long past time for settling down, according to Geraint. He is the Marquess of Ardwyn, and takes his responsibilities as head of our family very seriously, so is eager to assist me in making what he considers a good match.'

'Take the advice of someone who fervently wishes she had refused her brother's choice of a husband, and permit him to do no such thing.'

'There is no fear of that,' Ellis replied, with a sympathetic smile. 'I'm not interested in acquiring either a wife or a family. I enjoy my own company, and the freedom to choose how I spend my time, and where I spend it.'

'Save that you do not have the freedom to do either, do you?' Silvia pointed out.

'Ha! I'm a victim of my own success. I hadn't thought of it that way, but you're right.'

'You could say the same about me. I have achieved what I wanted, in that I am no longer married to Edward. He assuaged his guilty conscience by agreeing to pay me a very generous settlement, but, while I'm financially independent, my freedom is proving to be... I suppose, more constrained than I imagined.'

'In what way?'

She frowned, pouring herself the dregs of the coffee. 'The scandal of the divorce and all that I had to do in order to obtain it cost me every last shred of my reputation. In the first year or so after it was finalised, all I wanted was to hide away and lick my wounds.'

'I'm not surprised, after the very public ordeal you were forced to go through. Trial in the courts and by the press too,' Ellis said grimly. 'I remember thinking at the time how desperate you must have been to rid yourself of the man, to have endured such an ordeal.'

'I was desperate, though no one seemed to understand how much,' Silvia said, shuddering.

'Your family, surely...'

'As far as my brother, Clive, is concerned, I have no family.'

'What? He can't possibly blame you for the divorce, given your husband's track record? I am sorry to be blunt, but he was a notorious philanderer.'

'Not even my brother would deny that, though of course the proceedings required that it was I who was labelled the adulteress. If I had eschewed the various court proceedings, if I had been content with a formal separation, I would still not have been welcome in polite society, but I could at least have had my sister, Melissa, to visit. I could not be content with half measures though, and so, from the moment my former husband initiated the divorce proceedings at my urging, I became a social pariah. Clive warned me it would be so—he begged me to reconsider, right up to the point where the private Act of Parliament made the divorce final—but I *could* not.'

'I should bloody—I beg your pardon—I should hope not!' Ellis exclaimed. 'The toll Lord Merton's despicable behaviour was taking on you was clear to see that first night we met.'

'Unfortunately, the impact my divorce has had on my family is, they tell me, significantly worse. The shame of having a divorcee in the family—for I really am a very rare specimen in society, you know—is too much to bear. And so,' Silvia said with a tight smile, 'I am now the sibling who never was. Which I am actually perfectly happy to be as far as Clive is concerned. Melissa, however—well, I miss her. Our brother has instructed her to deny my existence, and she has always been one of those people who follow the path of least resistance. As *I* was, I suppose, for far too long,' she added, grimacing. 'It was how we were raised. However, unlike poor Mel, I am now answerable to no one. I live quite alone, in a farmhouse on the edge of the moors, a few miles from

Whitby. I love my home, because it's mine, my very own sanctuary, with neither visitors nor servants. Like you, I enjoy my own company.'

'In that sense, then,' Ellis said, touched by her bravery, 'we are kindred spirits.'

'In more ways than one. Like you, I have all I thought I wanted, and like you, I'm beginning to wonder—oh, not whether I should have remained married, but rather what I am to do with the rest of my life. I am bored, and at times I'm lonely. I don't want what I had, but I'm not sure what it is I do want.'

'Your fresh start has become stale, in other words?'

'That is one way of putting it. I thought what I needed was a change of scene, and so took myself off to York. However, a single woman without a companion or even a maid is horribly conspicuous, and intrinsically of dubious reputation, I discovered. I stayed one night in the hotel, and then decided to come home before I was asked to leave, which is why I am here. It made me wonder, for the first time, if my living alone as I do is always going to prove a—well, as I said, my freedom is more constrained than I had anticipated.' Silvia flashed him a smile. 'You know, this is rather an intimate conversation for two people who are virtual strangers to be having. You would have made an excellent confessor if you had taken holy orders.'

'Trust me,' Ellis replied, 'I have never felt less pious.' Their eyes met, and held in a sudden, unmistakable jolt of awareness that took him completely aback. 'Forgive me,' he said, forcing himself to look away. 'It must have been obvious to you that first night we met that I was attracted to you, but that was an entirely inappropriate remark to make.'

'It *was* obvious,' Silvia replied, 'and at the time, a welcome balm to my very bruised ego. Not that I would ever have considered—nor indeed am I suggesting that you would have…' She broke off, blushing.

'Unlike your husband, I had every respect for the marriage vows you had made.'

'Alas, so too did I. I was faithful to the very end. Even when I was being slandered for my infidelities in the press.' Silvia winced. 'And what's more, I have remained faithful, despite the fact that I am no longer married.'

'And are consequently free to behave as you please.'

'In theory. In practice, however, since I live alone, go nowhere, meet no one…'

'Save for me.'

He meant it teasingly, and she smiled in response, but their eyes met again and their gaze held as she smiled, and it was there again between them, unmistakably, that frisson of awareness.

It was she who broke the spell this time, making a show of checking a gold watch which she wore pinned to her gown. 'You are forgetting that the landlord may summon me to my carriage at any moment. And you—I hope you're not putting off your journey on my account?'

'I'd happily postpone it completely, to be honest,' Ellis said. 'I have some business to conclude in London, and then I'm due at my brother's house in Glamorgan for Christmas. The annual family gathering.' He shuddered eloquently. 'Two weeks of festivities, with the events of every day cast in stone, right down to the ritual family falling-out over which direction we will take for our constitutional walk. Why cannot each person go in the direction of their choosing, a rational person might ask?'

'A rational person such as you?'

'Ha! When I am with my family I become completely irrational. That is my role, the slightly eccentric younger brother who must not be taken too seriously. It's torture,' he said earnestly. 'On top of everything else, my brother has decided now that I have made my fortune I have no excuse for avoiding settling down and getting on with the task of providing his children with cousins. For the last two years, he has gone so far as to invite a suitable candidate to stay, despite my having told him that he's being patronising in the extreme, not to say downright cruel, in subjecting the said candidate to the ordeal, quite needlessly and often without her knowledge too. I'm sure he'll do the same again this year.'

'Good grief. Can't you simply spend Christmas at home?'

'Christmas alone! Heaven forfend.'

'What a pitiable creature you would be, to be certain.'

'Oh, Silvia, I'm sorry, I didn't think.'

'It's perfectly fine.'

'No, it's not. I'm so sorry.'

'I don't know why Christmas Day should be any different from any other day, but it is. My family always have a large, extended gathering and like yours they stick to the same rituals every year. I find some of them tedious, some ridiculous, and their determination to have everything exactly the same every year infuriating, so it is absurd of me to miss any of it, but I do. That first Christmas in the farmhouse, the reality of what it meant to be a social pariah was really brought home to me. I knew almost hour by hour what they'd be doing. I made myself pretty miserable, I can tell you. Last year, I decided to embrace the occasion. I cooked an elaborate dinner and put on an evening gown. It wasn't a success. This year, I think I'll go back to ignoring it all.'

'I wish I could join you. Then we'd both avoid spending Christmas alone, and I would be spared the annual ordeal at Geraint's.'

'What would you tell your brother?'

'That I have received an offer I can't refuse,' Ellis said, smiling.

'He would be scandalised if he knew the truth.'

'What you don't know, as they say, can't harm you.'

'Anyway, I haven't actually invited you.'

'Go on, then.'

She was smiling, but once again as their eyes met the mood changed. 'You're not serious, are you?'

He leaned forward impulsively and took her hand. 'There's only one way to find out.'

Chapter Two

Friday 23rd December 1825,
East Rigg Farm, North Yorkshire Moors

Silvia's farmhouse was a solid, no-nonsense affair set on the edge of the moors, about eight miles from the spa town of Whitby. Long, narrow outbuildings protected the house on two sides from the prevailing winds, forming an open courtyard. She kept a kitchen garden and some hens, but, aside from her horse and a trotting pony, no other livestock, renting the fields out to a neighbouring farmer.

The front parlour faced onto the courtyard, giving her a clear view of the sinuous road snaking towards town. There had been no traffic for some time, and it was now after four in the afternoon. Ellis had been due at noon. It was already nearly dark. She could safely abandon any lingering hope that he might turn up. He had clearly not taken their pact seriously. Or had had second thoughts, and who could blame him? What they had proposed was beyond the pale.

Silvia drew the curtains to keep in the warmth. Time

and again in the last few weeks she had questioned the sanity of inviting a complete stranger to stay, and now the decision of whether to send him packing if he did turn up had been taken out of her hands. A circumstance for which, she told herself, going upstairs to change, she ought to be grateful.

Her gown was bronze silk woven with a dark brown stripe, with fashionably puffed sleeves tapering to a narrow cuff, and a deep ruche around the hem. It was far too grand for a farmhouse anyway. She pulled on a grey woollen smock and a pair of thick bed socks, then went back downstairs to curl up in her favourite wingback chair. The novel she was reading lay on the side table beside her, but she didn't pick it up. The fire crackled in the hearth. She had chosen every single object in this room, from the curtains and rugs, the comfortable sofa and chairs, to the little writing desk which sat in the corner. The bookshelves were filled with her own choice of reading material, and the one painting, of Whitby harbour and a stormy winter sea, had been her choice too. This was her little haven, and she didn't need anyone to share it with her.

Silvia leaned back in the chair, closing her eyes. That chastening trip to York had unsettled her, and the very strange conversation she'd had with Ellis had stirred up all sorts of mixed emotions. She was free of Edward, she had been set adrift by her family, her friends and society, but she was still living as if they were casting a condemnatory eye over her, as if she had a penance to pay, a crime to atone for. They would never welcome her back into the fold, and even if they did, she didn't want to return.

She didn't *need* or want anyone to share her home, but

she had been looking forward to having Ellis's company. Looking forward to behaving just a little bit scandalously. She smiled to herself. Actually, more than a little. She had never flirted in her life, but there had been a spark between them that she knew she had not imagined. The way he looked into her eyes, the touch of his hand, had woken her body from a long, deep slumber. Desire was another thing which had unsettled her, a longing not to be loved but to make love.

The doorbell clanged. Silvia jumped from her seat, her heart pounding. It could not be Ellis, but who else could it be? All her doubts came flooding back to her. She could simply refuse to answer the door. Or she could answer it, and tell him unfortunately she'd changed her mind, which would be the most sensible thing to do. And the most cowardly? Would she then spend her Christmas regretful and alone? And safe, she reminded herself as she made her way along the hall, hesitating with her hand on the latch. Safe and virtuous.

Silvia opened the door. Ellis was standing on the bottom step. 'I'm sorry I'm so late. The weather,' he said, indicating the sleet which was swirling around him. 'I've kept the post-chaise waiting, in case you've had second thoughts. Which you have, by the looks of it,' he said, taking in her odd attire. 'Did I rouse you from your bed?'

'Round these parts this is considered the height of fashion for a cosy night in alone, I'll have you know.' Her heart was still pounding, but it was with excitement now, and not fright. Ellis was here. She barely knew him, yet her instincts told her she could trust him, and her body was making its wants very clear indeed.

Silvia opened the door a little wider. 'Come in, Ellis; it's a filthy night.'

'Are you sure?'

She laughed. 'I've been assailed by doubts from the moment I issued my invitation, but I can't bring myself to send you away, now you're here.'

He smiled, making no attempt to disguise his relief or his pleasure. 'Give me a moment to pay the driver.'

An hour or so later, Silvia, flushed from the heat of the kitchen, took her seat at the little dining table, and Ellis sat down opposite her, feeling awkward. 'You shouldn't have gone to so much trouble.'

'It's no trouble; I like to cook,' she said, slanting him a tremulous smile as she served him a generous helping of grouse pie and creamed onions. 'I promise I won't poison you. At least, not fatally.'

'I'm not worried about that.' Ellis took a forkful of the food. 'It's delicious.' He meant it, but his appetite had deserted him. He had been so focused on seeing Silvia again, he hadn't given a thought to the reality of the situation. The intimate moments he had imagined were torrid and tempestuous, and did not include sitting politely making small talk over dinner. Had it been a mistake to come here? She seemed to be as uncertain as he was.

'You're not eating,' Silvia said, setting down her fork. 'Either the food is terrible, or my company is.'

Ellis too set down his fork, deciding that it was best to confront the issue. 'If someone could see us through the window, they'd think we were simply a husband and wife having a cosy dinner together.'

'This is the first time I've ever eaten dinner alone with any man, and I don't feel remotely cosy.'

He laughed shortly. 'I'm not exactly at ease either.'

'It's too late to leave now, but in the morning I'll drive you to the posting inn at Whitby.'

'I didn't say I wanted to leave, Silvia.' In fact, he felt strongly, now that it was mooted, that he wanted to stay. 'It's odd, that's all, being here with you, so completely alone.'

'I did tell you that I don't have any servants.'

'I'm perfectly capable of looking after myself and helping out too; it's not that.' Ellis topped up their wine, smiling ruefully. 'We are the opposite of what we appear to be. Not husband and wife having a quiet dinner together, but two strangers in a highly unconventional situation.'

'Highly scandalous, you mean?'

He thought carefully before he answered this. 'Scandalous in the eyes of the world, but, since no one will ever know, that's hardly an issue. Provided we are happy with the situation, then I can't see that it's anyone else's business.'

'And are you?'

Once again, he took his time to think carefully. 'Yes, provided you are. And I think we should both agree,' he added when she nodded, 'that if either of us changes our mind at any point, we should say so.'

Silvia smiled, holding out her hand across the table. 'That's a deal.'

He laughed, taking her hand and pressing the lightest kiss to her fingertips. 'I think I might manage to eat some of this delicious dinner now.'

Silvia watched with pleasure while Ellis ate, but she made no attempt to finish her own meal. Now that they had cleared the air, she was less on edge but even more conscious of the strangeness of the situation.

'Tell me more about your family,' she said. 'What are you missing out on today at your family Christmas gathering?'

'I can tell you exactly,' he replied, grimacing, 'since guests are presented with a schedule of events on arrival. Though I don't know why, for it is the exact same every year, right down to the menu for Christmas dinner.'

She picked up her wine glass, surprised to find it was empty, and held it out for him to refill. 'What is on the agenda for this evening?'

'Dinner, which will include a game pie.'

'Oh, no! I am so sorry. If I'd known I would have made something different.'

'As long as you are not planning devilled kidneys for breakfast...'

'I can think of nothing more revolting. And after dinner tonight?'

'Games and quizzes. Geraint, my brother, divides everyone into teams, and has a complicated system of scoring that no one understands save himself. My theory is that it is designed in order to ensure that he is always on the winning side and his wife's brother, who of course is not a Wyn-Jones, is always a loser.'

'It sounds to me as if our brothers would get along extremely well. Clive thinks that as head of the family he is entitled to come first at everything.'

'Geraint is exactly like that! One of the other traditions at Ardwyn House is to have one of those large dissected maps—you know the ones that are pasted onto wood and cut into pieces?'

'Actually, I gave my eldest nephew one for a birthday gift a few years ago.'

'Well, my brother has a new one made each year as a Christmas puzzle for his guests. It is set out in the morning room, and guests are encouraged to try to fit the pieces together. But Geraint always keeps one piece back so that he can be the only one to complete the picture.'

'Good lord, I can't imagine being very pleased if it was the one piece I was looking for.'

'Ha! Just one of the many contributions to the Grand Family Argument, which is never on the schedule, but which always takes place, none the less, usually a couple of days after Christmas, when the goodwill and peace to all men is starting to wear a little thin.'

'Christmas wouldn't be Christmas without an argument, or so my sister always used to say. She believed it cleared the air, but I have never understood how bickering does anything but give one a headache. Let us agree not to argue.'

'That is easily done,' Ellis said promptly. 'I cannot imagine wanting to argue with you.'

'You say that now, but after two or three days of my undiluted company, who is to say how you will feel about me?'

'Curious. Admiring. Wanting more.'

Silvia, to her consternation, found herself blushing. 'You seem very certain of that.'

'Yes, I am.'

His eyes met hers, and her breath caught at the heat smouldering there, but before she could become uncomfortable he broke the contact to pour the last of the wine. 'What shall we do tomorrow?' she asked.

'Why don't we wait and see how the mood takes us?'

'Very well. What do you like to eat for breakfast?'

'Silvia, I didn't come here to be waited on hand and foot. We will share the kitchen duties.'

'Can you cook?'

'Not as well as you, but I can follow instructions, and I'm a first-class dish-washer. I won't break anything or get under your feet, I promise. Let me help. It might even be fun. At least it will be something neither of us has done before.'

'That's certainly true.'

'I could help you to make a Christmas cake.'

'You could, if you'd been here a few weeks ago. All those nuts and dried fruits require regular tots of brandy, I'll have you know. Talking of which, would you like a port?'

Ellis shook his head. 'It's getting late.'

'Yes, I suppose it is,' Silvia agreed, surprised to see that the clock read almost eleven. 'I hadn't realised. I'm usually tucked up with my book long before now.'

'I've kept you from your bed. I'm sorry.'

'No, no, I didn't mean that. I've thoroughly enjoyed myself tonight.' Though the awkwardness had returned. 'Why don't you go up—or is it too early? I will just put the leftovers in the pantry,' she said, getting to her feet and picking up a dish, which she immediately set down again. 'When we discussed your coming here, we didn't discuss...'

'Any boundaries,' Ellis said, smiling faintly. 'Shall I be frank?'

'I think that would be for the best.'

'I admire you, Silvia. You intrigue me. If we could enjoy each other's company over the next few days, that would be more than enough for me. But you must know, and I think I have made it perfectly obvious, that I am very attracted to you?'

She could feel herself blushing, but she would not allow herself to look away or give the ludicrous impression that she was some simpering miss. 'The attraction is mutual.'

'I want you to believe me, though, when I say that I expect nothing more from you than companionship, and I would never...'

'Oh, I don't doubt that. But if we wanted to—become more than just friends,' she said, colouring furiously, 'I would welcome that, if you would.'

'Oh, I would. Very much.'

The smile which accompanied his words made her forget everything save the desire uncoiling inside her. She closed the gap between them, and he put his arm around her waist. His kiss was soft, not hesitant but allowing her time to make up her own mind. She put her arms around his neck, already decided, and opened her mouth to him. He groaned. And then they kissed. Slow, sensuous kisses, which took her by surprise, for her body was already racing and clamouring for what would follow the kisses. But Ellis refused to be rushed, his hand smoothing down the small of her back to the slope of her bottom, his mouth slow on hers, his tongue tasting, not thrusting, and her body stopped clamouring and began to melt.

Her eyes drifted closed. She nestled into him, feeling the hard length of his erection through her smock, and he moved slightly, holding her close but not pressing her to him. His hand stroked rhythmically from her back down her bottom, and his kisses mimicked the rhythm, kissing her softly and then more deeply, softly and then deeper, until she felt as if her bones had truly melted, a phrase she had often mocked until now.

And then the kisses came slowly to an end, and she opened her eyes to find Ellis smiling, a smile that exactly reflected her own, drowsily aroused. 'We have plenty of time,' he said. 'There's no need to rush, and I want you to be certain. I know you think you are,' he added when she would have spoken, 'but you've never done anything like this before.'

'You are the only person in the country who believes that. Even Edward, in the end, began to believe—though he should have known better. But I have never...'

'Silvia, I know that. You don't have to justify yourself or explain yourself. You went through hell to get out of that marriage. It cost you your reputation. For me, that tells its own tale.'

'Thank you,' she said, suddenly on the brink of tears. 'It's sad and pathetic, isn't it, that no one else has ever said so to me?'

'Hush. No more talk of the past.'

'Not another word.' Silvia smoothed her hand over his cheek, smiling softly. 'Goodnight, Ellis,' she said, kissing him softly. 'Sleep well.'

He laughed, releasing her with a flattering reluctance. 'The last thing I want to do is sleep, but I shall do my level best. Goodnight, Silvia.'

When the door closed behind him, she sank back into her seat at the table, smiling softly to herself. Her body still thrummed, but in a blissful, almost sated way, quite unlike anything she had felt before. Edward had been an accomplished lover, but there had always been a purpose to their lovemaking that at times left her feeling like an efficiently serviced mare. Though not, she thought sadly, efficiently enough.

She would not allow the past to intrude. She would put what was left of their dinner away. She would retire to her bed, knowing that Ellis was sleeping in the bedroom opposite. She would relive tonight, their laughter and their kisses, wondering if he was lying awake doing the same. And she would imagine what would be the next stage in their romance—for romance, she thought, smiling again, was precisely what this was. Albeit a very short-lived one. A gift they would share, to be unwrapped slowly, and relished, at each and every step.

Chapter Three

Saturday 24th December 1825,
Christmas Eve

When Ellis woke he was surprised to discover, squinting at his watch in the gloomy light, that it was gone seven. He had slept deeply and, for him, late. He lay for a few moments, stretching out in the comfortable bed, listening to the thick blanket of silence. Was Silvia still sound asleep in her bedroom opposite? She had been almost an hour later than he in climbing the stairs. He could hear next to nothing through the old oak doors, but that hadn't stopped him imagining her getting undressed, unpinning her silver-blonde hair, snuggling under the crisp sheets and warm wool blankets, her little toes reaching for the warming pan which she must have placed in each bed unnoticed by him at some point during their meal.

The kisses they had shared had been even more delightful than he could have imagined. His drawing back when they became too passionate too quickly had been instinctive, but it had been the right thing to do. This little world of their own was a precious moment out of time, the pleasure he was already certain they would discover together of the type to luxuriate in and draw out.

When had he become so fanciful? Ellis shook his head ruefully. Silvia was a paradox, the type of woman who looked too fragile to survive, and yet here she was, alone and self-reliant, flourishing. She would not relish his primal and misplaced male instincts to shelter and protect her, that was for sure. But that didn't mean she would be averse to being spoiled, just a little.

He pushed the bedclothes aside and shivered, for the room was icy, despite the fact that he had banked the fire up last night. He washed quickly in the cold water and ran a wet comb through his tousled hair. He would shave later. First, there was breakfast to be served.

'Good morning. You must have been up with the lark,' Silvia said, coming into the kitchen.

'And before the chickens,' Ellis said, grinning. 'Your ladies took umbrage at my disturbing them in search of breakfast ingredients.'

He was dressed in breeches and boots, a waistcoat and a white shirt rolled up at the sleeves to reveal sinewy forearms, with neither coat nor cravat. His hair was damp but he hadn't shaved, and his teeth looked very white against the dark stubble.

'I see your foraging was successful though,' Silvia said. 'Can I help?'

Ellis shook his head, waving her towards the table. 'I've just made a pot of tea.'

The kitchen was warm, the eggs smelled buttery and delicious, and the tea which she poured was precisely the right strength. The dishes from last night were stacked on the wooden drying frame. And Ellis, with his back to her, concentrating on his cooking, had a very appealing leather-clad rear. What would his beard feel like against her skin, if he kissed her? Was it preposterous that at the age of thirty-six she had never in her life been kissed first thing in the morning by an unshaved man? She was tempted to find out, but lacked the nerve, and, when he served her a perfectly fluffy omelette, happily distracted.

'This is delicious,' she said, as he took his seat opposite her. 'And you washed last night's dishes too; you are the perfect guest.'

Ellis grinned. 'I aim to please.'

'You have succeeded.' She meant the breakfast, but as their eyes met she knew that he was thinking, as she was now, about their kisses. It was ridiculous to blush at her age, but she could feel her cheeks colouring. 'Would you like to go for a walk on the moors after breakfast?' she asked. 'We'll need to wrap up, but I promise I won't argue about which direction we should take.'

He laughed. 'It's only Christmas Eve, and the Grand Family Walk doesn't usually take place until St Stephen's Day…besides, we agreed last night we wouldn't quarrel. This is your neck of the woods. I shall happily follow where you lead.'

The sky was a clear, wintry blue as they headed out onto the moor, but, though the sun was weakly shining, there was an icy breeze. Wrapped up snugly in her favourite red wool cloak with a long scarf, mittens and stout boots, Silvia lifted her face to the sky, relishing the feel of the cold, bright air on her skin. 'When I was growing up, my mother drummed it into me that a complexion exposed to the weather was the kiss of death to a young lady's chances of making a good marriage. The habit of shielding my face from the elements was so ingrained, I never questioned it. Only when I moved here did I realise what I was missing.' She turned to Ellis, smiling broadly. 'I shall be as wrinkled and wizened as a walnut in a year or so, but since I could not marry again even if I wanted to—which I don't—that's hardly an issue.'

'Could not?'

Inside her mittens Silvia's fists clenched, for the injustice of it still riled her. 'Legally. Edward is permitted to take a new wife, but I, as the appointed guilty party, am not permitted to remarry. As I said, it's not an issue, since the very last thing I would ever consider would be marriage.'

'Not even if you fell in love?'

'One sure and certain way to destroy love is to get married,' Silvia said scornfully. 'As a wife, a woman is entitled to no respect, no consideration, no say in her own life. She becomes, quite literally, her husband's property, and when he treats her with contempt she is expected to endure, and endure, and endure. You are a man. You can have no idea what that is like. It wasn't so much that Edward was a philanderer, but that he flaunted his indiscretions. You saw him yourself that night. I suffered that for years. Latterly, I felt as if I was quite literally shrinking, and it's very difficult to have any confidence in yourself when everyone pities you, and you know they have cause to. I am still, in the eyes of a great many people, a pitiable creature, but not to myself.' She paused shakily, wiping her eyes with her mittened hand. 'I'm sorry, I didn't mean to sound so—I didn't mean to get upset.'

'I asked the question.'

'I know that not all men are like Edward, but it almost doesn't matter. I have suffered a great deal to obtain my independence; I would never risk losing it again.'

Ellis smiled warmly at her. 'Put simply, you are your own woman.'

Silvia nodded, smiling. 'That is it, exactly. I am my own woman, and that means everything to me.'

'I understand that, I assure you. That's why I have never married.'

'You don't think you might change your mind, if you fell in love?'

'I'm thirty-eight and it's never happened. I reckon I'm too set in my ways now, to want to change.'

'And a wife and family would get in the way of all those inventions you still have to dream up.'

Ellis laughed. 'If I ever get the time. This is quite a climb. Where are we headed?'

'To the Wainstones. They are huge sandstone crags—I believe the highest on the moors. There are a couple more steep inclines, but the views are worth it. It's about two miles, and we can shorten the walk by coming back the same way, but if you don't mind adding another mile or so we can come back by a circular route.'

'I hate walking back the same way as I've come,' Ellis said.

'Oh, me too, though I learned through experience that it can be dangerous not to do just that if one doesn't know the path.'

'Have you managed to get yourself lost?'

'Several times, but I know my way around now. You must be very fit—this is quite a steep section.'

'And yet you yourself are barely out of breath.'

'I could, as they say in these parts, barely walk the length of myself when I first came to Yorkshire. Here we are at the top, and now you can see the Wainstones in the distance. Isn't it beautiful?'

Ellis shielded his eyes from the sun, scanning the view. 'You can see for miles.'

Silvia feasted her eyes on the moors, her spirits lifting as they always did, at the sheer elemental beauty of the vista. The Wainstones stood on the next ridge, from this distance looking like a huge ruined building, the tallest of the stones resembling a large chimney stack. All around them the moors unravelled in folds, brown heather and dead bracken alternating with patches of farmland, the whole dotted with sheep. 'In August the heather in full bloom is lilac and purple and alive with bees, though there's surprisingly little scent. You can see the path we'll take back—it's quite well marked. If you take a line from the stones—there, do you see?'

Ellis nodded. 'There's not another soul about.'

'I love that. All this beauty, and all that sky. It makes one feel so insignificant, you know, in the grand scheme of things? Oh, dear, I expect that's a terrible cliché.'

'But it's true,' Ellis said, pushing his hair back from his face. He had, like her, dressed for the weather, with a thick greatcoat, gloves and a muffler, though no hat. 'It's humbling, all this beauty. I'm used to much more rugged scenery back home in Wales, but all the same, there's no denying this is a lovely wilderness.'

A gust of wind whipped Silvia's cloak around her, making her stagger backwards. 'Lovely and wild, certainly,' she said, laughing. 'We should press on; we're not even halfway yet, and the light goes very early at this time of year.'

* * *

The wind whistling through the gaps in the crags greeted them when they arrived at the Wainstones. Silvia, red-cheeked, her eyes sparkling, brushed ineffectually with her mittened hands at a long strand of hair blowing about her face.

'Here, let me,' Ellis said. Steering her into the lee of the crags, he took off his gloves and tucked the silky tress back into the loose chignon from which it had escaped. She was smiling up at him, exhilarated from their last climb, and she looked so lovely, he could not resist kissing her. Her face was icy cold, but her lips were warm on his. It was the lightest of kisses. But when it ended and Silvia didn't move, her eyes locked on his, they kissed again, softly but more deeply. He wrapped his arm around her waist. Her body shaped itself against him, and her mouth opened to his, and their kisses deepened until the wind, tugging at their clothing and their hair, brought their kisses to a close.

They smiled at each other, and warmth spread through him, a feeling of such contentment and well-being that it took Ellis a moment to realise it was simple and pure joy, made all the more delicious for seeing it reflected in Silvia's face. Then of one accord they turned and set out on the path which would circle back to the farmhouse.

'I've never been to Wales,' Silvia said, breaking the silence after they had covered about a mile. 'I've never been to Scotland either. In fact there are huge swathes of our country I've never been to, and a whole world beyond that I have never seen.'

'Do you have a yen to travel more?'

'I tried to, as you may recall, and baulked at the first hurdle.'

'They didn't actually ask you to leave the hotel in York though, did they? You don't think you were being overly sensitive?'

'I really don't think so. I don't *fit*, you see. My appearance, my voice, my manners are perfectly genteel. And I look like a lady,' Silvia said sardonically. 'But by my insistence on living alone, or travelling alone, claiming the independence I fought so hard for, in other words, I am proclaiming myself to be anything but a lady.'

'You should have had the sense to set yourself up as a merry widow.'

She laughed. 'Perhaps I will, the next time I reinvent myself.'

'Next time?'

'When my dissolute ways are discovered, and I am hounded out of Yorkshire.'

'You don't have any dissolute ways. You told me so yourself, remember?'

'I am remedying that now, though. Don't worry, Ellis, I'm not being entirely serious. It's Christmas Eve, and if I'm not mistaken we are about to have some very seasonal weather.'

She had barely finished speaking when the first flurry of snow began to fall. Behind them, the horizon had all but disappeared, and above them the sky was iron grey and blanketed with clouds. Silvia pushed back her hood again and lifted her face to the sky. 'I wonder if it will lie? We had very little snow last year. Perhaps we'll be able to build a snowman. Or is that one of those family traditions we want to avoid?'

'Why don't we build a snow woman instead?' Ellis suggested.

Her eyes lit up. 'Now, there's a challenge. Shall we give her a fan instead of a pipe?'

'And straw for her hair.'

'Goodness, it really is coming down heavily.' They had reached the farmhouse, but instead of hurrying inside, Silvia stopped, her arms wide. 'We shall have a white Christmas.'

'If you stand there for another five minutes, we won't need to build a snow woman,' Ellis said.

She laughed, twirling around, her arms still outstretched, her red cloak flying out around her. 'I forgot to look on the moor for holly, but I don't suppose that there was any. I wanted to make a wreath for the fireplace. And a log! Oh, Ellis, we don't have a yule log to light.'

'I didn't see many trees out on the moors either.'

'No, and anyway, we said we wouldn't follow tradition, didn't we? I forgot.' She shivered, pulling her cloak back around her. 'It's freezing, and I don't know about you, but I have worked up an appetite and am more than ready for my dinner. Shall we go in?'

'You go. I'll make sure your hens are inside and feed your horses. Go on, I won't be long.'

Chapter Four

In a rush to prepare dinner, Silvia barely noticed the time passing, but it was quite dark outside when she took off her apron. Where was Ellis? So much for not being long. She discovered the lamp in the hallway by the front door had been lit, and the fire in the dining room was ablaze, so he was definitely back. Then the door to her parlour opened and he emerged. 'What on earth have you been up to?' Silvia demanded. 'Your hair is soaking wet.'

He grinned. 'I've been foraging. I'm afraid you were right—there's no holly to be had on the moor.'

'Oh, no, you shouldn't have wasted your time.'

'I didn't,' he said, ushering her through the parlour door. 'What do you think?'

The mantelpiece was festooned with greenery, juniper and laurel tied and woven together to create a wreath that was perfuming the room. 'Oh! It's lovely!' Silvia exclaimed, touched and charmed.

'I was lucky to find both growing near by.'

'Thank you. I know I said that I didn't want anything to remind me—but it's not really Christmas without a festive wreath.'

'Or a yule log? Now, before you get too excited...'

But Silvia had already burst out laughing. In front of the fire on the grate stood a slender bough, not much more than a twig.

'And it's green wood,' he said ruefully, picking it up. 'I couldn't find a saw, or any sort of axe, so I had to break it off. It's a poor effort but the best I could do.'

'I love it! It's the perfect antidote to the massive yule log my brother will be lighting.'

'Ha! Geraint too—he has to have something that fills the entire grate.'

'Exactly like Clive. I am not sure that this will even burn,' Silvia said, looking doubtfully at the twig. 'Perhaps we should simply leave it in front of the grate, to play a more ceremonial role.'

'An excellent idea,' Ellis said, setting it down again.

'Thank you.' She reached up to kiss his cheek. 'Very much,' she said, and hesitated only a moment before kissing his lips.

His face was icy cold. He smelled of juniper and laurel, and of the fresh Yorkshire air. She shivered, partly with cold and partly with anticipation as he pulled her into his arms, her hands finding their way under his coat to smooth over his back and then down to the taut muscles of his buttocks. He already tasted familiar, but his body was that of a stranger. She had never known anyone but her husband. Ellis could not be more different, and that in itself was exciting.

She deliberately deepened the kiss using her tongue, curling her fingers into his buttocks, pressing herself against his erection, enjoying the way it made him groan, made his kisses more feverish. His hands roamed over her back, her bottom, the curve of her waist, and then onto her breasts. Silvia moaned.

'Too much?' he asked.

'Not enough,' she said, pulling his face back down for more kisses, astonished at her boldness, and at the same time aroused by it, knowing from his own response that he felt the same.

Her hair had come down. Ellis combed his fingers through it, spreading it across her shoulders, loosening the lacing of her gown enough to pull it over her shoulders. He kissed her neck, the hollow of her throat, easing her gown over her arms. He kissed the valley between her breasts, then he trailed kisses from one to the other above the line of her corsets, making her nipples ache for his touch.

The fire crackled, and Ellis moved her out of reach of sparks, turning her around to deftly unlace her corset. He was still almost fully dressed, having shed only his coat, while she was in her undergarments, her chemise and petticoat, her pantalettes and stockings, but when she tried to unfasten his waistcoat he shook his head. 'Hush,' he said, 'this is for you. I can wait.'

More kisses. Her mouth again, and then his entire attention was on her breasts, and Silvia moaned. His mouth and hands stroked and teased, he licked and sucked through the cambric of her chemise, and then, pulling that away, on her flesh. She shuddered and shivered, tense and tight with desire, responding with soft moans when he asked her if she liked this, or this, or this. Her wishes had never been consulted before. She had never before experienced such a delightful, blissful onslaught of caresses focused entirely on her needs, on her pleasure.

Her petticoat was untied and fell to the ground, and

Ellis slipped his hand between her legs inside her panta-lettes, and began to stroke her, his fingers sliding easily over her, and inside her, and his mouth still on her nipple, sucking and licking. She had never before experienced this slow, smouldering climb to a climax, the certainty that there was no need to rush, that he wanted her to relish it. And when she clung and teetered on the edge, he slowed, lifting his head to smile knowingly at her, kissing her mouth, slowly and deeply, his tongue echoing the slide of his fingers, and Silvia surrendered.

Her climax was deep and long, wave after wave breaking inside her, forcing her to cling to his shoulders, and when she thought it was over his gentle, insistent, knowing touch took her again, kissing and stroking, until she was in a mindless state of bliss.

She opened her eyes to meet his gaze, his eyes dark with passion but his smile teasing and oddly satisfied. 'Too much?' he asked again.

Silvia shook her head, smiling back at him, a bubble of laughter escaping her. 'Oh, no,' she said, starting to unfasten the buttons on his waistcoat. 'Not yet. Now it's your turn.'

Ellis had never been so aroused in his life, yet he wanted to stretch every single moment, to eke the pleasure out and make it last as long as he could. But that sated, teasing smile of Silvia's was playing havoc with his self-control. She was delightfully transparent when it came to lovemaking, though she had not, it was obvious, been encouraged to put her own desires first. It would have been enough, he thought vaguely, for him to end it now, knowing that he had pleased her, but then she slid her hands under his shirt and her palms smoothed over his nipples, and he changed his mind.

Their lips were in danger of being frayed by their kisses, but he couldn't get enough of them, and when her tongue licked into the corner of his mouth he groaned. Her hands roved over his skin, his chest down to his belly, around to his back and then once more to his chest. He wrenched his shirt over his head and Silvia replaced her hands with her mouth, kissing and licking, her hands on his behind now, and then on the fastening of his breeches. He kicked off his boots and stockings, snatching feverish kisses, and between them they freed him of his breeches and drawers. He was achingly hard. He wouldn't be able to bear it if she touched him. He was desperate for her to touch him. And dear God…

A long, guttural groan escaped him as her hand curled around his erection, tracing the length of it gently, carefully. She was watching him. 'Like this?' she asked, stroking him. 'Tell me, Ellis.'

Her words echoed his. The way she asked him, shyly and yet boldly, made him throb in her hand. This was as different for her as it was for him. He didn't want it to end, but if she kept doing that—and oh, dear God, he so wanted her to do that again. Their mouths met in a deep, drugging kiss, and he knew he couldn't wait any longer. Of one accord they sank to their knees, still kissing, and then onto the rug, still kissing, and then she pushed him onto his back and she rolled on top of him, her nipples brushing against his chest, until he had to plead, 'Now, Silvia, I can't—it needs to be now.'

She guided him in, holding him tightly as he slid inside her, easing him further and further, drawing a shuddering groan from him, a soft, murmuring sigh from her. She was so hot and wet and tight. He wanted her to move, but she sat up, looking straight at him, just holding him, rocking slowly, and he found he could get even harder. More rocking, then a slow lift and slide, and her eyes changed, and her smile changed, and her own climax began to drive her. Ellis knew her now, he knew how to touch her nipples, how to stroke between her legs as she moved, knew the moment she tipped over, and knew that he needed to go with her.

Silvia sensed it too, crying out and thrusting, finding the rhythm he wanted, lifting and sliding down, thrusting harder and deeper, faster at his urging, until he too tipped over and she freed herself just in time as he came with a deep, satisfied groan, curling into his side, her leg over his, her curtain of silver hair trailing over his chest and tickling his cheek.

They ate dinner in the kitchen, laughing together about how ravenous they were, blaming their long walk and the fresh air, the looks they exchanged telling a different story. Bathed in a sated afterglow from lovemaking, Silvia had never eaten such an intimate meal. She had never felt so simply content, nor so relaxed in anyone's company.

Too relaxed, too quickly? Ought she to be a little more on her guard? Not against Ellis, precisely—she trusted him—but against the effect he was having on her. But where was the risk? She was under no illusions as to the temporary nature of their liaison, and they had both made it very clear that neither of them wished for more.

'What are you frowning at?' Ellis asked, topping up their glasses.

'This,' Silvia said, indicating the remnants of their

meal, their dishevelled state. 'You only arrived here last night, but we are acting with the familiarity of having known each other for years.'

'I'd say it was quite the contrary. For my part, it's the unfamiliarity of it all that is so delightful.'

'And we will have no time to become too familiar,' Silvia said, reassured. 'Perhaps that's what made me so bold, earlier.'

'Not bold,' Ellis said, pressing her hand. 'Confident. What is wrong with telling someone what you like or what you want, when it enhances the pleasure for both of us?'

'I know that now, but I didn't before,' she confessed, blushing a little. 'I think if my pleasure had been enhanced to any greater degree, I would have fainted.'

He laughed, kissing her hand. 'That feeling was entirely mutual, I promise you.'

'Truly?'

His answer was another kiss. And then another. And then they fell apart again, smiling foolishly at each other. 'Have you had enough to eat?' Silvia asked. 'Would you like some Christmas cake and a glass of the port you brought with you? Strictly speaking, we should keep the cake for tomorrow…'

'All the more reason to have it tonight, then,' Ellis said, getting to his feet. 'I'll fetch the glasses and open the bottle.'

Silvia had set the cake on the table, and was returning with the cheese dish, when Ellis came back into the kitchen with a bottle in one hand and two glasses in the other. His look of astonishment when he saw the cake was extremely satisfying. 'You made this?'

She nodded. 'I baked it back in November, then fed it brandy every few days, and iced it last week.'

'This is a work of art. It must have taken a great deal of skill and patience.'

She had worked a design like lace into the thick icing to form a border, and then overlaid the top with snow-flakes and the sides with snowdrops. The effect was exactly as she had hoped, both beautiful and wintry. 'Well, unlike you, I do have a lot of time on my hands. The proof of any pudding is in the eating, though,' she said, taking up the knife and cutting through the hard icing, then the moist but very dense cake. The nuts, peel and dried fruit were evenly dispersed, thankfully. She placed a thick slice on a plate for Ellis and cut a much smaller one for herself. 'Here in Yorkshire, the cake is tradition-ally eaten with Wensleydale cheese. I confess to having been dubious at first, but actually it's a very delicious combination, as the saltiness of the cheese offsets the rich cake. Will you try it?'

'When in Yorkshire,' Ellis said, 'why not?' He took a forkful of cake and a sliver of cheese, looking not at all convinced, but his expression changed immediately to surprised delight. 'You're right. It's delicious.'

Silvia raised her glass. 'Happy Christmas Eve.'

When they had finished their port, Ellis had insisted that she retire, leaving him to bank the fires and tidy the kitchen. Lying in her bed, Silvia listened for his step on the stairs. How many nights had she lain thus, pray-ing that Edward's step would not come to a halt at her door? She had never denied her husband, had never be-lieved she had that right. It was one of her most treasured memories, the first night after her divorce was finalised, lying in her own bed, knowing that he no longer had any claim on her body.

Ellis's footsteps did not falter. Ellis had no claim on her. But she was free to make her own choices now. She waited, giving him a chance to undress, gathering her courage, but when she finally tapped on his bedroom door it was with some confidence, for she knew she would regret it if she did not.

'You told me that I should ask if I wanted something,' she said when he answered, wearing nothing but a night-shirt. 'I want to spend the night with you. I don't want to wake up on Christmas Day alone.'

Chapter Five

Sunday 25th December 1825,
Christmas Day

It was still dark outside when Ellis woke to find himself nestled into Silvia's back, his arm around her waist, her bottom tucked neatly into his lap. He burrowed his nose into her hair, inhaling the scent of her skin and the faint traces of the love they had made, slow and languorous, in the middle of the night. He had never, literally, slept with a woman. He had always assumed that having another body in his bed would make him too edgy, too uncomfortable, too constrained, to let himself fall asleep. Yet last night, as they lay breathless, sweat-slicked and sated in each other's arms, it had seemed the most natural thing in the world to allow their slumberous kisses to lure them into slumber.

It wasn't real, he reminded himself as a warning bell clanged distantly in his head. The singularity of the situation, the clock ticking down on their limited time together, made everything feel more intense, that was all. Familiarity would inevitably breed contempt, no matter how unlikely he might think that now. He wasn't looking forward to leaving, but wasn't it better that he did so before this rosy glow had worn off? He should stop thinking ahead. All that awaited him was a return to the mundane world of commerce that had become his lot. He should concentrate on enjoying this one special Christmas with Silvia. Surely no harm could come of it?

Silvia stirred, muttered, and snuggled deeper under the covers. He kissed her hair and drew her closer. 'Merry Christmas,' he whispered.

'Merry Christmas, Ellis,' she replied sleepily.

It was light when Silvia awoke properly. Blindingly light. She slipped from the bed, pulling her nightdress over her head, and peeped through the curtains, to see a world that was completely white and starkly beautiful. It must have snowed for most of the night and then frozen, for the sun picked out glittering shards of icicles hanging from the eaves of the stable block.

Ellis looked to be soundly asleep, lying on his side, only the top of his head showing on the pillow above the tumble of sheets and blankets. She crept from his room to her own, making a very quick toilette before pulling on her bed socks and her scarlet wool dressing gown, eager to surprise him with breakfast.

She allowed herself a very necessary cup of tea before setting about her usual morning tasks in a rush, thankful that she had set a batch of muffins to prove yesterday. There were only two fresh eggs, and her poor hens were huddled in their henhouse, showing no inclination to go out in the snow, but Silvia was of a very different mind. Leaning on the courtyard gate, she gazed out at the moors, drinking in the sharp, clean, cold air and the huge expanse of sky. The snow lay in soft folds, covering everything, looking like the icing on her Christmas cake before she had carved any patterns into it, sparkling white and encrusted with frost.

Last year, Christmas Day had been overcast, the sky leaden like her mood. She had forced herself out for a walk, she remembered, but had given up halfway when the mizzle turned to proper rain, trudging back to her farmhouse soaking and dispirited, going straight to her bed. What a difference a year made. She closed her eyes, thinking of her sister, the peacemaker of the family, whose byword was compromise. She missed Melissa, but not nearly so painfully as before. Her sister had made her choice, as had she. Whether they would ever meet again was still too painful a question to be asked, but for now Silvia regretfully consigned her sister to the past.

The crunch of approaching footsteps made her turn around. 'Look at that view,' she said to Ellis. 'Isn't it wonderful?'

'Picture perfect,' he agreed, smiling at her.

He had shaved. His hair was damp. He wore a clean shirt and breeches with boots, but no waistcoat or jacket. She wanted to kiss him, but as she lifted her hand to stroke his cheek she changed her mind, alarmed by the tender possessiveness of the gesture. Ellis was her lover for a week. There was no place in their liaison for misplaced tenderness.

'Careful,' she said, stepping back. She was referring to the fragile eggs in her pocket, but she would do well to heed her own advice.

'We mustn't go too far,' Silvia said later as they stood on the edge of the moor. 'It's tempting to think we can find our way back by following our footprints, but it may well snow again, and besides, it's too easy to miss the path under the snow, and some parts of the moor are not much more than a bog.'

'We'll go far enough to justify our breakfast spread,' Ellis said as they set off into the snow.

'I'm sorry that there were no devilled kidneys.'

He laughed. 'I don't usually bother with breakfast at all, to be honest. When I'm working, I eat at all sorts of odd hours.'

'Don't you have someone to cook for you?'

'Oh, yes, I'm not self-sufficient like you, but I don't have any live-in servants. I like my solitude. I don't like to be disturbed when I am working.'

'Do you have a special room for your inventions? Tell me more about your life, Ellis; we've talked far too much about mine.'

'I'm not used to talking about myself,' he said, looking rather flustered, 'save when I am trying to interest someone in one of my inventions, and you don't want a lecture on the latest in steam technology.'

'What was the first thing you ever invented?'

'A sock warmer. It worked so effectively that it burned every single pair to a crisp. My first proper engine was a miniature steam locomotive that I built. It was intended to run down the middle of the dining table at Ardwyn House, delivering various condiments from the carriages. The problem was, it only stopped at either end, so if you were sitting anywhere other than at the head or foot of the table, you had to be quick off the mark.' He grinned. 'There was carnage, salt and mustard everywhere save on anyone's plate.'

Silvia chuckled. 'But seriously, tell me how you came

to turn an inventive mind into a successful business? You must have had some training, surely? Or—does one study invention at university?'

'No, but I did study mathematics for a while. Are you sure you want to know more?'

'I am not simply being polite, if that's what you're thinking. I have had years of making polite conversation and pretending an interest in matters that I found tedious, and I have resolved never to do so again. Please,' Silvia said, taking his hand, 'I do want to know.'

He needed to be coaxed, but she persisted, and soon he was talking enthusiastically and, as with the first time they had met, so lucidly and in such simple terms that she felt she could actually comprehend the subject matter. 'You have a real passion for your vocation,' she said. 'It seems such a shame that you no longer have time to devote to what you love best.'

'It's a compromise, but it's important to me to oversee everything personally,' Ellis said. 'My reputation has been built on doing just that, and for being honest, taking responsibility when something goes wrong. That way, people come back for more.'

'Perhaps you should take on an apprentice.'

'I've thought of that too, but…'

'You like to do things yourself, in your own way,' Silvia finished for him. 'You want to have your cake and eat it too.' They had reached the ridge, and both stopped to admire the view. The sky had clouded over a little and the sun was already low in the sky. Behind them in the distance, smoke could be seen trailing in a leisurely plume from two of the farmhouse chimneys. 'Can it be done, do you think?'

'Are you talking about me or you?'

'Both of us, I suppose. I wonder where we'll be this time next year? Will you be back at your brother's, another year older and wiser too perhaps, more amenable to the latest would-be wife he has presented?'

'That's not in the least amusing.'

'It's a possibility though,' she persisted. 'You will be almost forty, on the cusp of middle age, and thinking that you don't want to spend the rest of your life alone.'

'Is that what you're thinking? That you are at a crossroads in your life too? Where do you think you'll be next Christmas?'

'I have no idea,' she said, taken aback by the harshness in his voice. 'Perhaps I'll set myself up as a merry widow, as you suggested. Somewhere new, where no one knows me.'

'Or you could simply be yourself, and finally cast off the fetters of your divorce.'

'My divorce cast off the fetters of my marriage!'

'You're not acting as if you're particularly free, hiding away up here.'

'Talk about the pot calling the kettle black! You're fettered to your business. You're no more free than I am.'

Ellis flinched, opened his mouth to retort, then closed it again. 'You're quite right. I'm sorry.'

'No, I'm sorry. The simple truth is I don't know where I'll be or what I'll be doing.'

'Nor do I. Sounds like we both have some thinking to do.' Ellis sighed. 'Have we just had our Grand Family Argument, do you think?'

'Oh, no, that would require one of us to storm off. And besides, we agreed, didn't we, that was one tradition we'd dispense with?'

'So we did, but now you mention it, there was another we agreed to adapt,' he said, scooping her up into his arms.

Laughing, Silvia threw her arm around his neck. 'What are you doing?'

He fell down onto the snow, laying her on her back. 'Building a snow woman, of course.'

They dressed formally for Christmas dinner. Silvia, in a turquoise-and-silver confection of silk and lace, with a silver ribbon threaded through her hair, and a turquoise pendant glinting seductively in her cleavage, took his breath away. Ellis, in evening clothes, was once again reminded of the strangeness of the situation, and as a consequence was a little discomfited. He had been here two days, and in that time had shared more of himself, body and mind, than he had with any other woman. He was not accustomed to talking about himself or having his thoughts and actions questioned. He was used to thinking issues through by himself, making his own decisions. Out on the moor today, there had been moments when Silvia's challenging questioning was difficult to take, but he had to accept that she'd forced him to look more clearly at himself and given him a lot to ponder.

But it was Silvia he was thinking about as she carved the perfectly cooked goose and he poured the wine. Silvia, who, like him, was so determined to protect her independence, though for very different reasons. Silvia, who, like him, hadn't relished having her thoughts and decisions questioned and challenged. Silvia, whom he wanted to hold after they had made love, to cradle as they slept, to wake up with, and to share breakfast with. He had never wished any of those things before, never wished to blur the lines as they did, between making love and starting the day. His mind was starting to shy away from thinking about his impending departure. Maybe tomorrow it would be a good idea to claim some time to himself. It would be good for him to be on his own, remind himself what was real and what was an illusion. A very seductive one, but an illusion none the less.

They decided to drink their champagne in the parlour after dinner. Silvia was sitting in front of the fire, her hair down and her slippers off, when he returned with the glasses. The scent of laurel and juniper filled the room. She had tied her hair ribbon around the twig, which sat in pride of place in the grate. 'To give it a more festive look,' she said, smiling up at him. 'What do you think?'

'Much better.' Ellis poured two glasses of champagne, removing the parcel from his pocket before setting it down on the chair and joining her on the rug. 'I made you a gift.'

'A gift! But I didn't get you anything. You shouldn't have.'

'You've already given me the gift of inviting me here. This is a small token of my appreciation for making this a highly original and memorable Christmas.'

Silvia took the box from him, touching the tissue wrapping reverentially. 'Thank you.' She turned the package over, examining it closely. 'Not a book. Is it some sort of box?'

'Why don't you open it and find out?' he said, feeling suddenly nervous.

She carefully untied the ribbon and folded back the tissue. 'Oh!' She traced the gold inlay of the pattern on the silver lid, then the monogrammed 'S' in the central cartouche with delight, and then she lifted the lid. He had wound it up before he wrapped it. Her eyes widened with astonishment as the spring mechanism made the little enamelled bird inside sit up on its perch. The music box began its tinkling tune and the bird began to rotate, slowly spreading its wings, the movement reflected in the mirror he had fitted into the lid. She stared at it in awestruck silence, her eyes getting wider and wider as the tune ended and the bird completed its performance, tucking its head beneath its wings.

'He's gone to sleep.'

'He'll wake up again if you wind him up,' Ellis said, leaning over to show her the hidden mechanism.

'I have never seen anything like it,' Silvia said, after the bird had completed another display. 'It's enchanting. And so clever. I can't believe you made this for me. It must have taken hours.'

'I had a jeweller make the bird to my specifications, but the mechanics were my work.'

Silvia closed the lid and set the music box down on the table, as if it were a casket of precious jewels. When she turned back to him, her eyes were sparkling with tears. 'It's simply the best, most perfect gift.'

'I didn't mean to make you cry.'

'I'm being silly. It's only that no one ever gives me… not since…and I've never had anything like this made especially for me. Is that how you see me, as a bird unfurling its wings?'

'Learning to fly,' Ellis admitted, touched and a little embarrassed. 'A piece of whimsy, I know, but…'

'It's true. That is precisely what I am doing.' Silvia kissed him. 'Thank you for the best Christmas Day ever.'

Chapter Six

Tuesday 27th December 1825

Silvia opened the box and wound up the mechanism, watching entranced as the little bird began to perform and the music began to play. When it was done, she forced herself to close the lid. She had already played it three times today. Ellis had assured her that so long as she didn't overwind the spring she could not break it, but she worried that it would stop working from overuse. Best to keep it to play when he had gone.

Which was days away, so there was no need for her to feel melancholy. She placed the box back in pride of place on her desk. She and Ellis had made passionate love last night, in front of this very fire. They had shared her bed later, falling asleep curled up together, and had woken before dawn to make slow, languourous, morning love. It had been Ellis's idea for them to spend a few hours in their own company. The snow had melted, allowing him to take a walk on the moors. She had readily agreed. She was not the only one, it seemed, in need of a little breathing space.

She had grown accustomed to being alone with her thoughts, not only through living alone, but also before, in the painful latter years of her marriage as she steeled herself to act. She thought of herself as careful, a person who thought her actions through, who took the time to analyse the consequences, but the last few days with Ellis had proved her capable of impulsiveness.

Not only the last few days, she reminded herself wryly, heading for the kitchen to brew a pot of tea, for there was the small matter of her invitation to him, issued on the spur of the moment on the basis of a chance meeting and one conversation. Ellis brought out an aspect of herself that she hadn't known existed, a woman who acted on her instincts, who was bold in her actions, and confident too. The Silvia she had become in these last few days was not afraid to speak her mind, though she didn't particularly relish being under scrutiny herself. Ellis was too perceptive at times. Some of his insights made her uncomfortable, though she suspected she had the same effect on him.

She sat down at the kitchen table and poured her tea. The music box wasn't only a perfect gift, it was also the first gift she had received since—goodness, she couldn't recall. None of her old friends ever wrote to her and she had made no new friends. She had hidden herself away here on the edge of the moor, remote from the world which had rejected her and almost destroyed her. She went out only to buy vital supplies. She didn't join in the local gossip in the shops. She didn't read the newspapers.

She had licked her wounds. She had roamed the moors. She had learned how to be alone, and to relish it. And then, at precisely the point where she was trying—and failing—to break through the bars of the new prison she had created for herself, on that sad journey back from York, she had met Ellis.

He was the first person to congratulate her on her escape from her marriage. He understood as no one else had ever tried to what she meant when she said she was shrinking to insignificance. And he saw, back at the start of December, before she was fully aware of it, that she was now ready to spread her wings. That little bird was beautiful, but its creator's insightfulness was disturbing.

You're not acting as if you're particularly free, Ellis had flung at her yesterday, and he was right, but she had no real idea of how to change or what she wanted. She could bow to propriety and hire a lady's companion, and that at least would allow her to go out in the world a little more, but she didn't want a companion, a stranger in her house, eating at her table, sharing her thoughts.

Like Ellis! Silvia smiled to herself, indulging in the fantasy of having him as her travelling companion. Travel would be good for both of them. They would not make a Grand Tour, but they would settle for a few months here, a few months there. Ellis would be inspired to create new inventions, leaving her free to be herself, both of them just as they were today. But at the end of the day they would share dinner and conversation, and then later…

Enough! Silvia gave herself a shake and poured herself the dregs of the tea. She did not need a companion, of any sort. Whatever happened in this coming year—and yes, she was determined to make changes—Ellis would form no part of her plans. She would find a way to have her cake and eat it too, to start to enjoy the freedom she had fought so hard for, but that was the point of her freedom, wasn't it, to enjoy it alone?

Now was not the time to be making such world-changing decisions. Ellis was leaving on New Year's Day. They had five more days for them to enjoy this escape from the world and to indulge in the pleasure they took in each other and their lovemaking. And then it was time to get back to the business of real life. In five days she would be happy to have her bed to herself once again, and to be alone with her thoughts and get on with her life.

In five days. But not yet.

Chapter Seven

Thursday 29th December 1825

The morning dawned bright and fresh for their day's outing to Whitby. Leaving the pony and cart at an inn, Ellis and Silvia decided to climb the steps to the abbey, which stood on the East Cliff, dominating the town with a commanding view out to the North Sea.

'You were right—one hundred and ninety-nine,' Ellis said, catching his breath at the very top, where the wind threatened to whip his hat away. 'That was quite a climb.'

'But worth it though, don't you think?' Silvia's cheeks were flushed, her eyes bright. She was wearing her red cloak over a dark blue gown, and had pushed the hood back as she climbed. 'Look at that view.'

At the foot of the steps lay the oldest part of the town, with a marketplace and a warren of narrow cobbled lanes lined with cottages. The bottle-shaped harbour formed by the estuary of the River Esk was bustling with ships of all sizes, from colliers' barges to the few remaining whalers and the local fishing boats. A large sailing ship sat high and dry on timber props in one of the shipyards, while another was under construction at the next yard, no more than a huge wooden skeleton.

Behind them lay the church of St Mary, and towering over it the ruined Benedictine abbey, imposing and beautiful against the backdrop of the moors. 'It looks like we have the place to ourselves,' Ellis said. 'Shall we go and explore the site?'

Inside the solid walls, there was a sense of peace and calm, an eerie quiet once out of the wind. Sunshine dappled down on them as they walked from deep shadow into the light then shadow again. 'I love it here,' Silvia said, coming to a halt beneath the central tower, between the north and south transepts, exactly in the centre of the church. 'I don't know why, given its turbulent history, but I always imagine the monks must have been happy living their cloistered life.'

'Do you come up here often, then?' Ellis asked.

'I come into town to go to the market once a fortnight or so, and I usually wander up here first—though not in the summer, when it's much too busy. I'm not really a churchgoer, but there is a sense of serenity here that is good for the soul. I needed that, when I first arrived,' Silvia said, grimacing. 'I didn't regret what I had done, but I wasn't sure if I had the strength to survive on my own.'

'And yet you have done more than merely survive.'

'Yes, but you were right the other day, out on the moors, when you suggested I wasn't making the most of my freedom. The little bird,' she said, smiling wryly, 'has not yet fully spread her wings. Don't ask me how I plan to, for I have no idea, but be assured that I will.'

'I look forward to hearing...' He broke off, grimacing, shaking his head, and they made their way back outside to admire the view of the harbour again. 'I've been thinking about what you said to me too. It's time for me to make some changes, take a step back from the business a little.'

'And let go of the reins! Ellis, do you think you can?'

He grinned sheepishly. 'I don't know but I intend to try.'

As they descended from the abbey, Silvia's mood darkened. *'I look forward to hearing...'* Ellis had said before stopping himself, and she fervently wished he had not uttered the words. It was difficult enough to manage her own increasingly equivocal feelings about his pending departure from Yorkshire and from her life, without knowing that he too was struggling with it. She told herself once again that there was no point in wasting a moment of their precious time together fretting about the future. She ought to, as she had resolved the other day, try to enjoy every moment as if it were their last, until it actually was.

At the bottom of the steps, she slipped her hand into his arm and smiled up at him. 'I've been like one of those little barges out there, pottering along on a fairly even keel, but since you arrived I've been—what do you call it—full steam ahead?'

Ellis burst out laughing. 'Now you mention it, that's precisely how I feel. And it's delightful,' he said, his smile fading, 'but it can't last.'

'No.'

They walked in silence, lost in their thoughts, to the mouth of the harbour, where the River Esk separated Whitby into a town of two halves. The tide was receding, and the air was redolent with the smell of briny mud and damp seaweed. They watched the boats going out with the tide, and the smaller ones rush in, and then of one accord turned to make their way back to the inn, walking arm in arm.

'Lady Merton?'

Silvia's blood ran cold at the sound of her former name. Two women, who had passed them by a moment ago, were now retracing their steps. She slipped her hand from Ellis's arm, watching their approach with a sense of dread. She didn't recognise the elder woman, who was expensively dressed in furs, but the younger one she had once known well.

'Lady Merton, it is you. I could hardly believe my eyes when I saw you.'

'Lady Oliphant,' Silvia said, with a tight smile. 'What brings you to Whitby?'

'I am staying with my dear aunt, Mrs Bercow,' Lady Oliphant replied, while the older woman gave a very frosty nod. 'She was telling me all about the genteel lady who lives on the moors, who is considered quite an enigma here in the town. When she told me that she went by the name of Mrs Armitage, I did wonder briefly, for that is your brother's surname, of course, but then I dismissed it as being mere coincidence. And yet here you are, as large as life. Though I am not sure your brother would be particularly pleased—but then, you could hardly continue to call yourself Lady Merton, for that would be very confusing.'

'And wrong, since I am no longer married to Lord Merton.'

'Well, no, but what I meant was, it would be confusing for the current Lady Merton. You were aware that His Lordship had married, I presume? And only a few months ago was blessed with an heir too. The poor man; after being through such a dreadful ordeal, his name being splashed all over the papers with lurid headlines, we are all quite delighted for him. I take it you were aware of this very fortunate turn of events?'

Lady Oliphant's malicious little smile made it perfectly clear to Silvia that she knew she was not. The woman had always been a viper and never a friend. 'I was not aware,' she said, 'but I am very pleased for Lord Merton, for he always wanted a son.' To her surprise, she discovered she meant the words sincerely.

Lady Oliphant, too, was astonished that her barb appeared not to have stung as she had hoped. 'Life has not been so kind to you, I can see, but then, we reap what we sow, do we not? My husband would be appalled, I must tell you, if he discovered that I had spoken with you, but I have always been a good Christian, and charitable to the fallen.'

'As far as I recall, your chief attribute is to be a vicious gossip,' Silvia said, giving vent to her anger. 'And that's *me* being charitable.'

'Well! You have certainly given me plenty of new material for my return to London,' Lady Oliphant retorted with a twitter and a significant look at Ellis, 'since I know that your gentleman companion is not your brother—'

'Mrs Armitage,' Ellis interrupted, 'would not be seen dead in her brother's company. Mrs Armitage is a woman of discernment and most excellent taste. Which is why, madam, I am now going to remove her from your odious company. Good day.'

Deliberately taking her arm, he led her away. 'Ellis…'

'I'm sorry, I know you would have preferred me not to interfere, but I could not stand by…'

'Ellis, thank you. You put her in her place. And you were perfectly right about Clive too.'

'You're not angry?'

'I'm furious with her, but with you—no. I only hope and pray… But she has no idea who you are.'

'You hadn't heard the news, obviously…'

'About Edward? I really am happy for him.' Silvia wrinkled her nose. 'Or at least, not happy exactly, but it doesn't hurt as much as it should. Only if you don't mind,' she added, feeling suddenly rather faint, 'I think I'd like to go home now. I've had more than enough excitement for one day.'

Chapter Eight

Silvia couldn't sleep, and the more she tried closing her eyes and mimicking Ellis's soft, regular breathing, the wider awake she became. She eased herself from under his protective arm and out of her bed, then, grabbing a dressing gown, she padded downstairs, poking the kitchen fire into life. It was a beautiful, clear night, the stars sprinkling the sky like icing sugar.

An urgent need to be outside took hold of her. Throwing on an odd collection of clothes from the laundry, pulling on her boots, scarf and cloak, she let herself out of the back door. The air was still, and icy cold, stinging her lungs. She took great big gulps of it, immediately feeling better. The moor beckoned, frost glittering on the heather in the light of the half-moon.

Silvia walked fast, her anger flaring as she recalled the encounter with Lady Oliphant. It wasn't so much what the vile woman had said, but that her unwelcome intrusion had shattered the illusion she and Ellis had created, that they were in their own world. Seething, she marched on, her temper finally cooling, and came to a halt out of breath, realising that she had come much further than she had intended.

Perching on a boulder, she tried to order her thoughts. Edward's remarriage had clearly wiped his slate clean in the eyes of the world, leaving Silvia firmly entrenched as the scandalous wrongdoer for all time. It was a role, as today had proven, she would never entirely escape. The Whitby elite she had never attempted to engage with had been whispering about her. Wherever she went, there would be someone who knew her, or had heard of her. The scandal of her divorce would always haunt her. She could continue to hide from it, as she had been doing for the last two years, or she could embrace her tattered reputation and do what she had wanted to all along, and suit herself entirely.

There was no longer any question of her hiding away. The momentous decision which she had been avoiding ever since her trip to York was surprisingly easy to make now. Thank you, Lady Oliphant, Silvia thought, smiling to herself, for proving to me how little I care for your opinion or anyone else's of your ilk. From now on she would do precisely what Ellis had suggested. She would be true to herself, and herself alone.

Ellis. Her smile faded as she confronted the real reason for her sleeplessness. Lady Oliphant may have inadvertently set her free, but she had also destroyed any foolish hopes she may have had that Ellis could be part of her future. The chances of his identity being uncovered by either Lady Oliphant or the respectable Mrs Bercow were very slim, but it was a chance Silvia could not risk again. She was a fallen woman, and anyone who associated with her would be tainted as a result. Had he been the merest acquaintance, she would have been forced to cut the ties with him, and Ellis was very, very far from being that.

Another truth that Lady Oliphant had inadvertently forced her to confront. Silvia sighed heavily. If she were younger and more foolish, she would be in danger of thinking herself in love with him. A gust of wind made her shiver, and clutch her cloak more tightly around her. She would not allow herself to call it love, but what she felt was something very different from anything she'd felt before. Ellis had woken her sensual side and shown her the true meaning of intimacy. He had been on her side from the first, the only person to understand and support her decision to make a new life for herself. In fact, he'd seen before even she did that the new life had to be less bounded and constrained. Spread your wings, his gift said, and she would, because he was right; that was what she must do, even though it would preclude his presence in her life for ever.

It was too cold to continue brooding out here on the moors. She didn't need his presence anyway, Silvia told herself, beginning the trudge back to the farmhouse. She had battled for her independence, and now she had it she wasn't going to surrender it. Though Ellis felt that too, didn't he? In that sense they were kindred spirits.

Silvia sighed again, lowering her head against the wind. She was making too much of her feelings, and she didn't even know the nature of his. But once again, the encounter with Lady Oliphant prompted her into a reassessment. Ellis had leapt to her defence. He had feelings for her. Strong feelings which, if not managed, would get in the way of his future happiness. The time had come for them both to face reality, however harsh and painful.

* * *

Ellis was in the kitchen, wearing his dressing gown. 'I thought of coming to look for you, but I reckoned you wanted to be alone,' he said, getting up to take her cloak and usher her to a seat by the fire. 'Tea?'

'Yes, please.' Silvia wrapped her cold hands gratefully round the thick china cup. Ellis had pulled his chair up beside hers. 'You're wearing my bed socks.'

'Very alluring, aren't they?' he said, holding a foot out for inspection.

She smiled. 'Oddly, yes. In fact I think they suit you far better than me. Consider them a gift.'

'I'll treasure them, and I promise I won't put them in the sock warmer.' He leaned across to take her empty cup. 'That blasted woman has upset you, hasn't she? She knew fine well that you didn't know that your husband had remarried. I could see the glint in her eye when she told you. She positively relished it.'

'Our encounter has provoked a reaction in me, I won't pretend otherwise, but it's not so much about Edward— well, only a little.' Silvia smiled wanly. 'I don't ever regret severing my ties to him. If anything, I wish I'd had the courage to act earlier.'

'The courage it must have taken to act at all leaves me in awe.'

'I wasn't brave. I was humiliated, and miserable, and Edward wasn't happy either, you know.'

'It was his atrocious behaviour which made you miserable in the first place.'

'It's not as simple as that. It was foolish of me to expect him to be completely faithful, for in our world— his world—it was accepted that a man could have casual affairs. He told me they meant nothing.'

'Which proves how callous the man is, to treat both his wife and his many paramours with contempt!' Ellis exclaimed. 'It may be accepted, but that doesn't make it right, and when a man is as blatant in his dalliances as your former husband, it's disgusting. You were his wife. At the very least he owed you some respect.'

'I don't disagree, and perhaps he would have treated me better if I had given him an heir, but I could not. In his eyes I had failed as a wife, and in the eyes of polite society too, as my brother kindly informed me. Anyone who knew Edward would be perfectly well aware that it was he who had broken his wedding vows, but the worse, more heinous crime was mine, in failing to fulfil my part of the marriage contract. I had no choice but to play the guilty party in order to obtain a divorce, but, though I didn't realise it at the time, I actually did *feel* guilty, for failing in my fundamental duty as a wife.'

'Oh, Silvia.' Ellis reached over to press her hand. 'Did you wish for children?'

It was not a question she had asked herself, and so she took her time answering. 'I assumed that I would have them, for that was the purpose of my marriage. I'm glad now that we didn't, for I could never have left him if that had been the case. My marriage may have been less painful if I could have given Edward an heir, but it would never have been happy. I always felt—stifled, I suppose is the word.'

'Did you love him?'

Silvia shook her head firmly. 'I thought I did at first, but I was very young. My divorce was never about a broken heart.'

Unlike this pending separation?

She pushed the question firmly to one side. 'What I'm

really trying to say is that the news Lady Oliphant so desperately tried to rub my nose in, that Edward has become a father, has wiped away the last traces of guilt I didn't even know I had. I'm finally truly free of him, Ellis.'

'So now you can spread your wings unhindered? I am very glad to hear that.'

The words were so bittersweet, demonstrating exactly his innate understanding of her, and the reason why she must now put an end to any hopes either of them may have had for a future together. 'Thank you, Ellis, I knew you would be.'

'But that's not what sent you wandering out on the moors alone, is it?'

'Only partly.' Silvia took a breath. 'I'm not going to live a lie anymore. I'm not going to hide away here anymore. I am going to use my freedom to see more of the world. Not travel for the sake of it, but experiencing other places, other cultures. Living where I choose, moving on when I have had enough.'

'That sounds very appealing.'

Recalling her daydream of travelling with Ellis, once again, she felt his words were bittersweet. 'To be one who has no ties. No one to consult save herself. No family to care for. No business interests to worry about. No reputation to protect.'

'I see.' He got up to stir the coals, a heavy frown drawing his brows together as he sat back down again. 'In other words, Silvia, there is no place for me in your future, is that it?'

It was his pride that was hurt, that was all, she told herself. 'You are thinking me presumptuous, for we have never discussed...'

'You are not being presumptuous,' he said curtly. 'I have no desire whatsoever to end our—our...'

'Liaison.'

'Relationship.'

'A liaison, and a scandalous one, is how it would be perceived, Ellis. You saw Lady Oliphant's reaction.'

'I wish we had not met that damned woman.'

'It's for the best that we did though,' Silvia said, gently determined now, knowing that she was set upon the right course and knowing also that what she felt for him went a great deal deeper than it would be safe to admit. 'If your family or any of your respectable business associates ever got wind of our... If it was known that we were friends, never mind lovers, your reputation would be damaged, because your judgement in associating yourself with someone as notorious as I am would be called into question. Do you see?'

He opened his mouth then closed it again, drumming his fingers on the arm of his chair. 'It's so unfair. That you should be judged so harshly over something you should be proud of, standing up for yourself as you did— you should be lauded, not condemned.'

'Thank you. You have always understood that, and I am very grateful.'

'I don't want your gratitude,' he said with a twisted smile. 'What I want is—oh, I don't know. These last few days have gone a fair way to calling into question everything I thought I knew of myself. I didn't expect to feel like this, and I don't know what it might mean, but I do know I don't want to say goodbye, even though I know what you are saying makes perfect sense.'

She winced, for despite everything, his words lifted her heart. 'I wish you had not said as much.'

'We have been honest with each other from the start.' Ellis got up and set the kettle back on to boil. 'Tea,' he said with a wry smile, 'the cure for all life's ills. I hadn't counted on our—our connection having such a profound effect on me, but I'm not going to deny it.' He poured them both a fresh cup of tea and sat down. 'Would it be best if I left now?'

'Oh, no!' she exclaimed instinctively. 'Now that we have cleared the air...now that we both understand... Oh, no, I don't want you to leave.' Tears threatened to spill. She sipped her tea furiously, trying to regain control of herself. 'Can't we simply enjoy the rest of our time together, as we planned? Create a memory that we can treasure for ever?'

'Are you sure that is what you want?'

She didn't have to think about it. The possibility of him leaving now made her panic. 'I'm certain,' Silvia said, forcing a smile.

'Very well.' Ellis sighed, stretching his legs out to the fire. 'It's getting light. What shall we do with our day?'

'What would you be doing if you were in Wales?'

'It's the thirtieth, isn't it? Tomorrow will see the New Year's Eve play, which means most of today will be spent rehearsing, making costumes, building the stage.' He shuddered. 'Being Welsh, whatever the play is, there will be singing involved.'

'Can you sing?'

He laughed. 'I can't hold a note to save my life, which means, thankfully, I'm usually given the task of designing the scenery, and that suits me fine. What will your brother have in store for his lucky guests?'

'There will be a treasure hunt this afternoon, which Mel always organises because she's brilliant at coming up with clues. Tomorrow is Clive's *pièce de résistance*, the gr-r-r-rand Hogmanay ceilidh,' Silvia said, in an appalling Scottish accent. 'Clive's wife is from Edinburgh, which as far as I am aware is not in the Highlands, but for one day of the year, her accent takes on a Highland lilt and they deck themselves out in tartan. One year they even had a man playing the bagpipes, though when I say playing…'

'Like whisky, an acquired taste,' Ellis said. 'I worked with a real Highlander a couple of years ago, making some refinements to his still and whisky production process. He was so happy with the result he gave me a case of his best thirty-year-old malt. It tasted to me like something you'd be given by a quack to rub onto arthritic joints. I don't know if it was simply terrible stuff, or if it all tastes like that, but never again.'

'Fortunately, I don't have any whisky.'

'I'm thinking, though,' Ellis said, 'it might be fun to celebrate New Year's Eve with our own—what did you call it—a kaylay?'

'Ceilidh. It means dance, or party, in this case to celebrate the approaching new year. But there are only two of us, and we don't have any tartan, never mind a set of bagpipes.'

'Where there's a will, there's a way. What do you think?'

She laughed. 'Why not? I might have a plaid blanket I could turn into a kilt for you.'

'Have I the legs for it, do you think?' Ellis asked, holding one out for inspection.

'You'd have to take off those bed socks.'

He got up, pulling her to her feet. 'Why don't we go upstairs and you can take them off for me? These memories won't make themselves, you know.'

Chapter Nine

Saturday 31st December 1825,
New Year's Eve

Silvia put the finishing touches to her toilette, smiling at herself in the bedroom mirror. She had fashioned a tartan sash from her plaid blanket to drape over her blue silk evening gown, fixing it to the shoulder with a pin decorated with heather from the moor. She had with some difficulty woven more heather into her hair. The remainder of the plaid rug formed a runner down the centre of the dining table, where more heather formed a centrepiece. She and Ellis had gathered it on their walk this morning, at his request taking the circular route out to the Wainstones which they had walked on their first day together.

She had spent the afternoon in the kitchen, while Ellis was out in the stables. 'Inventing,' he'd said, smiling mischievously when she'd asked him what he was up to.

'Inventing,' she had retorted back at him, when he'd asked her what she was doing in the kitchen.

This would be their last night together. She was determined that it would be perfect. She wouldn't think about tomorrow or allow anything to spoil the few precious hours they had left.

Ellis was waiting for her in the parlour, freshly shaved, dressed in his evening clothes. Her heart gave a silly little leap as he stood up to greet her. 'I made use of what was to be your kilt,' Silvia said.

'It looks a great deal better on you than it ever would on me. You look quite lovely.'

'I'm afraid I smell of the moor.'

'You smell delicious,' he said, leaning in to kiss her. 'And you taste every bit as good, my bonnie Highland lass.'

She chuckled. 'Not nearly as tasty as the porridge I've made for our dinner.'

'Silvia, please tell me you're teasing.'

'Porridge to start, followed by a lovely big plate of haggis and neeps.'

'I have no idea what that is...'

'Boiled sheep's stomach stuffed with offal and pinhead oats, and mashed swede or turnip. That's what they'll be eating tonight at my brother's ceilidh, but in the spirit of being contrary, we're having something different.'

'Thank the stars. First, though, I think we should start the celebrations with a wee dram of champagne, which I've had chilling outside in the horse trough.' Ellis popped the cork and poured two flutes, handing one to her. 'To the most unusual and wonderful Christmas, which I have been privileged to spend with the most beautiful, courageous, enticing, clever, amusing...'

'Stop, Ellis, you're making me blush like a maiden.'

'Then I'll say simply the most wonderful woman I have ever met. Thank you, Silvia.' He touched his glass to hers. 'For everything.'

'And to you, Ellis.' She kissed him softly. 'Thank you for making this my most memorable Christmas. I doubt it will ever be bettered.'

The smell of the heather which they had gathered that morning scented the dining room. As he took his place at the table, Ellis couldn't help but think that this was the last time he would do so. All day, he'd been painfully aware of his looming departure, trying not to count down the hours to the arrival of his post-chaise. There was no point in revisiting the possibility of their seeing each other again, for they had said all there was to be said. It was simply not possible, for either of them, leaving him no other option but to say goodbye. Yet he couldn't quite quell his gut instinct, which was telling him he'd be making a huge mistake.

Hearing Silvia approach from the kitchen, he gave himself a shake and set about pouring the wine. He was not going to spoil tonight. Her cheeks were flushed from the heat of the oven. She was smiling nervously at him as she set the covered salver down. 'I have prepared an alternative Scottish delicacy, a Scotch pie.'

She removed the lid with a flourish, releasing a cloud of steam and the most delicious smell. The pie was golden brown, slightly oozing, and surrounded by a garland of carrots and winter greens. 'What is a Scotch pie?' Ellis asked. 'I've never had one.'

'Nor have I. It's my own invention. It's mostly diced lamb, with a little oatmeal to thicken it, and a red wine and mint jelly.'

She cut him a wedge of pie and served him the vegetables, taking care, as was her custom, to arrange the plate neatly. After she had served herself she waited, as she always did, for his verdict on the food, biting the corner of her lip, a tiny, anxious frown drawing her brows together. Knowing how much it meant to her, he took his time to savour it, enjoying the way her smile broadened, her eyes lighting up when he told her, in an equally atrocious Scots accent that it was 'Braw!' Only then did she allow herself to taste it.

The phrase domestic bliss had always filled Ellis with terror, for he'd imagined himself hounded and constrained, perpetually performing a role he didn't want. With Silvia, domestic bliss entailed sharing a meal, including the cooking, and even clearing up afterwards. It was talking as they did, teasing, or being quiet without any need to talk. It was being able to say *I'd like to be on my own now*, and having that quietly accepted. It was the undercurrent of awareness that was there every time they looked at each other, the tantalising possibility of lovemaking, but also the comfort and pleasure of simply lying together in one another's arms. He would miss all of this desperately.

After dinner, they returned to the parlour where the yule twiglet sat, by now slightly singed, in the hearth. 'My brother's wife gives everyone a broom or a duster around about now,' Silvia said. 'It's apparently a Scottish superstition, intended to sweep the house clean of malevolent spirits.'

'She'll never accomplish that until she throws her husband out.'

'Clive is selfish and arrogant, and I don't think he actually cares very much for anyone other than himself, except perhaps his eldest son, but he's not evil.' She smiled mischievously. 'I must confess, though, I would love to see his wife attempting to shoo him out of the ancestral home with a broom!'

'I find it difficult to believe that all over the Highlands, there are hordes of men and women sweeping evil spirits out of their cottages.'

'No, I've always thought that one was an invention of Clive's wife. I reckon they will all be dancing reels and drinking whisky.'

'It will all come to an abrupt end on the stroke of midnight, though,' Ellis said. 'That's one thing I do know—the Sabbath is sacred. When I was working with my Highland distiller, he attended church three times a day on a Sunday.'

'You would have to wait until Monday to travel back to Wales if we were in the Highlands, then.'

'Tomorrow's a long way away,' Ellis said, getting to his feet. 'We have a reel of our own to dance first.'

Silvia's smile returned as she got up. 'We've no music.'

'Aha! That is where you are wrong.' He retrieved the instrument he had constructed from behind the sofa. 'If you would be so good as to take your place, madam, I will now play you a tune I have written especially for the occasion.'

'Ellis, what on earth…? Is that a pair of old bellows?'

'It *was* a pair of old bellows. Now it is a set of Yorkshire bagpipes.'

He began to pump the bellows. The noise started as a low drone, and then, as the instrument took in air, became a high-pitched whine, the 'notes' formed by the reed he had fashioned, and the length of pipe with holes drilled in it which he had attached. Silvia's face was a picture of astonishment turning to mock-horror as the wailing became a semblance of a tune. To his delight, she picked up her skirts and daintily executed a few steps and a twirl, before dissolving into laughter.

'Oh, Ellis, that is quite extraordinary, and actually not far off the sound of the real thing. What is your tune called?'

'"The Bonnie Maid of Yorkshire Moor".' He set his invention down with some relief and took her into his arms, humming a more sedate tune. They danced a slow waltz. She laid her head on his shoulder and followed his lead. He smoothed his hand down her back to rest on the slope of her bottom, and she slid her hand under his evening coat to echo the movement. He ached with the need to say something of his feelings, to tell her—what, that he loved her? Bloody fool, Ellis thought, for those were the very words he'd been refusing to allow himself even to think. Now they were there, in his head, as they circled slowly together, and the sinking feeling in his stomach contrasted with the lightness in his heart. He did love her. Maybe not for ever, but now, in this moment, he loved her.

The clock on the mantle made a tinkling noise and began to chime. Silvia lifted her head. 'It's midnight.'

Ellis poured the last of the now warm champagne into their glasses, and as the last chime finished they raised them together in a toast. 'Happy New Year, Silvia.'

'Happy New Year, Ellis. Here's to the future.'

Her tremulous smile made the urge to speak almost unbearable, but what would be the point? He had no idea if her own feelings were as strong as his. If they were not, she'd be embarrassed. If they were, it would make their remaining few hours together agonising. He could not speak, but he could act. Setting both their glasses down, he took her into his arms again, and kissed her.

* * *

Silvia wrapped her arms around Ellis and pressed herself tightly against him. She didn't want there to be any space between them. She returned his kiss, letting her body tell him what she would not even permit herself to acknowledge. Of one accord they reined in their passion, wanting their lovemaking to last, knowing it would be the last time. Their kisses were slow and lingering. She murmured his name, because that was all she could allow herself to voice, and he repeated hers back to her, softly, in a manner that no one else had ever used when they spoke her name.

They kissed their way out of the parlour and onto the stairs. They kissed their way up to her bedchamber, and there were more kisses as Ellis kicked the door shut. They shed their clothes slowly, an item at a time, taking turns to unfasten and to kiss each new bit of exposed skin. She kissed his neck and his throat and his chest. He kissed his way down her spine, and then turned her round to kiss her breasts. They touched each other with the confidence of familiarity mingled with a new, tentative tenderness, wanting to rouse, but not too much, not yet. They kissed as they lay entwined, naked, on the bed, still murmuring and stroking and touching, and there were more kisses as she took him inside her, shivering, clinging on to her self-control, their gazes locked as they began the final climb together in a slow and steady rhythm that only became frantic at the end. Her climax shook her to the core, triggering his, making them both cry out and cling to each other, to make this one last moment of complete togetherness unforgettable.

I love you. The words refused to be tethered any more as they kissed again, though Silvia didn't speak them.

She loved him so much, and all she could do was to show him in her kisses, in her touch, in her gaze. I love you, Ellis, she said to herself as she kissed him one last time, as he pulled her close against him, wrapping his arms around her, and she laid her head on his shoulder. I love you, Ellis, she thought. I love you so much.

Chapter Ten

Sunday 1st January 1826

They spent the night entwined in one another's arms, talking and kissing, making silly jokes, sometimes lying quietly together with their thoughts, but not sleeping. The first day of the new year dawned to a winter wonderland of fresh snow and a crisp azure sky. After breakfast together they went for a last walk on the moors. The air was sharply cold, but there was no breeze. Their strides matched on the path, their boots crunching in time like drumbeats on the fresh snow, silent now, both of them, locked in their own internal musings.

'There is something I have to say,' Ellis said as they reached the boulder that marked the turning point on this now familiar walk. 'I have been trying all night to persuade myself that there's no point, and maybe there is not, but if I don't speak now, I know in my bones I'll regret it for the rest of my life.'

Silvia, who had concluded much the same in the course of the night, but lacked the courage to act, stared at him mutely, terrified and, against all odds, hopeful.

'I love you,' Ellis said, taking her mittened hand in his. 'I have never been in love before, but I know that's what I'm feeling. I love you, and I simply cannot bear the thought of never seeing you again.'

Tears sprang into her eyes. Her heart felt as if it was swooping and soaring. She knew that nothing had fundamentally changed but oh, it felt as if everything had. 'I love you too,' she whispered, finding huge relief and pleasure in finally being able to utter the words she had forbidden herself to think. 'I love you so very much.'

She was in his arms in a moment, kissing him frantically, telling him over and over how much she loved him, and he was telling her over and over that he loved her too, so much, so much…

But then reality forced its way in, and their kisses stopped, and they gazed at each other, stricken and smiling at the same time.

'Oh, Ellis,' Silvia said, 'what are we going to do?'

'I haven't the faintest notion,' he answered, running his fingers through his hair, shaking his head ruefully, 'but I'm determined we're not saying goodbye for ever.'

'What else can we do?'

'Would you marry me if you could? Truthfully, Silvia?'

'I don't know; I've not thought about it,' she said, beginning to panic. 'I don't want to give up my freedom, but I don't want to give you up either. Yet what else can I do, for being with me will ruin you?'

'In the eyes of the world, perhaps, but I don't give a damn about that.'

'You should. You do. You will.'

'Maybe. I don't know. I do know that you'll make my

life a great deal happier if we can find a way to be together somehow.'

'But you don't want a wife, Ellis. Your independence…'

'Is as precious to me as yours is to you, I know that. But more precious still is your company. I wasn't lonely before I knew you, but I'll be lonely without you now.' He took her hands in his. 'I'd never treat you as he did. I love you. I want only you, but I wouldn't ever want you to stay with me save for one reason, and it's nothing to do with a marriage contract.'

Tears tracked down her cheeks. 'Only love?'

He nodded. 'Only love.'

'That doesn't sound like marriage at all.'

'It sounds like our form of marriage. We've made Christmas in our own image,' Ellis said; 'why not do the same with our marriage?'

'How can we do that?'

'I don't know, my love. The question is, do we want to try?'

Despite herself she smiled. 'Oh, Ellis, you make it sound as if it's almost possible.'

'I have to believe it is,' he said fervently, 'because I can't contemplate the alternative.'

'I don't want to either, but I can't see—do you really think it might be possible?'

'I'm not going to start out by making promises I can't keep. I can promise to try, but you must do the same. You have been through so much, and come so far alone, I don't want you to feel I've rushed you or compromised you. We're talking about the rest of our lives here, and it's far too important a decision to make on the basis of a week together, much as I want to.'

'I know you're right,' Silvia said slowly. 'It would be

foolish indeed of me to risk all that I have fought so hard for on the basis of one impulsive week. How long do you think we need?'

'You must take your time. Learn to fly on your own first,' Ellis said, kissing her hand. 'You might decide you like it.'

Up here on the moors, the morning after that encounter with Lady Oliphant, Silvia had decided to do exactly that, but that was before Ellis proposed...what? She had no idea what he was proposing. 'I don't know. You're right. I owe it to myself to try to spread my wings, I know that. Oh, but I don't want to say goodbye, only I can't imagine how—are we deluding ourselves, do you think?'

'We'll find out, one way or another. Next Christmas, Silvia—by then we'll have spent almost a year apart, that's more than enough time for us both to work out what we want, what we don't want, find a way to be together or not, for we must be honest with each other if we change our minds. Unless you are already having second thoughts?'

'No! I love you. I know that for certain.'

Ellis smiled, pulling her closer. 'And I love you. We'll hang on to that, shall we, since that's more important than anything else?'

She nodded, on the brink of tears again. 'Your carriage will be here soon. I don't want to watch you go. Let's say goodbye here.'

'Not goodbye,' he said, taking her into his arms and kissing her hard. *'Adieu.'* Then he turned away and began to walk swiftly back towards the farmhouse.

She watched him for a moment before she turned away and began to walk quickly in the opposite direction.

Chapter Eleven

Monday 25th December 1826,
Christmas Day

Silvia opened the music box and wound the mechanism, marvelling as she always did as she watched the little bird spin and take flight before it once again closed its wings and fell asleep. It was exactly a year to the day since Ellis had given her the present. She set the box back on the shelf and opened the long French doors before stepping out onto the terrace. The sun was just peering over the verdant, gently rolling hills which lay to the east of the villa. She breathed in the salty tang of coastal air, leaning on the balustrade bordering the terrace which provided her favourite view down to the golden sands of the cove below. There was still a chill in the air, but by midday it would be warm enough for a swim.

She had left Yorkshire last February, sailing to Italy, where she spent three months in Florence living alone, discovering, amongst other things, a passion for the cuisine and for the sunshine which made the produce in the markets so ripe and colourful. She had chosen the location deliberately, knowing that it was a popular destination with tourists from England, and wishing to test herself. She had been snubbed and patronised and propositioned. She had been reduced to tears. But her resolve to be true to herself had not once faltered, nor had her heart.

She had left the city only because she was ready for a change of scene, spending two months in Nice, then two in Valencia. It was when she left Spain to sail for Greece in October that she had written to Ellis. Their year had not yet been up, but she knew she wouldn't change her mind. She had been content, at times happy in her own company, but she had never stopped missing him, and absence, in her case, made her heart grow ever fonder. She loved him. She would continue to be happy without him, but life with him would be immeasurably happier. When the year had expired, if he was prepared to make the required leap of faith, she would be ready.

As it happened, he hadn't waited until the deadline, arriving in person last month, delayed only because of a last-minute hitch relating to the sale of the patent for his steam lathe. She was aware of him now, even before he padded onto the balcony, turning around to meet him.

'I thought I'd find you here.' Ellis pulled her into his arms and kissed her soundly.

'I woke up early, and thought I'd watch the sunrise. You're already dressed. Goodness, very well dressed too.'

'An example I think you ought to follow. Delightful as you look in your dressing gown, I think the occasion calls for something a little more formal.'

Half an hour later, wearing her favourite gown of cream silk adorned with forget-me-nots, Silvia, now thoroughly intrigued, followed Ellis down the steps to the beach. 'Where on earth are we going?' she asked for the third time.

'It's a surprise. Not far to go now,' he said, leading her across the sand towards the outcrop of rocks which bordered the cove.

'I hope you're not expecting me to clamber over those—I'll ruin my gown.'

'No clambering required,' he said. 'We're here.'

They were at the entrance of what she had assumed was a narrow cleft in the rocks. Ellis picked up the lamp, taking her hand and encouraging her through the gap. She followed him warily, though the sand was soft and dry, the cave clearly well back from the high tide mark. After a few steps, the passageway turned sharply, and Silvia stopped short in astonishment.

The cave, or grotto, twinkled by the light of what appeared to be hundreds of candles. The walls were elaborately decorated with shell mosaics, patterns of stars and a moon above a sea filled with exotic-looking fish. Silvia traced the shapes with her fingers, marvelling at the intricacy of the work, the variety of seashells used. 'What is this place?'

'I have no idea. Some sort of shrine dedicated to fishermen, I would think.'

'It must have taken years and years to do. What a wonderful surprise. And this,' Silvia said, joining him; 'it looks like an altar. Ellis?'

'The law won't permit us to formally declare our love, but we don't need a piece of paper to demonstrate our commitment to each other.' He dropped to his knees in front of her, taking her hand. 'I solemnly vow that I will always respect you, never take you for granted, and that I will love you, with all my heart, to the end of my days.'

Utterly overwhelmed, her heart almost too full for her to speak, Silvia dropped onto the sand beside him and, stuttering with emotion, repeated the vows he had made. The ring he placed on her finger was not a plain wedding band; instead it featured two tiny birds soaring, wings outstretched. 'It's perfect, just like you. I love you so much,' Silvia said, throwing her arms around him and kissing him. 'I said last Christmas would never be bettered, but it just has been. Being with you is the best Christmas present imaginable. I don't think I could ever love you more.'

In answer he kissed her back, smiling wickedly before getting up and pulling her with him. 'I very much hope to prove you wrong, my love,' he said, scooping her up in his arms and heading out of the cave. 'I might have given up my business but I'm still an inventor at heart, and I've had almost a year to apply myself to inventing new ways for us to make love. I reckon it's time to advance a few of them to the practical phase of the process.'

* * * * *

If you enjoyed these stories, you won't want to miss these other Historical collections

Invitation to a Cornish Christmas *by Marguerite Kaye and Bronwyn Scott*
Snowbound Surrender *by Christine Merrill, Louise Allen and Laura Martin*
Tudor Christmas Tidings *by Blythe Gifford, Jenni Fletcher and Amanda McCabe*
Christmas Cinderellas *by Sophia James, Virginia Heath and Catherine Tinley*
A Victorian Family Christmas *by Carla Kelly, Carol Arens and Eva Shepherd*

Historical Note

Before the 1857 Divorce Act was passed in England, divorce was extremely rare. Since women were not recognised as having any legal status, a wife could not sue for divorce, no matter how atrociously her husband behaved.

The process was complex, drawn-out, expensive and scandalous—which is why there were so few occurrences. First a hearing in an Ecclesiastical Court was required, which the husband had to instigate. This was followed by a hearing in the Common Law Court for 'criminal conversation'—commonly referred to as 'crim con' in the scandal sheets—during which the husband accused another man of stealing 'the property of his marriage'. In other words, accusing his wife of adultery.

In Silvia's fictional case, as in so many real-life cases, the adultery was staged, with 'reliable' paid witnesses conveniently positioned to gather evidence. If the criminal conversation was proved, and damages awarded, a husband with power and influence could then bring about a private Act of Parliament to finalise the divorce, which in some cases would allow him to remarry.

A wife had no right to defend herself at any stage of

the process, and nor was she ever permitted to remarry. An allowance could be awarded to her, but this was entirely at her former husband's discretion. Children, as property of the marriage, remained with the husband.